A
Photographic
Death

A DELHI LAINE MYSTERY

JUDI CULBERTSON

WITNESS
IMPULSE
An Imprint of HarperCollinsPublishers

EPub Edition MAY 2014 ISBN: 9780062296351
Print Edition ISBN: 9780062296368

10 9 8 7 6 5 4 3 2 1

To Emily and Drew who astonish me with their creativity and love.

Prologue

"ARE YOU COMFORTABLE, Jane?"

Karl Lundy looks at my daughter with the smile of a chef about to garnish his favorite piglet. It makes me want to grab her wrist and head for the door.

Yet Jane looks comfortable enough, her hair golden against the navy worsted fabric of the chair, her mouth slightly open in anticipation. Dr. Lundy seems excited too. His gray eyes keep blinking behind gold-rimmed glasses. His hand plays with a paperweight on his desk, a rose trapped under glass.

When I approached him last week and told him what we wanted, he explained that he rarely did one-offs, that he hypnotized people over the course of months for therapeutic reasons. But he didn't refuse. Jane must be an interesting change from people trying to stop smoking or lose forty pounds.

"You need to understand that hypnosis is serious business, Ms. Laine."

"Call me Delhi. And I'm happy to hear you say that."

Yet I'm still uneasy, shunted off to one side on a straight chair like a husband in a dress shop. Is it too late to say we have another appointment and walk out? What if Jane is about to be traumatized for life? Whatever we learn is going be a shock, I know that. We will find out either that my youngest daughter, Caitlin, may still be alive, or that Jane stood on the riverbank and watched her drown nineteen years ago. *The lady or the tiger. Dear God, don't let it be the tiger crouching behind the unopened door.*

Restless, I search the room for clues as to what's going to happen, but it is a typical doctor's office that gives nothing away. The vanilla scent is meant to be calming, as are the paintings on the walls—country scenes of red barns and golden haystacks, mountains reflected in turquoise lakes. I wonder if someone Dr. Lundy knows painted them. The bookcases hold the kind of academic volumes that I, as a book dealer, have little interest in. I would not rescue *them* in case of fire.

"Jane, I'm going to put you in the light trance I told you about, and we'll gradually regress you to the age of four. You'll be back in the park in England on the last day you visited there." He looks to me for confirmation and I nod. "Is there anything else you'd like to work on in your life?"

She laughs. "You mean like getting up early and going to the gym every day? Or not spending so much time in clubs?"

"Any area of your life you'd like to improve."

"You can tell me not to buy any more expensive purses and shoes. Seriously," she adds, seeing his expression.

"All right. Now sit back and get as comfortable as possible."

Dr. Lundy has been standing behind his desk all this time. Now he moves to the chair on Jane's left. They can glance at each other, but don't have to. He is as bland and comforting as the vanilla cookie scent of his office, from his gray-and-sky-blue argyle sweater to his solid gold wedding ring. His soft Midwestern voice reminds me of Garrison Keillor telling a story.

In the pre-hypnosis interview, he gave me the facts meant to reassure me: That Jane would not be unconscious or asleep. She would be alert and attentive, able to bring material from the past into awareness. He promised he would not cross-examine her or make any suggestions he knew would be contrary to her wishes. If she became uncomfortable, she could raise her index finger and he would move away from what was upsetting her. He managed to make hypnosis sound as interesting as watching water boil.

It was what an apprehensive mother needed to hear.

"Do you want me to close my eyes?" Jane asks.

"If that makes you feel relaxed, certainly."

"Okay." She does, pressing deeper into the chair.

"You're becoming very relaxed," Dr. Lundy drones. "When you're completely relaxed, your right arm will feel as light as air. The lightness will start in the fingers and spread up through your wrist toward your elbow. The arm will become so light that it will lift into the air on its own."

Oh, sure, I think. And for two or three minutes nothing happens. But then her arm eerily starts to rise, the gold bracelet sliding back against the cuff of her sweater. My stomach jumps. What have I gotten us into?

Her arm floats in space until Dr. Lundy says, "As you go deeper and deeper, your arm will gradually lower back to the chair rest. When that happens you will be fully in a trance state, ready to explore the things that have happened to you in the past."

He continues to make the same suggestions, stating them in slightly different ways. My own lids start to droop and I have to fight not to sink into the past with Jane. Both she and my other daughter, Hannah, have the ability to close their eyes and be immediately asleep, napping until a change in the atmosphere startles them. I used to be the same way.

Then I am jerked awake, as surely as if Dr. Lundy had slapped me. Before my eyes, Jane is turning into a little girl. It's in the way she twists in the chair, mouth slightly open in wonder. Her eyes are open now too, but they are not seeing the room we are in.

"Where are you now, Jane?" Dr. Lundy wants to know. "Are you in the park?"

"In the park," she confirms. "We brought bread to feed the ducks. They ate all of it!"

"Who is in the park with you?"

"Mommy. And the twins. And the new baby. But we can't see her yet."

Dr. Lundy tenses. "Why not?"

"She's still in Mommy's tummy." None of us knew then that the baby would turn out to be Jason.

Dr. Lundy smiles sheepishly, gets Jane to tell him where everyone is in the park, then summarizes for her: "So your sister Hannah is asleep and Mommy is taking photos of people in boats on the river, and you and Cate are playing. What happens next?"

"That lady comes."

What lady? I don't just tense, I pull back in the chair, galvanized, electricity running haywire through my body. I actually lean toward Jane before I remember that I am forbidden to interfere.

"Jane, I want you to look at this lady and tell me about her. What kind of clothes does she have on?"

"Her nurse clothes. She always wears her nurse clothes."

What could she be talking about? Jane sounds as if she is used to seeing this woman in the park—how could I not have seen her, not even once?

"Does she have on a white dress like a nurse?" He waits for her to nod. "What color are her shoes?"

"Her shoes, her shoes." She actually seems to be looking down at someone's feet. "Her shoes are brown like Daddy's shoes. But she has on these funny stockings. With bumps."

"Is she as old as Mommy?"

No answer.

As old as Grandma? I want to demand. *What kind of funny stockings?* My hands are gripping the metal seat edge as if I am high on a ski lift with no restraints around me. He's not asking her the right questions! I lift an urgent hand to catch his eye, but he is focused on Jane.

The smell of vanilla in the room is making me nauseous.

"Is the lady talking to you?"

"She says—she says, 'Go pick that yellow flower for me and I'll give you a toy from the carriage.' "

So the nightmare begins.

Chapter 1

WHEN PATIENCE CALLED with last-minute Thanksgiving details, she reminded me not to bring anything.

"I could make Mom's cranberry sauce," I teased. Actually, that was one of the few things our mother—God rest her soul—knew how to cook. I remembered her bent over the vintage stove in the old parsonage, patiently stirring water, sugar, and tiny red globes until the cranberries burst their skins. When the concoction cooled she would add mandarin oranges and chopped walnuts and we would snack on it till it was gone.

That is, if there was any of it left after dinner. My father always invited a handful of homesick Princeton students, the odd parishioner—no shortage of those—and several local eccentrics to share our feast. The conversation was always interesting.

"Don't bring anything!" Patience repeated. "The Golden String Bean does a cranberry mold to die for."

I tried not to laugh. "The Golden String Bean?"

"Only the best caterer in Southampton. I had to book months ahead to get them."

"Just for us?"

"We're not worth it?"

We were, of course. Worth the long, slow crawl through Long Island traffic to Southampton, worth the ornate sterling and Waterford goblets, the endless pourings of fine wine and the mandatory walk on the beach afterward to admire the ocean. There would be exquisite desserts.

But this year the thought of having to endure the ritual made me anxious. The day before, along with all the mail a bookseller gets, there had been a blue tissue envelope with English postage stamps. I couldn't think of any recent orders from Britain where they would be sending me a check, but I sliced the envelope open carefully.

The note inside turned my world upside down.

"Delhi?"

"I'm still here. Just thinking. I could always bring chocolate." Scarfing down candy was one of my twin's few weaknesses. I had learned early to hide my Easter basket and trick-or-treating stash.

"Godiva's always welcome."

"I'll be sure to bring her along." Patience's idea of sufficient Godiva cost more than a turkey and all the trimmings from Stop & Shop, but I didn't begrudge it to her. Not with the Golden String Bean on the job.

"Is Colin coming?" she asked.

"He's coming." My husband, Colin, had moved out a year ago, looking to recapture the glories of his youth, though lately he had been hinting about moving back home. The problem was, I wasn't sure there was still room enough for him. Colin took up a lot of space, emotional as well as physical, and it meant an adjustment I wasn't sure I wanted to make. "He's bringing the wine," I added.

"And the children?"

Hardly children now. I thought of yesterday's note and shivered. "Not Jason, just the girls."

It should have been our usual Thanksgiving celebration, one more turn of the calendar page. But I already knew it would not be.

Chapter 2

AUTUMNS ON LONG Island seem to be getting warmer and warmer. Red and orange leaves cling stubbornly to the trees, their tenacity reminding me of tag sale signs left behind on telephone poles—signs that were crucial to me until last month. Through October, I spent weekends waiting in line to buy the books I sell in my Internet business, Secondhand Prose. Like a squirrel, I need to amass enough volumes to carry me through the winter.

Finding books was getting harder. The golden days of online bookselling had tiptoed quietly out of the room when no one was looking. At least once a month I snapped awake in the darkness, wondering what my life would be like in five years. I reminded myself that books were not ephemeral like LPs and videotapes. No matter the popularity of e-books, physical books were *eternal*. Who could live in a world without them?

Today, Thanksgiving, was close to fifty degrees outside. We were dressed for that weather. Jane looked perfect in a rust-colored crewneck, brown velvet blazer, and a gold 1896 dollar medallion around her neck. Hannah, who had arrived late last night, was dozing in the backseat next to her sister, still in the same grimy Cornell sweatshirt and cargo pants.

Beside me Colin was dressed like the college professor he is, in a houndstooth jacket whose pattern dwarfed his Phi Beta Kappa key. Underneath his blazer was a sweater the color of Jane's. Despite his generous size, his white beard and regal bearing made him look dapper at the wheel of his ancient green BMW. One could imagine him in Merrie Olde England, wearing a flat cap and driving on the wrong side of the road.

I say, old chap, Happy Thanksgiving!

I had not been able to decide what to wear. I needed to be taken seriously when I told people about the note, but I did not have many clothes to choose from. Because I'd never had a real job, my work clothes were mostly sweatshirts and jeans. Finally I'd settled for my most serious thrift shop outfit, black slacks and a black turtleneck. But I couldn't resist adding my vintage red Mexican jacket embroidered with an hombre in a sombrero sleeping against a cactus on the back. It had been a rare find at North Shore Thrift. I knew it was politically incorrect, but I couldn't let it go. Colin had rolled his eyes when he opened the front door and saw me, but did not comment. Evidently what I wore to my sister's on Thanksgiving didn't merit a fight.

Jason, if he were here, would be dressed like Jackson Pollock in paint-stained jeans and sweatshirt. I wondered if he had any plans for Thanksgiving, alone as he was in Santa Fe. The thought of him by himself made me sad. But given the choice of coming home now or for Christmas—I could not afford the airfare for both— he had chosen Christmas. Colin refused to give him any money at all until Jason capitulated and returned to college.

I wondered what Jason would think if he knew about the new chapter I hoped to write in our family history. When I thought about it, my stomach bucked and churned like the old washing machine we'd had in the parsonage. Placing an extra blanket on Hannah's bed yesterday and tidying up Jane's old room in the farmhouse, I'd rehearsed what I was going to say and tried to imagine how my daughters would respond.

I couldn't. Not really. I decided I would wait until after dessert, until after a prodigious amount of wine had been consumed by everyone except my little nieces. By then they would be away from the table anyway, texting their friends or playing Angry Birds.

As we drove farther east on Sunrise Highway, traffic started to thicken like the gravy I had spent years trying to get right. Other cars boxed us in; I pictured them fragrant with the smell of apple pie and pumpkin bread. The large gold box of chocolates I was balancing on my lap gave off its own scent. To keep from obsessing over what I planned to say, I let myself listen to "Appalachian Spring" on NPR.

Everything about the holiday made me miss my parents. They had both died much too young, in their early seventies. They should have been here with us, enjoying the food and the conversation and their grandchildren. Sometimes it felt as if Patience and I were teenagers, trying to act like adults without them. Today especially I needed my parents to tell me what to do.

Finally we were turning onto Dune Road, driving past gazillion-dollar beach homes. Patience and Ben's vacation house came into view, a gray-shingled cottage with white trim and a wraparound porch. "Cottage" was a Hamptons word, a coy description of a house like theirs with seven bedrooms, four bathrooms, and cathedral ceilings. The pool was tucked off to the side, so as not to interfere with the view of the ocean out the front.

"I'd rather have a house in Amagansettt," Jane said airily, though at twenty-four she could barely afford the rent on her Manhattan apartment.

Colin snorted. "Save us a balcony room."

I laughed.

"Oh, brother," Hannah groaned, finally awake. I turned and saw she was scowling at the caterer's van parked in the circular drive. On its white side a carrot, a lamb, and an asparagus stalk joined hands in a jig.

Hannah was upset by the lamb dancing to its doom, and I wondered if all pre-veterinary students were vegetarians. At least today there would be a wider choice for her.

My own stomach was jumping, making me wonder how much I could eat myself.

Chapter 3

PATIENCE WAS AT her best when she had to do nothing more than be the perfect hostess. She appeared in the driveway as soon as we opened the car doors and hugged each of us warmly. Her light hair was swept back in its perfect French braid, and she had on a black cashmere turtleneck that emphasized a handcrafted silver necklace. I noticed how slender she looked in pin-striped slacks and wondered if I should get a pair.

When we were standing in the slate-tiled foyer, she asked if she could take my jacket for me.

"No, it's part of my *ensemble*."

"Of course."

When we were growing up in the parsonage in Princeton, we had people for lunch every Sunday after church. Twice a year Bishop Morrison and his wife came for Confirmation. When Patience and I were twelve and David Livingstone (no one ever called our brother just David) was ten, Mrs. Morrison tried to draw us into the conversation by asking what we wanted to be when we grew up.

I told her piously that I was going to be a missionary to Darkest Africa. I wanted to travel and I didn't know how else to get there. David said he was going to be a stunt pilot, and then she turned to my sister.

"And what do *you* want to be when you grow up, Patience?"

Pat smoothed the napkin in her lap. "Rich."

Of the three of us, she was the only one whose wish had come true, though David Livingstone seemed happy making weird films in L.A. and I had traveled the world with Colin.

My sister moved us toward the fieldstone fireplace and the wineglasses arranged on the coffee table in rows like a marching band.

"Where's Ben?" I asked.

Mild exasperation. "Upstairs taking a shower. He just got back from playing squash."

"On Thanksgiving?"

"You know how compulsive he is, Delhi. He has to play every day of the year no matter what. Come sit down."

I still didn't move. "Where are the girls?" Usually they would be there by now, admiring their older cousins, and all over me.

"Tara and Annie Laurie?"

"You have others?"

"They had an invitation to go skiing in Vail for the long week-end."

"Vail, Colorado?" I couldn't imagine letting my daughters, especially when they were barely teenagers, fly halfway across the country and miss a major holiday.

"They were *thrilled*." Our eyes flashed, then she said briskly, "Red or white?"

"I'll start with white."

Colin and Jane moved right into the Cabernet Sauvignon, and Hannah didn't drink, though today I wished she would. She was the one who would be most affected by what I had to say.

"This Chardonnay is lovely," I tempted her.

"*Mo-om*. You know I don't like wine."

"It's something you develop a taste for. As an adult," Jane said.

"As I can see you have," Hannah snapped.

"Exaggerate much?"

"Come on, girls. It's a holiday." *And you're not in junior high school like your cousins.*

"You got here!" Ben appeared, his dark curly hair damp, a white towel around his neck. He bore down on us like a city bus.

"You're not even dressed." Patience looked askance at his T-shirt and sweatpants.

Ignoring her, he came over to where I was warming myself by the fire. As always, he ran an appreciative hand through my long hair, using it to pull me toward him for a kiss. "Hey, beautiful. I don't know why Pat didn't get these curls."

"We both had straight hair when we were small. I don't know what happened to mine." I knew Ben fussed over me to irritate my sister, and sometimes I was glad. Though today, I didn't want to upset anyone. "How's Brooklyn?"

"Still there. Glad I bought it when I did."

Shorthand for Ben's shrewdness as a young man in guessing which areas would gentrify fastest and buying up whole blocks. Having a father willing to put up seed money had helped.

"Prices coming back?" Colin asked as Ben strode over to shake his hand.

"Yeah. I was lucky. They never dropped into the catastrophere."

Then he was hugging Jane and Hannah and complimenting

them, asking about their lives. Ben was their favorite uncle, albeit their only functioning one. Colin's sister had never married, and we rarely saw David Livingstone. We'd taken the children to see his magnum opus, *The Tomato That Ate Akron*, but they had not been impressed.

"Time to eat," Pat announced. "Ben, go get dressed! We're paying String Bean by the hour."

What was it about the very wealthy that let them spend a fortune on something extravagant, then suddenly decide they had better economize? It was like buying a yacht as big as an ocean liner, then refusing to sail it anywhere because fuel was so expensive.

THE TABLE WAS arranged in front of the window like Leonardo's *Last Supper* so that we all could have a view of the choppy gray-blue ocean and empty beach. As the hosts, Ben and Pat to the corner seats, so that they had to turn their heads to look out. Instead of saying grace as the twelve apostles might have, we lifted our glasses and toasted each other for being the people we were, then fell upon the miniature crab cakes. Two young women in white jackets and houndstooth pants next served us pumpkin bisque with corn sticks.

The main course was everything that Patience had promised: succulent turkey, sweet potatoes molded in the shape of a pumpkin with lines of pecans for the ridges, and a turkey-shaped cranberry mold. He kept his head, but tipped over as people dug into his sides.

A few bites and my appetite was gone. I decided to test the waters. "People are always telling me I look like someone they know. Their sister-in-law's sister or someone they met on a cruise. We must be a popular genetic type."

Patience and Jane looked surprised, but Hannah said, "It happens to me all the time. The first week of classes, this guy came up and gave me a big hug. *He* looked like Leonardo DiCaprio."

"Wow," Jane said. "Was it?"

"Naw." Hannah stabbed a broccoli floret. "But I wasn't who he thought either. Someone he met sailing right around here a couple years ago."

That jolted me. "Did he say what her name was?"

"Probably. But I don't remember."

"I have an opportunity for you," Ben broke in, helping himself to more oyster stuffing and grinning at me. "A friend of mine has an investigative agency, the largest on the island."

Of course, the largest. Ben only dwelt in superlatives.

"He's looking to expand into stolen artwork and books, so I was telling him about you. How smart you were and how you know everything about rare books. Do you have a business card I can give him?"

"You hate my business card." With Ben and the job opportunities he came up with for me I never knew whether he honestly believed I was the best for or if he just felt sorry for me.

A look of pretend disbelief infiltrated his dark eyes. "You still haven't gotten a new one?"

"I'm working on it." *A lie.* I happened to like my card with its image of my Siamese cat, Raj, sniffing at several leather-bound volumes, and the caption, "Got Books?" My pertinent information was on the back.

"Well, when you get something that looks professional, send me a few. No hurry, he won't be putting it together for a few months."

"Okay. Sure. Thanks." Although I didn't need anything else to do—I was busy with my book business and helping out when I was needed in my colleague Marty's bookshop—the idea of tracking down lost books instead of always trying to buy them to sell had a certain appeal.

"Would this be full-time?" Colin was looking for a way to get me gainfully employed with retirement benefits. I had already turned down his suggestions of being a food demonstrator at Trader Joe's and assisting at the university day care center. Since Colin had assured the director that working with small children was my first love, he had taken that refusal hard.

"*I was only trying to help you.*"

"*Do me a favor; don't help me.*"

Since he had been considering the possibility of our getting back together, he had been pressuring me to finish the B.A. he'd interrupted when I was nineteen.

"Of course it would be full-time," Ben assured him.

"Nothing wrong with that." The two men grinned at each other.

I drank more of the red wine I had switched to with the main course. When I was in college, I went to the boardwalk in Ocean City with several friends and visited a fortune-teller. I was already seeing Colin, a teaching assistant and fledgling archeologist, but was wondering if he was in the cards—so to speak. The Gypsy, a young woman who did not express herself well in English, said, "You will always be surrounded by people with money, but not you—you will never have any money yourself." It was not what I had come there to hear, but so far it had been true.

She had also promised me that love was waiting for me to claim it, a prediction that emboldened me to leave Douglas College at the end of my sophomore year and marry Colin. She hadn't predicted how long love would last.

When the dinner plates were being cleared, Patience pushed back her chair with the look of a gym teacher rousing a bunch of slugs. "Time for our walk!"

The tradition was to walk a mile or two on the dramatic winter beach, then come back and have dessert in front of the living room fire. When we were done, Colin, Ben, Jane, and the little girls would go outside and shoot baskets and the rest of us would nap.

I knew that once everyone was scattered, my chance would be past. "We can't. Not yet!"

Now that I had everyone's attention, I stared out at the ocean for inspiration. "This is all wonderful, but someone is missing."

"He could have been here if he weren't so stubborn," Colin said grimly.

"Not Jason."

"If you're talking about my daughters—" Trigger-happy as ever, Patience was ready for the fight.

"No, no, not the girls. I know they're off having fun. I'm talking about Caitlin."

A silence as palpable as the mist that was gathering at the edges of the beach, fell over the room.

"Who's Caitlin?" Hannah asked, bewildered.

Chapter 4

IN THE SILENCE I could hear the rattle of the dessert cart in the hallway and smell fresh-brewed coffee. Evidently Patience had not told them there would be a break between courses.

We sat as still as a photograph in a glossy magazine.

Then Colin came to life and grabbed my arm. "What are you *doing*? Why are you bringing this up now?"

"Who's Caitlin?" Hannah repeated.

"No one." Colin looked around me to our daughter. "Forget it, Hani. Your mother's just getting maudlin. She's had too much to drink."

"I'm not getting maudlin." I turned to Hannah on my other side, frantic to get the words out before Colin silenced me. "A long time ago you had a twin sister. She drowned when you were two—or so we believed. Jane was four and I was pregnant with Jason."

"I had a *what*?"

Colin groaned, a sound so primeval that I jumped. "Don't do

this," he hissed into my ear. I turned and our eyes locked, mine imploring, his unyielding. In that look were years of challenge, disappointment, and love.

In the momentary silence, the caterers emerged from the hall-way with the dessert cart. It was as if they had been lying in wait for a pause. We turned to stare at the cheesecake, pumpkin pie, and chocolate-dipped strawberries.

The young woman carrying a silver tray with the coffeepot and china cups gave me a curious look.

I could not imagine any of us eating dessert, but Colin and Ben helped themselves to everything. The rest of us agreed to black coffee.

As soon as the caterers had retreated to the kitchen, Jane looked around Colin at me. "I don't remember anything like that."

"We never talked about it. It didn't happen here; we were in England for six weeks. Dad was in an archeology program. We went to the same park every day."

Surely she was too young for the wrinkled lines creasing her forehead. "Were there swans and boats?"

"You never told me I had a twin?" Hannah broke in.

"We weren't trying to hide it from you . . ." Yet that was exactly what had happened.

I waited for Colin to explain to Hannah why he had insisted on our never mentioning Caitlin, why he hadn't wanted them to grow up under the shadow of death.

But he was staring out at the beach.

"What happened?" Jane asked.

I gave Colin a rapid glance, but he wasn't trying to stop me. "That day in the park everything was the same as always. Hannah was napping on the bench and you and Caitlin were playing. I was taking photos and—I got distracted. Caitlin suddenly disappeared and people thought she had fallen into the river."

Colin clattered his fork on the plate, startling everyone. "At least tell the *truth*. You were napping too."

I turned to look at him. "No. I wasn't. I know I said that but—it was all so crazy. I was afraid if I told you I was taking photos, you would have killed me."

In those days photography had been my passion, my way of escaping from the endless round of dirty diapers and runny noses and tears. At home, as soon as the children were in bed, I'd fled to my darkroom, working into the early hours printing and tinting photos. The quiet darkness was an addiction. As sleepy as I was during the day, I came alive in those night hours. It was the woman I would have been if I had never met Colin.

Growing up I had never daydreamed about having a family, of being surrounded by children. I'd read endlessly, imagined myself in exotic places, even saw myself as an archeologist or explorer. I loved the children fiercely, they were mine, but they were something I had taken for granted.

Until I lost one, due to my preoccupation. After that I never took another photograph.

"You thought falling asleep sounded *better*?" Colin was menacing beside me. I felt he might grab my shoulders and start shaking me.

I realized that I should have told him about the note first, that we should not be having this conversation in front of everyone. "I—yes. And after I kept saying it a part of me started believing it. When I finally admitted the truth and told someone else, she pointed out that if I was standing right by the water, I would have heard a splash or seen Caitlin fall in. And I was right by the edge of the river. I—"

"But I thought the police had investigated everything." Patience couldn't keep out of it any longer.

"Of course they did." Colin's voice was too loud for the alcove. "They interviewed everyone who'd had been in the park that day. We even hired a private detective. Who found nothing."

Through the miasma of wine and coffee I tried to remember what had been in the detective's report. Surely, for all the money we borrowed from Colin's parents to pay him, he had turned up *something.* "But the police never found her. They said that was unusual for that part of the Avon."

"But not impossible." Colin held up a professorial hand, a gesture he would have used to silence a classroom. Everyone looked at him, waiting. He addressed the girls first. "I'm sorry you had to learn this from someone in a drunken stupor. It's something that happened long ago. We didn't want you to grow up thinking something terrible would happen to you too. We didn't want it to overshadow your childhood. Losing your sister was the worst thing that ever happened to us. But your mother has conflated another day when she was taking pictures with the day it actually happened. Her memory is unreliable."

I was so furious that I couldn't think of which lie to address first. I was *not* in a drunken stupor. I was not mixing up the days. My memory was as good as anyone's. I told myself to calm down. I needed to explain why I was bringing it up now. "What I was doing that day isn't the point." I reached in my Mexican jacket pocket and pulled out the fragile blue envelope. "This is the point."

A rustling, a squeaking of chairs, as people shifted to look.

It was addressed to "Mr. and Mrs. Fitzhugh," which was odd

for two reasons. First, no one who knew Colin would address him as anything but Dr. Fitzhugh. Second, I had never taken Colin's name, keeping my own name, Laine, right from the start. They would know that, too. I had stared at the red and green stamps of Queen Elizabeth and a blurred postmark I could not read and been mildly curious. Curious the way someone would be when opening a letter from someone they did not know.

Now I pulled out the white paper inside, unfolded it, and laid it flat on the table so that the people closest to me could see. In large black letters it read:

YOUR DAUGHTER DID NOT DROWN.

When Colin and the girls had seen it, I passed it to Patience, who scanned it and gave it back so I could show it to Ben. "It came in the mail Monday," I said. "I can't tell what part of England it's from."

Colin picked up the envelope and studied it. Again, everyone seemed to be waiting for his official pronouncement. He did not disappoint them. "A mean trick. Someone's idea of a sadistic joke."

A sadistic joke? "But why now?" I argued, shocked. "Almost twenty years later? Who'd even know about it now?"

"Maybe they ran a story in the local papers," Ben said. "Maybe the detective who investigated the case is retiring or something."

"It wasn't like that," I said. And why would anybody track us all the way over here? It's not like it was a criminal investigation or anything. No policeman would be remembered for it."

"Maybe that's what the story was about then, people drowning in the river." Ben brightened as if he had solved the problem. I reminded myself he wasn't trying to be cruel. He just liked to fix things.

"They'd hardly go to the trouble of finding Delhi and Colin's address in another country," Patience said. "It sounds like they definitely know something."

"Can't we have the handwriting analyzed?" Jane interrupted. "Or have it dusted for fingerprints?"

Colin sighed, playing with a small glass salt shaker that had been left on the table. "It's hardly a criminal matter. Why would the police get involved? Besides, we're missing the point. Even if Caitlin survived, which she didn't, too much time has passed. It's too late. It's like an adoption, it's final."

"No!" It came out of me as a wail.

Patience gasped. "It is *not* like an adoption. If your daughter didn't drown, then she was kidnapped! She has every right to know her real family."

"Patsy"—Colin lapsed into her old nickname—"it's not that simple. You can't assume something as sinister as a kidnapping. If she didn't drown, she probably wandered off and someone found her."

"Daddy, what are you talking about?" Jane grasped his forearm. She was flushed, probably with Cabernet, and furious. As close as they were, she often lost her temper with Colin. "People don't keep lost children. They find a policeman and get them back to their parents! It's not like a stray kitten you decide to take in."

"No, Daddy's right," Hannah looked up from where she had been tormenting a cuticle. "How would you feel if someone contacted us and claimed after nineteen years that I had been stolen and was part of *their* family? That everything I'd thought was true was a lie and they wanted me to come live with them. Anyway, I don't want a twin. I'm fine just as I am."

Colin pushed back from the table. "I think it's time for us to go."

"But we haven't had our walk," Ben protested. "We have to take our beach walk!"

Poor Ben. If he'd been on the *Titanic*, he would have demanded his nightly whiskey as the ship went down.

"Yes, go on your walk. I have to show Delhi something of our mother's that I found. We'll catch up," said Pat.

I knew we wouldn't.

"Can I see?" Jane asked eagerly.

Patience and I exchanged a look.

"Sure," I told her.

Chapter 5

I HAD NOT been in Patience's bedroom in years. A king-sized bed was positioned to face a balcony with a view of the sea. Except for a Fairfield Porter painting of geraniums in a blue jar on the wall, everything in the room was white.

Pat gestured at the coverlet, puffy as marshmallow foam, and Jane and I sat down side by side on the bed. She pulled up a boudoir chair opposite us. We were so close that I could see the faint lines starting to surround her blue eyes like crazing on china. "So?"

I sighed. "To begin with, I didn't 'conflate' any memories. It was stupid to lie to about being asleep, but—it was all so horrible, everyone blaming me, I didn't know what I was saying half the time. I was already soaking wet from jumping in the river trying to find her." I suddenly remembered a man, shocked at my swollen stomach, trying to hold me back. Me screaming, "My baby fell in!" and wrenching away from him to plunge into the murk with no idea of how deep the water was.

The horror and devastation had faded until a few years ago

when I read a short story about a young woman who went down to the English seaside for vacation, a single mother with a toddler son. She met a young man who was renting a cottage with his mother, and they were attracted to each other. One night they were down by the water with her little boy in tow, and finally fell passionately into each other's arms. After several minutes, she remembered her son and pulled away to find him. But all she could see was the endless ocean. The story had brought everything crashing back, the sense of helplessness, the blame.

Was I really being given another chance?

"People must have seen her fall in," Pat said.

I shook my head "Jane was the only one. And then she changed her story."

Beside me the bed jolted. "*I* did?"

"You came running up to me and told me she was in the water. Then that night you said a 'bad lady' took her and kept talking about a bunny."

"What bad lady? What bunny?"

"I don't know, sweetheart."

"Why can't I remember?" Jane agonized. "Something so important? And why didn't you ever talk about her?"

I sighed. All I wanted to do just then was lie back on that puffy bed and sleep. I pictured myself pulling part of the comforter over me like a cocoon. "You heard what Dad said. He didn't want it hanging over us, defining your childhood. Mourning her at every holiday, the fact that she wasn't there and we could never be complete as a family. He didn't want us to be like those people whose little girl was kidnapped in Portugal, the McCanns, who've given up their lives to try and find her."

Patience was nodding, but Jane seemed appalled. "And you agreed with him?"

"Jane, I was your age. I felt so guilty about letting it happen, I would have done anything he asked. Sometimes I wondered if *he* had been the one responsible, would I have forgiven him. I don't know." Did Colin's years of refusing to treat me as an adult—his moving out last year—all go back to Caitlin?

I struggled on. "When you and Hannah stopped asking about Caitlin, it just seemed easiest not to bring it up. Dad wanted to put it behind us and move on." It sounded heartless, but there were precedents. After Teddy Roosevelt's young wife died of childbirth fever, he never spoke her name aloud again. Henry Adams's beloved wife, Clover, who killed herself, was never mentioned in his memoirs, making him seem a lifelong bachelor. Men who felt they had a purpose in life, who kept their emotions private . . . "He wanted to keep it from hijacking your childhood." I put my arm around her and hugged her against me. "Was that so bad?"

"No. I had a great childhood. Something was always there though, something melancholy that I couldn't quite remember, but I just thought that was normal. Did you feel the way he did? About wanting to forget it?"

I knew what she was asking: *If it had been me, would you have forgotten me and moved ahead with your life?*

I told her the truth. "I never got over it, not really. I was busy, we had some wonderful times, but it never went away. If I'd thought it was upsetting you, I would have talked about it."

"I always wondered why Colin told us never to say anything," Patience said. "I just thought it was because it was so horrible he

didn't want any reminders. My girls don't even know. But now—
that note makes it sound like she could still be alive."

"I know. Bianca Erickson was the one who pointed out that if I
was standing by the river I would have heard something."

Patience knew Bianca socially. *I* knew her from analyzing her
father's book collection and finding out that what had happened
to Nate Erikson and Bianca's daughter had been deliberate, not a
tragic accident. It had taken the murder of another family member
to shine a light on the darker corners of the illustrator's family life.
My final encounter with the murderer had brought me perilously
close to my own death.

"And what Hannah mentioned happening to her at Cornell," I
went on. "It's not the first time."

When Hannah was twelve, a friend of mine had called, excited.
"I didn't know you were skiing in Colorado too."

I had been in Denver once, but never on skis.

"We could have gotten together for dinner!"

"Diane, we weren't in Colorado."

"You must have been. We saw Hannah on the slopes. On the
chairlift actually."

"I don't think so."

"I *know* it was Hannah. She always ducks her head in that cute
way when she laughs. I looked for her when we got to the bottom,
but I never saw her again. I never saw any of you either."

"Because we weren't there."

"Huh."

Yet her insistence had lit a tiny flame. *What if . . .* What if Caitlin had somehow miraculously survived. If the Stratford-upon-
Avon police could speculate that she must have gotten caught on a
branch and been held underwater so that her body never surfaced,

I could imagine her somehow staying afloat, being carried downstream and rescued by someone in a boat. My fantasy had broken down at that point but it didn't matter. Since then I had never lost the sense that she might somehow still be alive.

I had questioned Diane extensively, trying to get her to remember any other details, any passing impressions. "You said she looked like Hannah when she laughed. What made her laugh?"

"Oh. The man on the bench with her, I guess. I was surprised that it wasn't Colin, but I thought you must be there with friends. He was about Colin's age, but that's all I remember."

About Colin's age . . .

It was probably nothing at all.

"I guess I should have told Colin first. But I was afraid he'd react, well, like he did."

"I don't get him at all," Patience said.

"He doesn't like to have his life upset. Especially when there's no guarantee of anything."

"Mom and Daddy warned you about Colin."

What was she talking about? "Only that they thought I was too young." I was transported back to the parsonage where my gentle parents begged me to stay in school.

"If he loves you, he'll wait."

But I knew he wouldn't.

"They didn't like that he didn't believe in God."

"They didn't like that anybody didn't believe in God."

Outside the French balcony doors, dark clouds were moving in. "I'm really surprised at Hannah," I said. "I thought she'd be excited to find out she had a twin. Remember it, I mean. I know *I* would have been."

But it occurred to me as I said it that growing up I would have traded being Pat's twin for any decent offer—a cheeseburger, say, or a new headband. She must have been thinking the same because our eyes met and we smiled. How could we share the same genes and been so different? We had been like puppies trapped together in a burlap sack, fighting to get out.

"Why don't I have a twin?" Jane said plaintively. "Now everyone has one but me."

It was so absurd that Pat and I started to laugh. "We'll find you one," I promised.

But our laughter died as if we had remembered at the same time the reality of the situation. What if, miracle of miracles, Caitlin were really still alive—my bright, inquisitive baby, the child Colin called "the city that never sleeps." Caitlin who would slow down long enough only to crawl into my lap and be cuddled, lifting her head so I could kiss her downy hair. A wave of nausea, a threatened upheaval of everything provided by the Golden String Bean.

"We have to look for her, Mom."

"I know—but how?" There were seven billion people in the world, millions and millions in the United States alone. And if she didn't even know she needed to be found . . .

"You'll find a way."

I'll find a way? "Wait. Just wait. It can't be just me. If I could do this myself, I already would have."

"I don't mean just you." Jane straightened up and leaned over to press my hand. "I'm in."

Patience moved over and put her hands on top of ours. "Me too."

Chapter 6

As soon as we were back in the car driving home, Hannah leaned forward and demanded, "Why aren't there any pictures of me with this 'twin'?"

I turned in the passenger seat so I could see her. Hannah's face had filled out since the summer; I thought she looked prettier now. "There are. We put them away."

I couldn't remember all these years later if Colin had ordered me to store the albums, tiny dresses, and Caitlin's special toys in cartons, or if I had been unable to bear coming across them.

"I want to see them." I couldn't tell if she was eager or still skeptical.

"We'll look at them as soon as we get home." I could picture exactly where the boxes were, hidden in the barn behind the farmhouse where I stored the six thousand books I had listed for sale on the Internet. I spent most of my time there at my worktable, describing a book's physical condition, its printing information and content, and pricing it for sale, then uploading it to the bookselling sites, AbeBooks or via Libri. The barn was my comfort zone, heated in winter and sweltering in summer, furnished with a worn couch and Oriental rugs from my parents' home. When I'd claimed, it I'd put art posters on the rough walls of artists I liked: Magritte, van Gogh, Fairfield Porter.

"*Delhi*," Colin warned. It was a voice meant to bring me to my senses.

"What? What? It's not a secret now. It's her twin, for God's sake!"

Colin paused, turning onto Montauk Highway. "I agree that she should see the photos, but as a tragic event from the past. Where it's going to stay buried."

"I thought you were an archeologist." A silly thing to say.

"I uncover artifacts to learn about past civilizations, not to destroy innocent lives."

Jane broke in immediately. "That's crazy! Whose life are you talking about?"

He turned and gave her a stern look. "A young woman just like you who probably isn't even alive. But if she were, this would devastate her world. Not to mention that it's perfect fodder for the tabloids. Talk about destroying people's lives."

"Is that all you can think about?" I broke in. "How it would inconvenience *you?*"

"At least I'm doing some thinking."

"*I'm* thinking. It could have a happy ending."

"Trust me. It won't."

He sounded so certain that I pressed my arms against my ribs, chilled. What did he know that I didn't? "Colin?"

In the darkness I saw him focus on driving. "The subject is closed from now on. Show the girls the photos if you have to. But we're dropping it after that."

"No. We're not. Unless you know something you're not telling me."

"We're dropping it because Hannah doesn't want to pursue it. Do you, Hani?"

I turned and stared at my younger daughter pressed sullenly into the corner of the backseat. I tried to read what was behind her slow head shake.

I didn't know. But I would have to find out.

AFTER COLIN LEFT us at the farmhouse and went on to his rented condo, Hannah wanted only to sleep.

"Don't you want to look at the photos?" I asked.

"Tomorrow."

"I have to be at the bookstore during the day. It'd have to be at night."

"I want to see them *now*," Jane protested.

"We'll do it as a family. Tomorrow night." Suddenly that suited me. I needed more time to prepare myself to see Caitlin's tiny dresses, her silver baby cup, and God-knew-what-else was stored with the pictures that I had forgotten about. It would be a painful, tearing-the-scab-off experience.

"I can't tomorrow night. I have plans in the city."

I gave Jane a look.

"Oh, okay. I'll stick around. Do I have a choice?"

Hannah had already scooped up Raj, our ten-year-old Siamese cat, and was cuddling him. "Who's my baby?" she crooned, bringing her face down to his. Raj swooned.

Miss T, our larger, younger tabby, looked up from the doorway. She jumped into my lap once in a while but would never allow the liberties Hannah took.

After Hannah and Raj had escaped to bed, Jane and I sat in the kitchen, drinking coffee. Not one thing in the room had changed since Jane's childhood, not the scarred oak table we were sitting at, the white enamel sink on legs, or the harvest gold appliances that only worked when they felt like it. Patience had insisted that we take home pumpkin pie and half the cheesecake, and we filled our plates, ravenous now.

"Hani doesn't know what she's missing," Jane said, cutting another sliver of cheesecake.

"She can have some for breakfast."

"If there's any left."

"Why do you think she doesn't want to look for Caitlin?"

Jane considered, fork halfway to her mouth. "I don't know. But you and she have never been on the same wavelength."

I set my cup back down. How could she say that? It sounded tragic, a lifetime of missed signals. Was it true? I remembered all the times I had been impatient with Hannah's declarations, her overdramatization of the ways she was mistreated, her exaggeration of her own shortcomings or the plight of animals. When she was growing up everything had been either magic or tragic. There had never been any neutral ground between, any time when she just shrugged and said, "Oh, well." It was hard to remember times when she and I had felt bonded in shared feeling.

I took a sip of coffee and considered something else. Had I held her at arm's length *because* of Caitlin? Had that loss, instead of making us closer, made me afraid of losing her too? Or had I compared her diffidence to Caitlin's early charm? Had I ever felt, God help me, that the wrong twin had drowned?

I caged that thought immediately and tossed it down a ravine. Not true.

Chapter 7

THE NEXT MORNING I left before 9 a.m. to open Port Lewis Books. I was sorry I had agreed to spend the day in the shop. I felt too keyed up by everything that had happened yesterday and would go on happening. But I had promised my friend Susie Pevney that I would cover for her so she could fly home to South Dakota for Thanksgiving.

I still thought of the bookstore as the Old Frigate, which it had been known as until last July. The name had been a nod to our village's sailing history and to Emily Dickinson, whose portrait hung beside the door. The poet had had no connection with Long Island or sailing other than to write, "There is no frigate like a book to take us lands away," but she remained on the wall, pale and frowning, our patron saint. She might have been bemused that the village's historic streets were now filled with souvenir shops, yogurt stands, and tarot card readers, all meant to entertain day-trippers who took the ferry over from Connecticut.

I bought a large cappuccino at the Whaler's Arms next door, then unlocked the bookstore. The new owner, Marty Campagna, had wisely kept the former furnishings. The leather couch, Oriental rugs, and wing chairs arranged around the fireplace gave the room the look of a British men's club. Marty's best books were kept on the shelf behind the sales counter. His second-best spilled into the open bookcases, a few even stored in the room behind this one where my books were. Susie's books, which Marty couldn't bear to look at, were kept in the back room. Susie had suggested serving coffee, but Marty vetoed that. "Not around *my* books. Let them go to Starbucks if they're thirsty."

The shop was soon filled with visitors enjoying the festive holiday weekend. They entered merrily, red-cheeked from the wind off the water, rubbing their hands and moving toward the fire in the grate.

Just before noon, a young woman in a black cashmere coat swept in, trailed by two children in scruffy parkas and sneakers. The boy looked to be about six, the girl younger. The woman's black hair was lacquered around her face like a Japanese doll's, eyelashes thickly coated, lips a 1940s red. Somehow the look worked.

"Where's your children's section?" A burst of musky perfume.

I stepped around the counter. "We don't have a special section, but kids' books are kept in back. I'll show you."

Leading them into the last room, I pointed to two low shelves with a ragtag collection of picture books and grade school paperback series. Marty had scoffed when Susie brought them in, claiming that they demeaned the atmosphere of the shop, but Susie insisted that children needed something to look at while their parents browsed.

Susie had been right.

"You don't have any little tables and chairs?" The woman raised dark penciled eyebrows.

"No. I'm sorry." Perhaps, I thought, I should mention it to Marty and watch him implode.

"Doesn't matter. Okay, kids, pick out a book and get comfortable on the floor," she instructed. "I'll be back in an hour."

"Wait." I didn't move from where I stood in the archway. "You can't just leave them."

"They're no trouble. They'll just read."

"But you can't leave them here on their own."

"Why not?" Her expression told me to get a life. "They'll be fine. They're very responsible. If they'd come in alone, you wouldn't have thrown them out."

She had been edging toward me, and we were face-to-face now, so close that I could see that her red lipstick was two different shades, darker on the outside. I caught a whiff of that perfume again.

"Sorry, but I'm late." She tried to step around me. "I came over here specifically for this lunch date."

"If you leave your kids, I'll have to report it."

Where had *that* come from? On a different day, I might have settled the children on chairs in the front room, served them milk and cookies, and found them books they liked. I couldn't imagine making a phone call to the authorities. It was not like I had been Mother of the Year.

Yes, and you paid the price for it.

We weren't talking about a moment of inattention here anyway. I knew she would be gone at least an hour.

I stayed in the doorway like a bouncer at a Hollywood club.

When she could see no way to get past me, she said. "Oh, come on, kids. This mean lady won't let you stay. We'll find somewhere else."

"You said there'd be *toys*," the boy grumbled.

"We'll find some."

I wondered if she would try to take them up the street to Howard Riggs, the other bookshop in town. Compared to Howard, I was Mary Poppins.

She had a few words for me on their way out, the mildest of which were, "I'll tell everyone not to come to your shop. I'll post it on Facebook!"

I knew that would upset Marty not at all.

Chapter 8

I PLANNED TO pick up a rotisserie chicken and enough different salads that Hannah would not feel slighted but decided to stop at home first to see if the girls were in the mood for anything different.

Jane was in the living room in Colin's wing chair, frowning at her phone. The furniture was as soft and faded as a stage set from *Death of a Salesman*. There was a striped tuxedo-style sofa from Colin's parents, maroon and beige, several wing chairs, an oak rocker that had been in the farmhouse when we moved in, and portraits of my great-grandparents behind convex glass. The dry, dusty smell of summer attics was always in the room, though I tried to cover it with pine or citrus air fresheners when we were having company.

Jane looked up. "Ryan isn't happy that I canceled tonight."

"You called him?"

"Sent a text. We were going to a cast party."

"Where's Hannah? Upstairs?" I suddenly felt anxious about seeing her. She had had more time to process yesterday's huge revelation. Would she decide she wanted to find Caitlin after all? Would she blame me for carelessly losing her sister?

Jane shook her head so emphatically that her light hair bounced against her face. "She's having dinner with Daddy. He picked her up a few minutes ago."

"Are you kidding?" Then I added belatedly, "You could have gone too. I would have been okay."

"Nope. Wasn't invited."

"Really? He asked her and not you?" It was bad enough that Colin had co-opted Hannah in the struggle over Caitlin, but to ignore Jane was unprecedented. Evidently she was being punished for siding with me.

"He insisted she put on something decent, but she hadn't brought anything."

I sank onto the striped sofa. "What did she do?"

Jane grinned. "She found this thrift store upstairs."

"You mean my closet?"

"Well, I wasn't going to let her stretch out any of *my* things."

"You think she's put on weight?"

"*Mom.* I doubt that she's hiding bales of cotton under there."

"I just thought she looked healthy. I was thinking, I could pick up a chicken and some salads if you'd like."

Jane made a face. "What would you be having if I wasn't here?"

"After working at the bookshop all day? Probably something unhealthy."

"Bring it on."

TACO BELL HAD probably not intended for their burritos to be washed down with lime margaritas, but Jane insisted on stopping at the liquor store on the way home.

"After yesterday I'm sick of wine," she announced, and I didn't argue.

When we got back we ate sprawled on the old Oriental rug in the living room. Our plan to look at the albums after dinner was as tangible in the room as third diner. I was glad Jane didn't mention it. I thought of myself as easygoing, not given to emotional extremes or hysteria, but as I sipped the sweet fruity drink my emotions were running as wild as brats at a birthday party. If the girls decided they didn't want to see the albums after all, I would feel let down—and relieved. I knew I would be reliving every day, every feeling, behind each photograph.

When we were folding up the yellow wrappers, Jane said, "Let's get started."

"You mean with the albums? But Hannah's not here yet."

"We'll have everything ready for her." She looked at me with patient amusement. "You can't keep putting it off."

"I'm not putting it off."

"Yes, you are. We want to find Cate, remember, and we want Hannah on our side. Besides, I'm dying to see those photos!" She gave me a teasing, margarita-fueled look. "This isn't just about you, you know."

"I know." But going through those early years would be excruciating.

The albums and mementos were stored in two Del Monte crates with a blue-script logo on the side advertising canned peaches. I had hidden the boxes beneath cartons of books, classics that I would never get around to listing online. I had been certain that *The Three Musketeers* and *The Mill on the Floss* would discourage the curious from looking further.

Jane helped me carry the boxes in from the barn and set them down on the rug. We knelt down beside them. I stared at the way the cardboard flaps curled up, how shabby the cartons seemed. I could at least have stored them better. It seemed careless, disrespectful.

"Well, go on," Jane encouraged.

"I will." But my hand stayed where it was.

"It's okay to feel sad."

"It's more than sad. It's going to hurt."

"Come on, Mom. You *know* we're going to find her. Think of this as the first step in the process."

I thought of the billions of people in the world, both alive and dead. But I said, "You're right."

Still I teared up immediately, unpacking a tiny pink dress my mother had hand-smocked. By the time I came across a sweater that Patience had had made with "CAITLIN" knitted under a black Scottie, my eyes were streaming.

How different our lives could easily have been. If only. If Colin hadn't gotten that archeology fellowship. If only one of the girls had had the sniffles and we hadn't gone to the park that day. If only I had been paying more attention. The twins would have grown up together, we would have been an intact family; we would have known nothing but the ordinary joys and setbacks. We might even have had the additional children that Colin had wanted before it happened.

Could this be the chance—not to change the past, of course— but to make the future what it was meant to have been?

"They're so small," Jane marveled, running her hands over the pieces of clothing. "I can't believe we were ever that small."

"I saved your things too."

"Did you really? Funny, I don't think of you as sentimental. And you're certainly not a hoarder."

"I don't know what I am."

What I dreaded most was unpacking the worn white lamb Caitlin had insisted on sleeping with, though she usually left Sheepie home during the day. When I did unwrap the little animal from its white tissue slumber, I held it tightly against my chest, then brought it to my face to see if any scent still lingered. Anything from my little one at all—a sniff of baby powder or the sweetness of the graham crackers she loved. There had to be *something* left behind. But I could pick out only the dry, powdery smell that I identified with books long-stored in attics.

My tears dropped on the matted wool.

Sheepie was the key. If we ever found Caitlin, would seeing him stir any deeply buried memories? Would it reach down to the place where language had not yet existed and let her realize the truth of what we were telling her? Hannah hadn't had a favorite animal. She'd had a blanket she called Boo which she would never be separated from. She had been curled up with Boo on the bench the day everything happened.

I didn't wail or collapse on the floor, just let the tears continue to run down my face. It was as if I had been storing them up for years, waiting for the time I would be free to release them without Colin scolding me. Now and then Jane reached over and squeezed my arm.

The photo albums were in the second carton we opened. When I had crept home from Stratford with one less child—I gave birth to Jason a month later—I hadn't separated out Caitlin's photos from the others; I had just shoved all the albums into this box. So there were photos of themselves as little girls that Hannah and Jane had never seen.

Jane turned the pages wonderingly. "I can't believe how alike the twins looked. Did they act identical too?"

"No, not at all. Caitlin was always the adventurous, outgoing one. She loved new things, meeting new people. Hannah was more clingy." Whiny as well, but it sounded unfair to say after my conversation with Jane last night.

At the bottom of the carton were some eight-by-ten black-and-white photos that I had taken and developed myself. There weren't many of the girls, I had concentrated professionally on slice-of-life scenes from the world around me. The photo that wasn't here was my favorite, the twins sitting facing each other in the grass, gravely exchanging daffodils. I had let myself keep that one hidden in a portfolio in the barn.

Jane and I both jumped when we heard the kitchen door open, caught out, though we weren't doing anything wrong. I suddenly felt we should have waited for Hannah to be here before opening the boxes.

She appeared in the living room archway and removed her blue down jacket, revealing my black velvet blazer and white turtleneck. She looked fine in it. Only my black corduroy pants were suffering, straining across her thighs and unfastened at the waist. "Whatcha up to?"

"Where did you have dinner?"

"The Mexican place. Are those the photos?" She came over and knelt down next to me, then reached over and picked up the little dress. "*I* was never that small."

"Oh, yes, you were. I have an identical dress of yours in mint green."

Hannah's hand moved restlessly through the other clothes, then she picked up a photo album with yellow chicks on a baby blue background. Neither Jane nor I said anything as she turned the pages.

"Wow," Hannah said softly. "I can't believe what I'm seeing. We really *did* look alike. I didn't know what to think when you told me, but—I'm not even sure which one is me!" She turned the album around and showed me the pair of them in winter jackets at the top of a slide.

I knew immediately. Caitlin was the triumphant one in front, Hannah clinging to her sister's waist and looking terrified. In most of the photos I could separate the twins by their expressions.

"My hair is darker now," Hannah said dubiously, as if she was not sure she was the baby in the photographs. Over the years her hair had gone from dandelion fluff to a rich, wavy gold. She didn't treat it like the treasure it was, most of the time jerking it back into a careless ponytail.

"*Her* hair's probably darker too," Jane said. "I bet you still look alike though."

"I bet we don't."

"Why wouldn't you?"

"Oh—she's probably thin and gorgeous. She'd think I was disgusting."

"Stop eating dorm food then. By the time we find her you could lose twenty pounds."

"Jane, stop! Hannah, you look fine," I protested. "You're beautiful and healthy and that's what counts."

She pushed herself up. "It's not just that. What if you find her and she's the daughter you've always wanted? What if you love her more than me? You always did."

It was the kind of comment from Hannah that could make me crazy. But I held myself in check. "Considering you don't even remember her, why would you think I loved her more? And for the record, I didn't."

"Whatever. I have to study."

"But you do want to find her, don't you?" Jane asked.

"I *told* you. I'm not interested." And she was gone.

Jane looked at me over the pathetic little pile of memories. "Now what?"

Chapter 9

SUNDAY AFTERNOON HANNAH's ride came to take her back to Ithaca, and Jane took the train to Manhattan. There had been no more conversations with Hannah about Caitlin. I wanted to call Colin and ask him why he had excluded Jane from dinner, but I tried to pick my battles as carefully as he did.

Port Lewis Books was closed Sundays and Mondays so I did not have to fill in for Susie. It was just as well. People had already started ordering books for Christmas from Secondhand Prose: signed copies of John Updike and Kurt Vonnegut, first editions of Ayn Rand and John Steinbeck. I had gotten a gratifying number of orders to fill over the weekend. I tried to rein in my pleasure by reminding myself that December orders had to carry the lean months that followed, but even that did not dampen the relief the sales brought.

The orders also made me feel that I could do *something* right, that I was more than a person who wrecked families, who could not keep children safe. I let myself admit how crushing the last few days had been.

On Tuesday morning I stopped at Port Lewis Books before it opened to find out how Susie's Thanksgiving visit to South Dakota had gone and to let her know what had happened while she was away. I picked up my usual cappuccino from the Whaler's Arms, and we sat down on the leather sofa facing the fireplace.

"We should build a fire," Susie said dreamily, leaning back, her eyes closed. She was wearing a new Crazy Horse sweatshirt, and looked as radiant as sunrise over the mountains. Instead of her usual scruffy ponytail, her light brown hair fell in waves around her face.

"Everyone's good?" I asked.

"They're great. My sister's kids are getting so big! It's time to have one of my own."

It was Susie's yearning to move ahead with her life that had made me suggest to Marty that she work in the bookshop. After he bought it, he had decided he wanted me to manage everything and had taken it badly when I refused to give up Secondhand Prose. He had been resistant to Susie, but I knew she would be good—and needed the income.

Susie Pevney and her husband, Paul, were part of the Long Island bookselling community. They had unfortunately been nicknamed the Hoovers by the other dealers for their habit of arriving at the end of a sale when the remaining books were cheapest, and vacuuming up cartons of them. The books they scarfed up were the ones other dealers ran screaming from. Susie had been listing those books for pennies on eBay and spending the rest of her time at the post office mailing them. It was, she had claimed, like being a gerbil in a classroom cage.

Marty finally capitulated when I promised to be involved with the shop too. But Paul Pevney remained opposed to Susie working here, complaining as loudly as if she were selling her body on Harbor Street. He had been forced into working at Home Depot to keep from losing their home, but insisted it was only temporary, only until they got their bookselling business going. Paul believed that every book was worth something and would only appreciate in value. If it didn't sell on eBay now, wait ten years. Like a stubborn child with a broken toy, he kept insisting that all they needed to make it work was faith—and Susie working harder.

"Paul doesn't seem to have noticed that I've been squirreling away most of the money I make here. He has good health coverage through Home Depot."

"That's great." Traditionally booksellers didn't.

But she suddenly looked as if the sun had gone in. "All he wants to do is be a full-time bookseller and not worry about a family. He doesn't realize that I'm thirty-one and it's time."

I nodded and finished my coffee. I hoped it would work out for her.

Although I knew that Christmas orders were still piling up on my computer in the barn, I lingered in the bookshop, curious to talk to Marty. He had spent the weekend at a two-day book auction in Charleston, one of the most prestigious in the South.

He appeared at noon, pushing the door back with a bang. "My books get here yet?"

"The books you bought? When did you send them?" I was sitting on the leather sofa now, filling orders on my laptop.

"Yesterday."

"There you go. How was the auction?"

"Not too shabby. When they got over not wanting to sell to me."

I glanced at Marty in his scruffy black leather jacket, his red

"Cappy's Cadillac Repair" T-shirt showing underneath. He was tall and attractive, but his black-framed glasses were taped at the bridge, and his dark curly hair was overlong. Picturing him among the old boys' club of book dealers in velvet dinner jackets, I laughed.

They hadn't known—how could they—that Marty had inherited family money. His grandfather was one of the first cesspool pump owners in Suffolk County and had created his own chemical process to dissolve waste faster. At the perfect moment Mario Campagna had sold the formula to a national company. Campagna cesspool trucks still patrolled Long Island, showing a mischievous little king perched on a toilet with the slogan, "We turn your waste into gold!" Gold for the Campagnas in any case.

Marty sprawled in a wing chair, hands behind his head, looking pleased with himself. "This lackey followed me around while I was inspecting the books, then when the auction got under way and I started to bid, the head guy came up and asked me how I planned to pay."

"What did you do?"

Marty grinned. "Showed him the money."

I had seen Marty's wad of bills at sales and could picture him pulling the handful of folded hundreds from his jeans pocket. "One of these days you're going to get mugged."

"Not to worry, blondie."

With perfect recall, he went on to describe every book he had bid on and won. The prize had not been a book at all, but a letter written by Jefferson Davis.

"Funny thing for a Yankee to want," I said.

"It was a steal."

He stood up and moved around the counter to gloat over his best books. They weren't under lock and key, but were shown only to serious buyers.

"Hey, good. Somebody snapped up that history of the Kansas Regiments and the signed first edition *Kon-Tiki*. I should go away more often."

"No, they didn't." I would have noticed sales for over a thousand dollars. "But the *Tom Sawyer Abroad* sold for $325."

He waved that away as if it were a half-eaten bagel. "Did you move them somewhere else?"

"I haven't touched them."

"Did *she*?"

"Susie?" I called.

She came in from the next room where she had been straightening stock.

"Have you seen *Kon-Tiki*?" I asked.

"It's on the shelf. Or was," she added, seeing our faces.

We searched every shelf behind the counter. There were no obvious gaps where the books had been, though everything seemed a little more spread out.

"Who was working?" Marty demanded.

"Me. And I was in this room all the time." Yet that wasn't entirely true. I had been in back several minutes showing the woman from the ferry where the children's books were. Had it been a ruse? Maybe she had never planned to leave her children. Maybe it had only been a distraction while her accomplice pilfered the most valuable books. But if so, why only take two? You could get away with at least four without anyone knowing for days. Granted, you'd have to know where they were located, but someone could have scoped the bookshop out earlier.

Yet I had not heard the bell over the door chime when I was in back.

"What the hell? They were here when I left!"

I believed that. Marty's phenomenal memory was one thing that made him so successful as a book buyer. He devoured references and catalogs and never forgot a single detail of anything he read.

I stared at him, guilty. It must have been on my watch. Maybe I wasn't as competent as I had been reassuring myself. "Who would come in and steal just those two? No one was even behind the counter to look at books." But someone must have been. "They have to be around."

"They'd better."

Or else.

Chapter 10

WHEN I WAS thirteen I believed in reincarnation, that people could be regressed back to past lives. I had stumbled on *The Search for Bridey Murphy* on a library shelf and went on a quest, tracking down all the other past-lives books it had spawned. I was enthralled. The writers had traveled back through something called hypnotic regression. As I lay in the porch swing that summer, knees up supporting the book of the day, I was actually in famine-ridden Ireland or medieval France.

My father patiently pointed out why reincarnation was impossible.

Granted the Bible was his authority, but he was persuasive enough to make me give up my fantasy of being an Egyptian princess darting among the pyramids. What remained was the knowledge that people could be age-regressed to earlier times in their own lives.

I woke up thinking about it the next morning. Why had we never regressed Jane back to that day in the park? Probably because we hadn't thought of it. Even if we had, we would have felt that making her relive her sister's drowning would be too traumatic, too horrible for her. There had been no reason to doubt that that she had watched Caitlin go in the water and drown. Until now.

Even now the "proof"—five words from England—was as tenuous as a whisper overheard in an airport. We needed to find out what had happened that day.

Could we do it? Jane was an adult now, and if she was willing to undergo the experience . . . As the only eyewitness, she could tell us what actually happened that afternoon. If she had seen her sister tumble into the water, Caitlin would return to sad memory, at least known now to her sisters. Colin would be spared the notoriety he seemed to fear. Hannah could focus on finishing her senior year at Cornell without having to worry about a beautiful doppelganger.

And me? I would have to accept the inevitability that one moment of inattention could lose a rare book. Or a child.

But what if the outcome were different? What if Jane remembered that afternoon differently and could tell us more about the "bad lady" she had been obsessed with that night. I still had no idea how we would find Caitlin, but it might give us some clues.

THE FIRST OF December found me in Dr. Karl Lundy's office, asking him about age regression. Finding a good hypnotist—one that I felt comfortable about consulting—had been a challenge. I'd considered asking people I knew at the university for a recommendation, but was afraid it would get back to Colin. He would be furious with me, not just because I was pursuing the truth about Caitlin after he had declared the search off-limits, but because he scoffed at hypnosis, visualization, and healing by prayer or "pink light."

Most of all, he would be worried about the damage it might do to Jane.

So I turned to the Internet. I studied the qualifications of hypnotists in the area and finally called one who was a trained psychologist. He had gotten his doctorate from Columbia and had a collection of positive reviews. Even so, I planned to interview him thoroughly, to make sure I would not be putting this daughter in any emotional danger.

Karl Lundy was intrigued by what I was asking. He warned me not to tell him the details of the day it happened. "Subjects under hypnosis want to please. They pick up cues and say what they think you want to hear. If I knew what you were looking for, I might convey cues without meaning to."

"Is there any danger?"

He chuckled at that. "Not at all. Your daughter will be aware of what is happening the whole time. If anything, she'll probably be more relaxed and refreshed afterward than she's been in weeks."

"Is it okay if I sit in?"

"Not a problem, Ms. Laine." He went on to tell me a story about a young woman who was so short-tempered with her children that she and her husband sought counseling and then hypnosis, suspecting her abusiveness had roots in her childhood. As her horrified husband watched, she was regressed to age eight when she had brought home a stray kitten and her father had beaten her and strangled the cat.

"She had no conscious memory of that," Dr. Lundy said. "But when she remembered, she knew it was true and she was able to redirect her anger at her father, not her kids. It gave her husband a better understanding of what was going on."

I shivered. "Do a lot of people have things they don't remember?"

"A lot," he agreed. "Most of us, in fact."

I tried to imagine what mine could be.

JANE WAS ENTHUSIASTIC when I called her. "I never would have thought of that. Can we film it?"

"I don't have a camcorder."

"No, on my phone. I want to be able to watch it afterward."

Would she really want to see it if it confirmed that she'd watched her sister drown?

But we asked anyway. Dr. Lundy said that he would audiotape the process, using built-in, state-of-the-art equipment, since videotaping it would be too distracting. "You can get everything you need by hearing the process."

I doubted that, since gestures and facial expressions are so crucial. But I would be there to see it. I didn't know how living through that terrible day again would make me feel, but I reminded myself this was not about me.

I picked up Jane at the LIRR station in Port Lewis and we drove to Dr. Lundy's office. He explained the process to her the way he had to me, and she settled into the navy high-backed chair, took a deep breath of vanilla air freshener, and smiled at him.

DR. LUNDY TOOK her back to the park, establishing who was there, getting her to describe the woman who approached them, then asked what she was saying to Jane.

"She says, she says—" Jane's voice was piping and eager, the way it used to sound when Colin brought home a surprise. " 'Go pick that yellow flower for me and I'll give you a toy from the carriage.' "

What toy? What carriage? I put my hand over my mouth to keep from crying out.

"What does the carriage look like?"

"It's like our one at home." She said it impatiently, focused on the promise of a toy. Did she mean it was plaid? Or double-wide? But I couldn't interrupt her to find out.

Jane was fully in the moment. "I want . . . I want . . . the bunny! The bunny is *so* cute. He has a pink nose."

And then suddenly she slumped back in the chair, defeated.

I couldn't breathe. Something had happened; she was no longer in the park in Stratford. Where was she?

"Jane? Did she give you the bunny?" Dr. Lundy understood something had happened too, and asked the question as if it were in the past.

"*No.*" Jane was still a child, but with a difference. "I got the flower for her, the yellow one. But she wouldn't let me get the bunny out of the carriage. She said—she said—'Go and tell your mum your sister fell in the river. Hurry now!' "

I started to gasp. This woman had seen it all!

Unexpectedly, Jane was back in the park again, breathless from running. "Mama, Mama, Cate fell in. She fell in the river!" After a moment, her face contorted. "No, don't *you* fall in."

"That's enough!" My voice came from nowhere, ringing into the room like an alarm.

Dr. Lundy jerked his head to stare at me.

But I was back in the park myself. I had plunged into the river, thrashing around to try and feel where Caitlin might be, scream-ing her name over and over. *This can't be happening, it can't be, not Cate.* Then people were everywhere, some in the water with me, two men on shore horrified at the wet smock clinging to my baby-swollen stomach and reaching their hands to pull me out. My head was buzzing and Jane, crying and calling me from the bank, seemed very far away. An older woman had stooped down and was trying to comfort her.

And yet—had all that searching been for nothing? Jane had only been repeating what she had been told to say, not what she had seen. She probably believed that Caitlin had fallen in. Because when you're four years old, adults don't lie to you.

It all hinged on what that woman had seen.

Chapter 11

To Dr. Lundy's credit, even after my outburst he brought Jane out of her trance gradually, promising her that she would feel relaxed and well-rested. As she had asked, he pointed out that when she wanted to buy an expensive new purse, she would remember all the beautiful handbags she had in her closet, and put her credit card away.

Jane opened her eyes and smiled at me. She was a young adult again who looked as if she had just finished dozing over a book. "What did I *say*? Is it—okay?"

"You don't remember?"

"Something about a bunny?"

"You'll hear. It's wonderful."

"I'll give you the recording so you can listen to it." Dr. Lundy turned from where he was extracting a CD from a system built into the wall, but he looked shaken, his pale eyes startled behind his rimless glasses.

As I zipped up my jacket, I asked him, "What do I owe you?"

"Suppose we handle it this way: If you come back and let

me know how it all works out, we'll treat it as a teaching experience."

I could see how curious he was to hear the whole story. "Well—that's very generous."

He helped Jane out of the chair as if she were a frail old lady, then watched as she buttoned her coat.

As soon as we had closed the outside door, I grabbed her shoulders. I could barely keep from shrieking. "You didn't see her drown! Someone told you to tell me that."

"Really? Really? I was afraid when you yelled, 'That's enough.' it was because you didn't want me to go through it again."

"You heard that? No, I guess I didn't want us to live through all that agony again, if it wasn't really true." Yet now I felt sorry that I hadn't let it unspool. We might have learned other things, like what had happened to the woman with the stroller. "But you're okay?"

"I'm fine. Just excited."

"Me too." Part of me wanted to dance and whirl and scream my happiness to the stars. What stopped me was that there had still been an eyewitness to the drowning,

I unlocked the van and we climbed in. But rather than stay in the small industrial parking lot, I drove to my favorite pond just a few blocks away. There were no other cars this time of night. In summer I would come here to watch the red-winged blackbirds swoop in and out of the trees, chasing each other. But they were gone now, the trees as bare as ancestral bones.

As soon as I pulled into a parking space, I slid the disk into the player. Jane was pressed into the seat, her knuckles against her mouth. I kept the engine running, the lights on.

"Don't let it hypnotize you again," I warned.

She laughed.

As soon as we heard Dr. Lundy's soothing tones and I looked out over the pond, I realized what I had done. I had brought us to a place of more dark water.

As the CD ended, Jane said, "Is that how I sounded when I was little? Play that part again."

How could she focus on her voice when what she was saying might have changed our lives completely? Obediently I ejected the CD, then pushed it in again.

This time she stopped the recording before Dr. Lundy could bring her out of her trance, and turned to me. "That woman should rot in hell! How could she steal Cate? How could she walk out of the park with her? She must have put Cate in that stroller as soon as I wasn't looking."

"You think she had Caitlin in the stroller?" Belatedly I started to fit it together.

"Of course she did. That's why she wouldn't let me reach in and get the rabbit, why she sent me running to you with a message so she could get away."

"But she said she saw Caitlin fall in."

Jane put her hand on my arm. "Mom, think. If that woman had been legitimate she wouldn't have stood there calmly and watched a little girl drown. She would have rushed over to pull Cate out herself, or at least raised the alarm. Besides, there wasn't enough time. We were far from the water and it only took me a minute to pick the flower and run back. I wanted that bunny, remember? There was only enough time for the woman to pop her in the carriage and—I don't know—chloroform her?"

I couldn't speak. The thought of my high-spirited little girl being roughly grabbed, shoved down and knocked out, shocked me as nothing else had. What had been done to her after that? I saw her being wheeled out of the park, past the historical build-ings of Stratford, and then—

But Jane was still trying to prove her point. "I said she was dressed like a nurse, but she could have been a nanny. Dressed like one. Why else would she bring an empty stroller to the park with toys in it if she hadn't been planning something like this?"

"Had you seen her before?"

"When I saw her tonight, I recognized her. So yes, I guess so."

"But where was I? I couldn't have been *that* oblivious." I had been a worse mother than I thought.

"She didn't let you see her. She'd planned it all out, I'm sure she had. I think she wanted people to get used to seeing her in the park so they would not remember her as something unusual from that day."

I nodded. "No one would have noticed a nanny with a carriage in the park. Even if they heard Caitlin crying, they wouldn't have thought anything of it. Babies cry."

The moonlight shone on Jane's face through the windshield. "I didn't really believe it before. But this means she's alive some-where. My sister's alive!"

She sounded so sure.

I wanted to believe it. I almost believed it. And then I thought of the note: YOUR DAUGHTER DID NOT DROWN.

Could it have been sent from the nanny herself, a deathbed confession to try and make things right?

An explosion of reds, yellows, and blues seemed to light up the sky around us. The fireworks felt so real I could see them reflected in the water. But the lifting of great guilt can cause that. An unfa-miliar lightness, a feeling as tangible as throwing off a heavy coat and welcoming the sun.

"Daddy and Hannah will have to believe us now," Jane said.

"I hope so."

"We should post Hannah's picture on Facebook. You know, 'Have you seen this woman?' " Jane said. "If they're identical twins, someone has to recognize her."

"But not without Hannah's permission. And I thought you could only post pictures to people who were your 'friends.' "

"That's true. But we can ask them to send it to their friends. You know how things go viral on the Internet."

A car came along the main road, its headlights playing over the pond.

Jane kept thinking. "The nanny said to tell 'mum,' so she was probably English. She had a British accent, I know that."

I thought of something else. "If she came to the park on more than one day, I may have photographed her as part of a group scene. I took a lot of photos trying to get a few good ones."

We stared at each other.

"Really? You think so? That would be amazing. Where are those pictures?"

"Packed away as rolls. Not developed." I prayed that I had brought all the film back with me, that I hadn't tossed it out in a fit of remorse. I told myself I wouldn't have done that since those rolls would have also held my last pictures of Caitlin.

"You don't have a darkroom anymore."

"No. But I think there's still one at the university."

"Great! Drop me at the train," Jane ordered, "and go find that film."

Chapter 12

IT TOOK ME until midnight to find the film from our last week in Stratford. The basement was cold, and with the overhead bulb burned out, I had to use a flashlight. I finally located the three undeveloped rolls wrapped in a yellow plastic supermarket bag, hidden under a stack of tax returns. I held the tiny yellow canisters against my chest and closed my eyes. *Dear God, make them still good. Make them have the pictures we need.*

It wasn't a prayer, not exactly, but more than a passing thought.

I was up again at dawn, sipping espresso and wondering how to safely develop the film. It was so *old*. If I still had my own darkroom and chemicals—but as soon as we returned from England I had turned the room into Jason's nursery and flushed the chemicals away. It hadn't seemed safe to keep them around.

Asking Colin for access to the university darkroom was out of the question. The only person who could help me, I decided groggily, was Bruce Adair. Bruce, a long-tenured literature professor with a specialty in the Victorians, was the smartest man I knew. He was a giant in the poetry world, a kingmaker who could, with one favorable review, set a needy young poet on the path to a Guggenheim. He had been congratulatory when Colin's second volume of poems, *Voices We Don't Want to Hear*, was shortlisted for the Pulitzer, but I wasn't fooled. The two men circled each other like rival chieftains.

Asking Bruce for help brought certain complications, but I decided I could live with them.

I wondered if 7:45 a.m. was too early to call him, then decided to take the chance. Sometimes I suspected Bruce lived in his office, keeping his cottage on the sound only for seduction. He was a quintessential bachelor and ladies' man, despite severe scoliosis that had curved his back and kept his height at under five feet.

He answered his office phone on the first ring. "Delhi!"

"How did—you must have caller ID."

"I prefer to call it Scottish second sight."

"Whatever. Listen, I need a favor."

"What a surprise." But he chuckled to soften the blow. "Do you want to stop by? My first class is at 9:10, but I'm here afterward. We could have lunch."

"No, I need to see you before then."

"What are you mixed up in now?" Bruce had been immeasurably helpful when my friend Margaret, the original owner of Port Lewis Books, had been attacked, helping me interpret clues I didn't understand.

"It's nothing like that. I just need a favor."

"Oh, is that all." He laughed again. "See you in ten."

IT TOOK ME closer to twenty minutes to reach the campus, park in the visitors' garage, and get to the literature department. When I entered Bruce's beautiful office, I saw that he had set out two cups, a teapot, scones, and jam.

"Bruce! You didn't need to—"

"This is my usual pre-seminar snack." He came around his polished desk and kissed me lightly on the mouth. Then he indicated the shellacked wooden chair across the desk from his own. "Sit."

I sat down and watched him pour me a cup of tea and nudge the sugar and cream close. He made sure the butter was also nearby. His caretaking brought me close to tears. When you've spent your life making sure everyone else has what they need, being cosseted this way will do that to you. That, not having gotten much sleep, and feeling emotional about what you're going to ask.

I looked around his office and found a lead-in to our conversation. Two hand-tinted photographs from the south of England that I had taken on an earlier trip hung above the waist-high bookcases that ringed the room. I had been given a show in one of the small gallery rooms in the library and Bruce had insisted on buying them.

He reached over and set a box of tissues next to my scone.

I looked at him. We already had napkins.

"I keep them for girls who claim I've ruined their lives by giving them a D. You have that look. Is it Colin?"

"Oh. No. No more than usual." I put down my teacup and told him the story of Caitlin, from her imagined drowning, Jane's hypnosis, and my certainty that she was alive. Because he was expecting me to, I managed not to break down.

Bruce listened gravely, nodding once or twice.

"So I need to use the darkroom."

"You need to do a whole lot more than that, Delhi."

I nodded meekly.

"I always wondered why you stopped taking photographs, but I didn't know you well enough to ask. I just assumed you'd moved on to better things, and the next time we talked it was rare books. What I don't understand is why you let this situation drag on so long."

His clear blue eyes were stern. I was that student deserving of a D.

"Because we believed what the police told us. Colin wanted us to just get on with our lives and I went along. The story of my life: I just went along."

"I don't believe that." He glanced at his understated but expensive watch. "I'll walk over and show you where the lab is. It's in Staller."

"Wait!" My voice cracked with panic. I already knew where the darkrooms were. "You said there were other things I needed to do."

"There are." To my relief, he settled back into his chair. "You need to go to Stratford-upon-Avon, back to where it happened. You have to talk to the police and find out everything you can about their investigation. Read all the newspapers. It won't be pleasant. Ask a lot of questions. See if you can locate this so-called nanny. Most of all you have to find out who sent you that note, and why."

"I'd thought about going to Stratford when it came." I'd also wondered how I was going to pay for a plane ticket at premium prices, and accommodations. My finances were nearly on empty and would only sink further as revenue from my book business decreased while I was away. Maxing out my credit cards wouldn't be that hard.

The boardwalk Gypsy's prophecy came back to me then. I *was* surrounded by people with money and didn't have any myself. Ben and Patience, Marty Campagna, my friend Bianca Erikson. Even Colin had some reserves. Why not me? Had the Gypsy's words become a self-fulfilling prophecy? Why couldn't I have found my passion in the stock market?

"Have you made plans yet?"

I sighed and told him the truth. "Being a bookseller is like being a poet. Long in satisfaction, but lacking in cash. I'll find a way to pay for it though."

His blue eyes in his rosy, white-bearded face were sympathetic. "Well, *I'll* give you fifteen thousand dollars. No strings."

"You can't, Bruce, you're Scottish." I meant it as a joke, which I assumed his offer was.

He laughed. "I'm serious. I live modestly and I have more money than I know what to do with. Who do I have to leave it to? Besides needy poets. I might as well do something interesting with the money while I'm alive."

"I can't take it."

"I said, no strings. You don't even have to invite me over for a down-home meal." There had been a brief time last summer when Bruce had become amorous, thinking we would make an engaging pair. I had been briefly tempted at dinner one night, imagining us as an artistic couple floating in a gondola down the Grand Canal. Me in white organza, Bruce in his straw boater. We were both relieved when it didn't happen.

I knew I should refuse the money. But I couldn't.

Chapter 13

"I HAVE TO meet someone at Staller. I'll walk you over with you, but I don't know anything about getting into the lab. I have a feeling it's just for faculty and students."

"That's okay. I know where it is. I'll be fine." But I was disappointed; I'd imagined Bruce as so powerful, so all-knowing, that he could say the magic password and get me into the darkroom. If I couldn't get in to develop the film myself, I would have to find a specialist somewhere. The film was too old and too important to mail it to some Internet site and hope for the best.

As it turned out, Bruce ran into a colleague outside the Staller Center for the Arts and I went on into the plain concrete building. I saw by the directory that the darkroom was on the fourth floor, and the photography department on the level below. I went to those offices first and found one that was dark, its door locked. The name on the placard outside said "Annalisa Merck."

When I reached the brighter, open area, a secretary was just arriving. "Oh—you startled me!"

"Sorry. Is Ms. Merck in yet?"

The secretary, younger than I was, consulted a schedule. "She has a studio class at noon. You could try a little before twelve."

That gave me three hours. Maybe.

Feeling the way I had when I was in junior high about to steal a lipstick from Rexall Drugs, I climbed the stairs to the fourth floor, and worked my way through the pale green cinder-block corridor. What was I *doing*? If I got caught sneaking into a darkroom . . . If they found out I was Colin Fitzhugh's wife . . .

Before I reached the reception area, I came to a door that I was sure led into the darkroom. I moved to it and tried the knob. *Locked*. But of course it would be. They couldn't risk people opening the door by mistake and spewing light everywhere.

Like riding a bicycle, darkroom techniques are second nature once you've learned them. I was sure that the past twenty years had brought new techniques, new chemicals that could ruin fragile celluloid, but how hard could developing this film be?

As my father used to say with a chuckle, "Fools rush in and don't know what to do when they get there."

I entered the reception room and smiled at a young Japanese student who had papers spread out on the desk behind the counter. He jumped up and came over to me.

"Is Annalisa inside?" I asked.

"Ms. Merck? No, not yet."

"I'm developing some sensitive film with her. Very old." I showed him, and his eyes widened at the dented yellow canisters. "Is it okay if I go in and get started?"

He hesitated. "You should wait for her."

"I'm in kind of a hurry. I'd like to get things started."

Come on, come on, come on.

"Are you in her class?"

"No. Just a colleague."

Perhaps because I looked old enough for that to be true, perhaps because he couldn't imagine any other reason for me to be there, he asked if I needed take-up reels.

"Yes. Three, please."

"Sign here." He pushed a clipboard with a lined page toward me. Mine would be the first name.

I wrote "Delhi Laine" as illegibly as I could and dated it.

He handed me the black plastic reels and then I was standing in front of a life-sized tube, the type you stepped into to be X-rayed.

"A gift from the medical school," he said with some pride. "Total darkness so you can extract the film. I guess."

Holding the empty reels, I stepped inside the cylinder. I knew I wouldn't like the narrow tube, but it was worse than I expected—as bad as waking up in a coffin and realizing there were several tons of dirt on top of you. No wonder George Washington had left instructions not to bury him for three days after he died.

I fumbled around for the end of the film in the first canister and couldn't find it. I couldn't see my hands or the reel either. Pushing everything else into my jacket pocket, I concentrated on bringing one hand to the other. With shaking fingers, I managed to find the piece I needed and wound the first roll of film onto the empty spool.

You won't die. Just do the other two.

I finally threaded two more rolls of film onto the reels, then was shaken by a new fear. How did I get out of here? I ran my hands along the smooth surface but could not feel a handle. Eventually Annalisa Merck and her class would come to use the darkroom and find my crumpled, oxygen-depleted body. Frantically

I started trying to slide the partition in front of me to one side and finally created an opening. Breathing hard, I half-fell into the darkroom. It was blessedly familiar. No lights except for the usual red bulb that glowed as dimly as a signal at the end of a runway. In its glow I could see nine or ten enlargers, several sinks, and other apparatus.

Moving to the center of the lab, I felt exhilarated. I was back in a darkroom, the place I belonged, the place where I hoped today to discover something crucial. If only we had all come safely back from England and I had gone on with my own photographic visions . . .

No time for regrets now. I had to work fast.

I raced mentally through the steps. Pour developer into a tank, agitate the unrolled film, swish it around with plastic-coated tongs. Lay the film in the first bath for ten minutes, then into the stop, the fix, and a final rinse in the sink. The acrid smell of the chemicals calmed me. *I can do this.*

Before I put the strips of film in the drying cabinet, I craned my neck to look at the tiny negatives. I could tell there were photos, real images, though I didn't know how clear they would be. Several seemed to be of the little girls, their faces inverted dark as coal miners with eerily lighter eyes, and I realized the pictures would show what Caitlin was wearing that last day. I braced myself the way I had when we'd opened the cartons at Thanksgiving, but at least now I had hope.

It was hard to see if any of the strips showed a woman dressed as a nanny.

When I was sure the film was dry, I took the negatives out and brought them to the light table. The photos that showed people rowing on the Avon ambushed me with sadness and guilt. Why hadn't I been paying attention to what truly mattered? I'd been so anxious to capture the two old ladies in frilly white hats and the young man at the oars that I'd ignored everything else.

I plowed on. One photo, just one, seemed to hold a woman in a white uniform at the edge of the frame.

My hand was shaking again as I cut the strip of negatives to fit in the enlarger. Why had I taken only one of her and so many of that damn statue of Shakespeare? The one photo I had would be blurred. The woman had evidently turned her head when she realized she was in my sights. She must have been constantly aware of where I was, what I was doing, knowing when to approach the girls. No one but me would have paid attention to a kindly nanny talking to them.

I placed the negative strip in the slot, turned on the machine, and waited. *Come on, come on.* The red light buzzed above my head, and I breathed in the chemicals. Waiting for the images to develop on the paper was excruciating. One precious hour was already gone.

When there was enough deep contrast, I took the photo through the steps of stop, fix, water. Almost there. I prepared myself to be disappointed. Discoloration could have crept in or white spots speckling everything. The woman could be too blurry to be identifiable. There were a hundred ways to go wrong, and only one to go right.

I let myself look down at the eight-by-ten photo. The nanny was off to the right. Dark curly hair. A white uniform with a cardigan around her shoulders. Some blur when she realized my camera was focused on her? At least I had her profile. But I was shocked.

She was so young and pretty. I had been imagining her as a cari-
cature of a nanny, somewhere past middle age and using a falsely
sweet voice to entice little children.

She looked barely forty. Had she been a desperate childless
woman masquerading as a nanny to find a child of her own? I had
heard of kidnappers dressing as nurses and stealing babies from
hospitals, but what had happened in those cases was discovered
almost at once. The disappearance of a child from a park with a
river was open to interpretation.

I had captured only a corner of the stroller, only enough to see
how high its plaid sides were.

Moving rapidly back to the machine, I enlarged her face further. I knew it would be grainy but I had no alternative.

A dryer in the corner of the darkroom, shaped like a pasta
maker, looked newer than the other equipment. I knew it dried
resin-coated photo paper more quickly than hanging the print up
the old-fashioned way. I hesitated. I had never used one. Suppose
I singed this picture? Yet time was an issue. If Annalisa Merck
arrived early and was told I was waiting inside for her . . . I didn't
want to imagine the scene.

Holding my breath, I slipped the paper through the narrow
slot and waited. It came out the other side clear and dry and gave
a better sense of the woman. Her nose was sharp and distinct.
There was a dark spot below her lip that could have been a beauty
mark or a flaw in the film. But I was sure I was looking at the
woman who I now believed had stolen my daughter. Jane's argu-
ments about the timing and the way a normal person would have
reacted had finally persuaded me. The plaid stroller she was rest-
ing her hand against seemed to clinch it.

We've got you now.

Was there time to print up a photo of Hannah and Caitlin? Caitlin had been wearing red corduroy pants and a striped shirt with a smiling goldfish appliquéd on the front. If I'd let her, she would have worn the shirt every day. I wanted that photo.

But I heard voices in the hall outside the door. It could have been anyone, just students passing, but I felt a flare of panic. I had what I'd come for. I had to get out. Covering the two prints I had made with tissue paper and wrapping the negative strips quickly, I slipped everything into my woven bag. Then I pushed open the outside door.

As I did, a fair-haired woman close to my age, passed me and gave me a startled look. Was it Annalisa Merck? I smiled and walked quickly toward the stairs.

Chapter 14

Outside in the early December air, I stopped and took several calming breaths, then started back toward the parking garage. I couldn't wait to call Jane. Yet when I saw the brick social sciences building, I decided to see if Colin was in his office. I thought of Jane's prediction, "Daddy will have to believe it now!"

Fingers crossed.

Colin's division, archeology, was part of the larger anthropology department. I rode the elevator to the fifth floor and walked to the Institute for Long Island Archaeology, not stopping to look at the color photos of local excavations. I knew they would show mostly Native American sites. There was a race to discover them before they were lost forever under developers' machinery.

Colin's office was empty, so I sat down in a cushioned alcove to wait.

I had taken out my phone and was about to press the button to connect me to Jane when Colin came around the corner, accompanied by two worshipful young women. The student in red tights was asking him what appeared to be a life-or-death question.

He stopped abruptly, seeing me. "Delhi! What—is everything okay?"

I knew his first thought was always the children.

"It's fine. I was on campus and thought I'd come by. We have to talk." It felt good to be the one using that phrase for a change. When Colin said, "We have to talk," it was never to find out what I wanted for my birthday.

He frowned, and the students melted away. "This isn't a good time."

"It won't take long."

"I have fifteen minutes before I'm meeting a grant representative."

"That will work."

"Not here. I'll walk you to your van." *And make sure I get into it?*

THE WINTER SUN played over the benches on the quad, the grass a pale, defeated green. There was a deep chill whenever you crossed into the shade. Students eddied around us on their way to the library or their next class.

"We'll get coffee," he decided.

"Is it private enough to talk?"

"Upstairs."

We bought our coffee in the cafeteria. I looked longingly at the cupcakes, decorated with red and green holiday sprinkles, but I had already eaten a scone. I remembered Patience in her pinstriped pants and left the cupcakes on the wire shelf.

As Colin had predicted, we were the only people on the second floor. The long room was dedicated to musicians who had performed on campus, and we sat down underneath a Janis Joplin poster.

He glanced at his watch. "So what brings you to campus?"

"I needed to develop some film in the darkroom."

"You're taking photos again?"

"No. These were some old rolls."

"I hope you didn't use my name to get in."

"No." I took a sip of coffee and looked at him. "Why are you so against trying to find Caitlin?"

"Because it will only lead to more frustration." He sighed. "I don't have time to go through my reasons again. Is that why you brought me here?"

"No." I cast about for the most persuasive way to tell him about last night. "Jane remembered what really happened that day," I started. "Remember how she kept talking about a 'bad lady' who would get her too? Well, it turns out there *was* a woman, someone dressed up like a nanny who talked to the girls. She asked Jane to go pick a flower for her, then hid Caitlin in a carriage when Jane's back was turned, and told her to tell me she had fallen into the water. That's what she was trying to tell us that night!"

He flinched as if resisting being pulled back into that scene. "And she suddenly remembered it all? All those details?"

"Well," I admitted, "she had some help."

"Some help? Delhi, no! Please don't tell me it was under hypnosis or some damn thing like that." He gave me a disbelieving look. "Next thing you'll tell me, she went to a séance."

"It was nothing like that. This was a psychologist from Columbia University. He's hardly some quack."

Colin set his mug down hard on the table, making me jump. "I don't care if it was Sigmund Freud resurrected from the dead. You let someone play with her mind?"

I leaned toward him. "It was perfectly safe. Really. You have no idea what hypnosis is like."

He closed his eyes, exasperated. "Do you know how many false memories it generates? All those abuse allegations about the day care centers? You subjected Jane to that!"

"It wasn't like that at all. Nobody coached her. He took her back to that day and she told us what she saw. That's all."

"What she wanted to see." He was momentarily distracted by two students who passed our table and spoke to him, then said, "Speaking of memories, you have a short one. Don't you remember what happened the last time you tried second-guessing the British police? You turned into their prime suspect. It's a good thing I was down at Boxgate that day or they'd have accused me too."

"That's crazy."

"Oh, really? They questioned the woman who ran the hostel to make sure you went out that day with all three girls. They asked her questions about whether or not you were abusive." He picked up his cup, changed his mind, and set it down more softly. Apparently something in my face made him add, "You really don't remember?"

I shook my head. I had spent hours at the police station, answering questions. There *had* been insinuations about how overwhelmed I must have felt, being so pregnant and with three young children. Far from home without any emotional support. But I had mistaken their comments for sympathy.

"They really thought I had done something to her?" I felt sucker-punched.

"I don't know. No one actually thought you were abusive. They found people in the park who saw all three girls."

"They actually thought I had done away with her and made up a story," I said flatly. Against my resistance it was coming back.

"They had to check out everything when you insisted she

hadn't drowned. And you cost me my best friend," Colin said suddenly.

"Who? You mean Ethan?"

Ethan Crosley and Colin had known each other since graduate school. "After it happened, he and Sheila never spoke to me again."

"But why blame you? If anything they should have blamed me and sympathized with you. That doesn't sound like much of a best friend to me."

I remembered the Crosleys only vaguely. Ethan rangy and mocking with tight red curls, and a face that just missed being handsome. Sheila had been slender with Irish-black hair in spiky bangs around her porcelain face and large blue eyes, a woman so intense that I didn't remember her ever laughing. A woman always on the verge of grievance.

"They were upset that we were so careless. They were trying to have a baby themselves and it outraged them that you could let something so dumb happen. Especially when you were pregnant and could easily replace one child with another."

"What? That's outrageous! As if any 'baby' could replace Caitlin! That's *insulting*. It's a good thing you didn't tell me then. I would have punched them."

He shrugged.

"No one else felt that way."

Five American couples had been living at the residence while the husbands, archeological colleagues from around the country, visited nearby English sites. We socialized constantly, and the mothers exchanged toys and advice. Our children played together every day. When we lost Caitlin, they were quick to babysit and offer any support they could. It solidified my friendship with one of the other wives, Rebecca Deitz, who had lost a child to crib death. We were still in touch.

Should I try to contact Rebecca or the others now, to see if they remembered anything else? Unfortunately, none of them had been in the park with me that day.

"Delhi, I'm serious about not upending this girl's life—if she is alive, which I doubt. Not to mention what it would do to our own lives. Suppose she's psychologically damaged—we have no idea what she's been through. We'd end up taking that on too."

"But she's our child!"

"She *was* our child. For two short years, a long time ago. You have this sentimental idea that genes trump everything. I don't."

I gripped my cup as if it were the only means of escape from his words and stared at him. It was the coldest thing I had ever heard him say.

"Anyway, Hannah is against it. How she feels is the most important thing."

"No. It's not." Her fears of inconveniencing her life did not match my need for Caitlin. "I'm the one who gave birth to this child. I'm the one she was stolen from. And if I have any chance on earth of finding her, I will!"

"Delhi." He reached across the table and stroked my lower arm. "How can I make you stop picturing her as a two-year-old and realize she's an adult who doesn't know us at all? Who may hate you for blowing her world apart? I care just as much what happens to you."

Blindsided by his unexpected tenderness, I couldn't answer.

Chapter 15

I WAITED UNTIL Colin had kissed me good-bye and left, then took out my phone and pressed Jane's office number.

She answered right away.

"Janie, it's her. It has to be. But she's pretty!"

"I never said she wasn't."

"Oh." I had been the one seeing the nanny as a fairy-tale witch. "She's turning away from the camera, but I've got her in profile. I'm leaving the university now and I'll e-mail the photo to you as soon as I get home."

"She's real," Jane marveled. "I didn't make her up."

"Of course you didn't. But what I need to do now is go back to Stratford."

"Can I come? I'll pay my own way."

"Of course you can come. And I'm paying."

An intake of laughter. "You don't—"

"No, I mean it."

Easy to be generous with Bruce's money.

"I can go anytime, Mom. I never take vacations. My boss will just have to live without me for a week."

I had never asked about her relationship with her supervisor. Jane dated a parade of Lances, Justins, and Bryans—men her age and younger, whom she called her "guys." They went to clubs and sports bars, attended plays and art openings, and Jane exchanged them as often as she switched handbags. Though she was my daughter, I didn't really know where she stashed her deepest emotions.

"I'll make the travel arrangements," I said. "We won't need more than a week there."

"What about Hannah?"

What about Hannah? "She's still finishing up the semester. Besides . . ."

"Yeah, right. It's just she'll be upset that we're doing something without her. Does Daddy know?"

"Not yet." It was then I realized how pursuing Caitlin had the potential for splitting the family apart. Was looking for her worth creating bitterness that might never be resolved? I knew families who had not spoken to each other in years. Was I about to toss a hand grenade into the center of my own? How far could I go before realizing I had to abandon the quest?

"Mom?"

"I told him about your experience. He doesn't believe in hypnosis. I don't understand him. It's as if Caitlin is someone he knew briefly in the past and has no interest in meeting up with again. The idea of blood means nothing to him."

"Wow. He's so involved with the rest of us. He texts me all the time."

"He *knows* you. If he felt indifferent toward Jason, he wouldn't be so furious with him. If only he knew Caitlin." I stopped, choked up. It hadn't been *her* fault, my poor little girl, that someone had broken our connection as surely as if they'd disconnected a cell phone and thrown it into the sea. "Let me go now so I can scan the photo for you."

But sitting in the parking garage, I couldn't resist dialing my sister Patience's office number. I was excited to let her know everything we'd found out. Would she want to go to Stratford too? We hadn't traveled together since we were teenagers.

Pat was available, though her assistant first answered the phone.

"Delhi?" Patience sounded surprised.

"Yes, hi. Sorry to interrupt, but I wanted to let you know what's happening with Caitlin. We're actually making progress."

"Before you get into it, I've been thinking about the situation a lot. That, and talking to other people." She paused as if waiting for an army of them to get in line behind her. "I think you should just let things be."

"*What?*"

"You need to get on with your life. Keep living in the present. You said the police in England were satisfied with what happened, you believed it yourself when you came home. Why stir it all up again only to get disappointed?"

"Who have you been talking to?"

"Just people. No one you know."

"But now we know what happened that day. Jane remembers a woman telling her to tell me Caitlin had fallen into the river."

"And?"

"Think about it." I remembered what Jane had told me. "If you saw a baby fall into your pool, what would you do? Jump in and rescue her or at least raise the alarm. This woman just told her to tell me and left. Taking Caitlin."

"You know for a fact?"

"It's the only thing that makes sense. We even have a photo of the woman. I just developed it. All we need to do now is find her. Jane and I are going to Stratford."

"Now? Before Christmas? Is Colin going?"

Ask him yourself. But maybe Colin hadn't been the one to influence her. Ben had not seemed anxious to get involved. Besides, Patience was quite capable of changing her mind on her own, of turning oppositional just when I was feeling warm about having a sister. I'd had a lifetime of Patience in action, agreeing to do something with me, then getting a better offer and going with that instead.

"I thought you were on my side," I pleaded. "You said we were in this together."

"I *am* on your side. I'm telling you what I think is best for you."

Thank God I had not approached her for money. Was that the subtext here, that she thought I would ask her to finance the search?

"Good luck," she added, as if I were an acquaintance leaving for a new job.

That was all my twin was willing to give me.

Chapter 16

I booked a flight for Tuesday night, returning Sunday. It did not come cheaply. After looking at inns and bed-and-breakfasts online, I settled on the White Swan Hotel in the center of Stratford-upon-Avon. It was within walking distance of the river, the local newspaper archives, and the police station—a necessity since I didn't want to rent a car.

I was excited to be traveling again, to be leaving the country for England. I might have preferred India or Japan, but I felt the same kind of exhilaration I had in the darkroom, as if some long-hibernating part of me had started to stir and was coming back to life. One way or another, I would be changed by this quest.

Marty wasn't happy that Susie would be left in charge of Port Lewis Books for a week, though when pressured, he admitted she was doing an okay job. The stolen books had all of us on edge, scrutinizing whoever came into the shop, never leaving the front room unattended. My other worry, besides book theft, was Susie's plan for decorating the shop windows if I didn't get them done myself. Margaret Weller, the original owner, had always done a beautiful job, and I was determined to carry on the tradition.

My plan was to use beautiful books and vintage toys loaned from Dock Street Antiques. If I didn't finish the windows by Tuesday morning, Susie would bring in her ceramic village and Precious Moments figurines. She already was campaigning to set up a pink artificial Christmas tree with silver balls and could not understand why it did not belong in the upscale front room.

There was added pressure to create an old-fashioned Christmas look because the Charles Dickens Festival started on Friday night. The celebration filled the village with carolers dressed in costume, high teas, and readings from *A Christmas Carol*. There were concerts and a house tour. Port Lewis thoroughly enjoyed a past the village had never actually experienced, though that detail had never stopped us before. We had old-fashioned red telephone booths on street corners, though Victorian London had no more connection to our seafaring history than Charles Dickens himself. But everyone loved the festival weekend and I felt inspired to do my part.

I WOKE EARLY Tuesday morning and packed several changes of clothes. I had already arranged to stop the *Times* and given my neighbor's daughter a key to come in and feed Raj and Miss T, and was at Dock Street Antiques as soon as it opened. Jen, the owner, helped me pick out a china doll and high chair, a Steiff monkey, a spelling board with movable wooden letters, and, of course, a multitude of lithographed tin toys. My favorite was the Ferris wheel, which still circled slowly when wound. A discreet white card in the front of the display would explain that the toys were available for purchase from Dock Street.

When Susie came in at noon, she marveled at the decorated windows. There were never any hard feelings with her. She saw the world as good-hearted, a collection of people as eager to help their neighbors as her pioneer forebears had been. When I looked at her I saw wheat fields and hoedowns. I hadn't told either Susie or Marty why I was going to England, saying only it was a family matter.

"You want me to pick up some Shakespeareana?" I'd asked Marty.

He snorted. "In Stratford-upon-Avon? That would be like buying a watch in Times Square. You're better off looking in some old barn outside London. A sixteenth-century farmhouse where they used pages from his playbills to plaster the walls. Shakespeare is the most *discovered* author in existence."

"I take your point."

I doubted I would have much time for book hunting anyway. Yet like a drinker touring the Guinness factory, I knew it would be hard to abstain. I had already made a list of five or six promising bookshops in Stratford and left room in my carry-on bag for any finds.

JANE AND I met at the AirTrain at four. Our flight wasn't until nearly seven, but I'd heard so many horror stories about delays in getting through security that I didn't want to be caught in that web. It had been an easy ride on the Long Island Rail Road for me, and the subway for Jane. The AirTrain, no more than a collection of several silver cars, was arriving when we reached the platform and we were quickly at Terminal One.

Everything was going much too well. I wondered if the Virgin Atlantic flight would be canceled or delayed, but the departure board said it was scheduled to leave on time. That left only the 747 breaking apart over the Atlantic or overshooting the runway at Heathrow and ending engulfed by flames. Of course there was still the smaller connecting plane that would take us to Birmingham Airport. Everyone knew how dangerous little planes were.

Actually I loved flying. Yet each time the plane dropped its wheels like a weary traveler and cruised smoothly onto the tarmac, it seemed a biblical miracle. Not on the level of the parting of the Red Sea, perhaps, but at least as important as turning water into wine.

With wine in mind, we stopped at an Irish bar near our departure gate. I took half a Dramamine with my Chardonnay and nibbled at the potato skins Jane had impulsively ordered.

She took a sip of Sauvignon Blanc. "So what did Dad say about us going?"

"I knew there was something else I had to do."

"Mom! You haven't told him?"

"I figured I'd wait until we were safely on the plane."

"What—like he'd kidnap us in the terminal?" She wrinkled her pretty nose. "You give him too much power."

"Old habits die hard."

"And what about Hannah?"

"I sent her an e-mail this morning telling her I had to go to England and saying I'd call her when I got there."

Jane shook her head. "At least call Dad now. He has to know we're out of the country."

"Maybe he'll be teaching." I reached into my woven bag for my phone.

It was not to be.

"Hey-lo!" He always answered his cell the same way.

"Colin? It's Delhi. You'll never guess where we are."

Jane closed her eyes.

Chapter 17

THE LAST TIME I saw Warwickshire was in the lush flowering of an English summer when the gardens were rainbows fallen across the earth and fountains tossed up diamonds against blue skies. Every scene had been deserving of a calendar photograph.

December's grass was a patchier green. The bright hollyhocks and roses were a memory now, and the trees had relinquished their leaves. A few fall wreaths waited on doors to be replaced by evergreen boughs, and a haze of melancholy hung over the world as we drove from Birmingham Airport. Jet-lagged and disoriented, I felt this boded poorly for our quest. At least we had remembered to get pounds and silver at the airport ATM. Having the right currency made me feel marginally better.

"Coming for the Christmas Market, are ye?" asked our driver, a cheerful man of a certain age with rosy cheeks and a tweed flat cap.

I leaned back in my seat, not interested in talking.

Jane asked, "What's that?"

"Oh, they come from all over for it. Booths on Henley Street and everything done up with lights. Do all your holiday shopping near t'your hotel."

I wasn't interested in buying gifts here though I thought Jane might be.

"Your first time in these parts?" He was relentless.

"No. We came here once when I was a little girl. Not that I remember much."

When I'd told Colin about our pilgrimage to Stratford from the table in McDonough's Pub, he didn't get it at first. "Why Stratford? Why not London?"

"There's something I want to check."

"Oh. But why is Jane going?"

He must have had a hard day.

"She's doing a term paper on Shakespeare's finances."

"Delhi . . ."

"She needs a vacation. And I wanted the company."

"I hope she's not paying for this!"

"No. My treat."

"If business has been *that* good—"

Give it a rest, Colin. "You can reach us on Jane's phone if anything comes up." I pressed disconnect. "He's fine with it," I'd told Jane.

On the outskirts of the village, I pointed to our left. "We stayed over there, in a residence that had been a grand manor." Although it had appeared to still be a beautiful mansion from the outside, three stories with bow windows and porticos, the sixteen bedrooms on the second and third floors had felt like a dormitory. Besides the matrimonial bed, our room held a set of bunk beds and a tiny cot. I had been worried about Jane falling from the top berth, but she'd loved clambering up the ladder at bedtime and insisted she would be fine. The twins snuggled together in the lower bunk. In half a day, the cot was buried under a mountain of toys, clothes, books, and laundry soap.

The hostel catered to longer-stay academic conferences and assumed you would be happy just to have a place to stay. They didn't make the beds for you or clean the bathrooms, and served basic meals family-style. There had been a lot of brown meat in gravy, and at breakfast the odd choice of "Orange juice or corn-flakes?" But we had been young and relished sitting outside on the back patio in the evenings, draining pitchers of ale while the children played around us. It gave the academics who would become the archeological establishment of the next generation a chance to form alliances. I'd reveled in the communal-style living and friendships—right up to the moment when Caitlin disappeared.

"We'd walk along the river to Bancroft Gardens," I told Jane, "not quite in the center of Stratford. You always wanted to bring bread to feed the ducks and swans."

"Not allowed now," our driver butted in. "You must leave the wildlife alone!"

Jane and I burst out laughing.

THE WHITE SWAN Inn was located on Rother Street in the center of town, a half-timbered, white-stucco hotel. Check-in was a strict 3 p.m., so we left our bags with reception and wandered through the cobbled streets. The cold felt more assertive here than it had at home, a cheerless, leaden chill that took its right to dominate for granted. It knifed through our down jackets. People on the sidewalk moved briskly, not looking at anyone else.

Still the shop windows made you want to linger. We gaped at a toy shop scene of a happy family on Christmas morning, as elaborate as the Lord & Taylor holiday windows in New York City. The greenery arrangements in the florists' windows were exquisite.

Stratford-upon-Avon was a large and prosperous town, though civilization had made a few more inroads than I'd remembered. Jane pointed out a building that Shakespeare himself might have lounged in front of, except for the "Pizza Hut" logo over the door.

It made me suggest lunch.

She gave a longing look at a McDonald's—"I bet it tastes different here than at home"—but I steered us into a lovely, deliberately shabby pub.

The interior of British pubs hadn't changed in the past twenty years. There was still the heavy dark furniture, a dartboard in the back, and bad lighting. Fluorescent beer signs on the walls vied with forgettable art. We settled into thick pine captains' chairs. I could picture the loo with its mineral-stained sink, and the door beyond it leading to a small garden with summertime tables. The smell of frying food mixed pleasantly with beer and a piney scent though I couldn't see any evergreens. Most of the tables were filled with locals, predominantly men, chatting comfortably. A few tourists sat at the other tables looking pleased to be there.

We ordered potato-and-cheddar soup and Strongbow cider. I'd forgotten how much I liked English cider and how much I drank the last time we were here. I hadn't yet developed a taste for wine, and being pregnant I tried to give up alcohol altogether. Somehow cider had slipped past the censors.

We relaxed until our food came, too spent to talk.

"What should we do first?" Jane asked, dipping an experimental spoon into her soup.

I had a list of what we needed to do but hadn't put it into any order. I had found out as much as I could over the Internet beforehand so that we could move quickly once we were here. "Well, we have to look at the newspaper archives and visit the police station and see where that leads us." I planned on showing them the note first thing—*Your daughter did not drown*—and hoped they could analyze it. "We need to go back to where it happened, of course." That would be the hardest thing of all.

I'd brought photographs of Hannah at different ages, in case Caitlin was living in the area and someone might recognize her. The temptation to post them on an Internet site here was overwhelming. If it were local, a British site, Hannah would never need to know.

Across the table, Jane swirled a cube of dark bread through her soup.

The problem was, nothing on the Internet was local. Once it was out there it could never be retracted. More seriously, it was a breach of trust. I could not lose another daughter searching for the first. In the end, Jane had sent Hannah a text message from Heathrow to explain that she was with me, making it sound as if we were off for a brief jaunt so I could scout books and she could see London.

"We need to find a copy shop," I told Jane.

"WE'RE PUTTING YOU in the Hamlet Room." The young woman behind the counter beamed. "You're fortunate, it books years in advance, but we've had a cancellation."

I was sure she was trying to make me feel better about how much it was costing to sleep in the shadow of the melancholy Dane, but when I saw the room I was stunned. *Thank you, Bruce.* The white walls and ceiling, intersected by sixteenth-century dark beams, arched over a carved wooden bed, a leather sofa, and an intricately carved wooden desk. Next to the desk in a brick alcove there was a wood-burning stove. The bathroom was larger than many hotel rooms, with a freestanding copper-clad bathtub and a separate modern shower.

"I could live here," I told Jane.

"I saw it first." She collapsed in a chair next to the window. "This is the way to travel."

"I thought you loved camping in the desert."

"*Not.*"

Fighting the urge to curl up on the puffy white duvet and nap, I said, "Let's find out where we can make photocopies."

KOPYKAT WAS SEVERAL blocks away on New Broad Street. Borrowing a sheet of blank paper from the accommodating young salesman, I printed, "Do You Know Me?" across the top and my e-mail address asking for contact on the bottom. I explained that we were only here for a short time and were hoping to reunite with long-lost family members, but decided not to give our names. Then I arranged the photos facedown on the glass and placed the paper over them. One close-up showed Caitlin in her fishy shirt and corduroy pants. The others were of Hannah at several-year intervals, ending with last Christmas.

Color photocopies were pricey, but we made sixty to start.

I'd remembered to bring pushpins and tape, and Jane and I went off in separate directions, searching for shops with community bulletin boards, supermarkets, and launderettes. I left several flyers on a beauty salon table with the magazines, and taped a few to lampposts though I was sure they'd be quickly taken down. Churches and bookshops were a better bet, but that entailed telling the story, and I wasn't up to that now. I hoped that by tomorrow I would be.

We met back at the White Swan an hour later, took our coats up to our room, and came back down to the lounge. Mugs of Fuller's cider in hand, we nestled on a couch in front of an enthusiastic fire, under one of the ubiquitous paintings of swans. Gradually I was overtaken by the centuries of other lives lived in this village, the lamentations penned and tears shed, the echoes of laughter when nothing else would do.

Why should I feel exempt, different from people of five hundred years ago? Many of them had lost children. I remembered Shakespeare, whose own son, Hamnet, had died at eleven, evidently of bubonic plague. I had my own challenges, hopefully a longer life ahead, but my world held no guarantees. Before I finished the glass in my hand, I set it on the low table, leaned back against the soft headrest, and slept.

Chapter 18

EXHAUSTED FROM THE flights, we slept the next morning until almost eight. I'd wakened in the night feeling warm, pushed off the duvet, and dropped back asleep. Without opening my eyes now, I listened to the spatter of Jane's shower, then pushed out of bed. In the breakfast room we steeped ourselves in coffee, enhanced by muffins and fruit. No time today for the "full English breakfast."

The police station was also on Rother Street, down several blocks from the hotel. I had seen its picture on the Internet, a two-story brick building well-landscaped and set back from the street.

"Newer than everything else," Jane said.

"Shakespeare wouldn't recognize it," I agreed.

A young constable with tight fair curls smiled as we entered and approached the reception desk. His smile widened as Jane came closer. "Good morning!"

"Good morning to you."

"You're here to make a report?" He pushed a form toward us.

"A report?"

"Theft or harassment are the usual complaints. Don't feel you're the only ones it's ever happened to."

"Thanks, but we're here about something else." I moved forward. "Something that happened a while ago."

"How long ago was it?"

"Nineteen years?"

He recovered nicely, considering that at that time he had probably been watching *Sesame Street*.

"Is there someone from back then still working here?"

"DCI Sampson will be in at nine. He's been here forever."

"What's *your* name?" I asked.

"Constable Roderick Bradford at your service."

It was impossible not to love him. When we said we'd wait, he settled us on a wooden bench, then brought a tin of Danish Christmas cookies and mugs of tea. The mugs were not police issue. Mine was dark green with a bull outlined in gold, an advertisement for a livestock insemination service. Jane drank from a white mug promoting a group of estate agents.

WHEN GABRIEL SAMPSON walked into the station, I was blindsided by emotions I'd never expected. The tea rose from my stomach and became a burning acid. My heart began jumping and I had to put the cup down to steady my shaking hand. What did my body know that my mind didn't remember? All I could think was, *This isn't going to be pleasant.*

DCI Sampson looked older, his dark hair now salted with gray, but his face was still wary as a hawk's. The last time I saw him he had been wearing a blue constable's uniform, not an expensive tweed overcoat and cashmere scarf. Now he appeared to be running the station. As his eyes flickered over to us, I remembered he had been the one who pooh-poohed Jane's comments about a "bad lady." He had treated me as if the tragedy was only to be expected from someone sleeping on the job. I suddenly remembered how odd it had seemed that he was intent on proving that Stratford and the river had not been to blame.

I had wanted to talk to someone familiar with the case. *But not him.*

Was there anyone else?

"These lovely young ladies are waiting for you," Constable Bradford said gallantly.

DCI Sampson stared at us. "You've made a report?"

"It's not about that. I'm Delhi Laine. Caitlin Fitzhugh's mother?"

He didn't recognize me or the names.

"Can we talk to you?"

He didn't move a millimeter. Pushing up from the bench and coming close to him, I saw that he had developed gray flecks in his mustache. His aftershave smelled like clean laundry.

He saw that I was not going to go away. "What's this about then?"

I did not want to tell him the story standing in the middle of the lobby, but I understood he was not going to move. So we stood in the center of the room, the lights of a tabletop Christmas tree blinking erratically on and off, personnel edging around us, and I reminded him of what had happened nineteen years ago.

He blinked with impatience. I was making a poor job of it.

Quickly I showed him the note and envelope. "This is what made us come back!"

He looked at them, scrutinized the postmark, then handed them to me.

I felt disappointed that he did not keep them for a forensic examination. "Can you tell if the letter was mailed from around here?"

"Hard to read. It could be Rugby."

"Where is that?"

"Northeast of here. Larger than Stratford. But it could be any number of places in Britain."

"Well, we came back to see if there's anything we missed here."

DCI Sampson sighed. "As I remember, the investigation was thorough. We even brought in a police diver. The file was closed as death by mishap."

"You remember a lot about it," Jane said, as if admiringly.

He preened. "Only because it was an anomaly. We deal with few fatalities. Automobile casualties, of course, drownings now and then. The kind of kidnapping you're suggesting, never."

Get ready to have your world rocked.

"Do you have notes about the case we could look at?" I asked. "Wasn't there a detective on the case?"

"Our files are official property, madam. There would have been no detective assigned as it was a drowning, not a crime. The case belonged to another constable and myself."

The concept of ownership seemed odd. "Could we speak with the other constable?"

"He left soon afterward. He went south."

I heard Jane breathe in. "What was his name?"

He turned on her reproachfully, as if she should know better than to ask. "That isn't information we divulge."

I jumped in. "Not even his name? He was part of our case, after all. Anything he remembers would help."

"There's nothing for him to remember. It's all in the case file."

"Which we can't see." I tried to keep my voice calm. I didn't think acting pitiful or begging would work and in any case I was much too angry to be convincing. How could he be so officious when it was a matter of a child's life? "Could you at least look at the file to see if there's anything you're forgetting? We've come all the way from New York to try and find out what really happened."

He couldn't have cared if we'd flown in from Jupiter. "When you bring me some new evidence—something more substantial than a 'recovered memory'—I'll take a look at it. Otherwise it stays in the file. Enjoy your stay in Stratford." And he moved past us and into a hall.

"What about the note?" I called after him, but he kept walking.

Jane and I stared at each other. Had we flown several thousand miles at considerable expense only to be brushed off like a flake of dandruff from his expensive coat? Could he actually refuse to tell us anything more?

"Have you seen Anne Hathaway's Cottage?" Constable Bradford called consolingly from the desk. "It's not to be missed."

We smiled at him and left.

" 'Enjoy your stay in Stratford,' " Jane mocked. "He's hiding something. I know he is!"

"Not to even give us the constable's name," I agreed. I cast back into my memory, back to that time, to see if the name or the constable himself was lurking somewhere in the shadows. No one stepped forward. Truth be told, even the police station looked unfamiliar.

"I'll bet the constable who disappeared was in on it! Maybe the nanny was his wife, and as soon as they'd taken Caitlin they moved away so no one would find out. No one would suspect a *policeman*."

"We still have other things we can check out." I was upset too, but I saw that Jane was hitting the travel wall, that point of feeling overwhelmed when everything seems futile and you're sorry you ever left home. It usually came closer to the midpoint of a trip, but travel malaise can strike anytime.

"We'll check my iPad later to see if anyone's e-mailed about the flyer," I promised. "In a small town like this, someone has to know something. If that constable's from around here, he's probably come back for visits over the years, maybe with a cover story about where Caitlin came from—either that they adopted her, or that she was a friend's orphaned child." I stopped, hearing myself. On the basis of nothing, I was embracing Jane's theory as if it were a fact. "Let's go look at the archives."

"I need more coffee."

"Looking at the newspapers won't take long. The *Stratford Herald*'s a weekly."

She sniffed. "Where's this newspaper office?"

"Actually, the archives are kept at the Shakespeare Birthplace Trust, not at the paper."

"Can't they do anything logically here? How do you know?"

"I e-mailed them." Unlike DCI Sampson, my correspondents at both the newspaper and the archives had been extremely helpful. They'd explained where the older newspapers were kept and what we would need to do to be able to see them.

The Trust was on Henley Street in an impressive brick and glass building with a bronze abstract design—now gone to green—on one side. Inside was a fascinating mélange of exhibits and films, worlds of sounds and visuals that the Bard himself would have marveled at.

Shakespeare would have *loved* Hollywood, I decided.

We made a stop at the loo, then headed for the Reading Room.

I had forgotten to bring our passports, which were stowed in the room safe, but we had our driver's licenses and those served for identification. The librarian brought us to an oak table next to a large window to wait for the volumes. "Let me know if you get cold. Sometimes the wind breaks right through."

We were still wrapped in our winter jackets and I was wearing the heaviest sweater I had brought, but I promised to let her know.

"There's no daily paper?" Jane asked.

"No, just one from Birmingham. We'd have to go down there to see the archives and I'm not sure they would have given it any more coverage. Probably less."

The newspapers we wanted were in one oversized volume bound in blue leatherette. The accommodating librarian positioned it on a cushion on the table in front of us. I had—and had not—been looking forward to this moment, but now it was here. Although I was desperate for any new scrap of information, any hint of where we should look next, I was not anxious to come face-to-face with that pregnant, frantic girl who hadn't even known what she was saying. I had a hazy image of myself apologizing over and over—to Colin, to the police, and most of all to Caitlin, whose just-starting life I had brought to a close.

My fingers felt as if they were encased in heavy gloves. I was unable to get any purchase on the page edges. Jane finally reached over and found the first story:

TODDLER SLIPS INTO THE AVON, DROWNS

For a moment I thought, *How terrible!* before my mind admitted that the story was about us.

The newspaper had been published on a Thursday, the day after it happened, so the only photo was of swans on the river. The facts were basic, preliminary.

Then Jane said, "Look!" and pointed to the end of the story. A Constable Donnelly was quoted as pointing out, "The current can be tricky, even in summer. The water was not clear enough to see to the bottom."

"Well, we already knew that."

"*Mom*. His name."

"Oh!" I wrote it down in the tiny notebook I had brought with me, though I was sure I would not forget it.

The next week's paper gave more details about what had happened, focusing on police interviews with people who had been in the park that day. The constabulary requested that anyone who had seen anything "out of the ordinary" to please come forward—had that been to placate us, to try and verify Jane's claim of a "bad lady"? The story did not say.

I stared at a photo of the five of us taken at Easter, which I didn't remember giving them.

In that same story a Celia Banks from Worchester Cottage recalled often seeing us in the park. "Such a lovely family! Brilliant little girls, and such a young mum. It's a terrible tragedy, yes it is."

"She saw us," I told Jane wonderingly. "This woman saw us in the park." Somehow that verification made it seem real in a way I couldn't explain.

"Let's hope *she* hasn't moved away like the constable," Jane said.

I wrote down the information. I had no idea whether Worchester Cottage was the name of a neighboring village or an apartment complex.

The third week, there was no mention of the story at all. We scoured every page, then looked at each other.

"That's it?" Jane was crushed. "No one said anything about the woman I saw."

"The police wouldn't make it public if someone had. Let's keep looking."

But the next week's lead story was about a hit-and-run on the Birmingham road. The paper showed a photo of the deceased, a glamorous shot of a young, dark-haired woman. Evidently she had been an actress with the Royal Shakespeare Company. And DCI Sampson had insinuated nothing violent ever happened in placid Stratford. A "drowning" that no one witnessed and a fatal hit-and-run within a month of each other?

I heard Jane breathe in next to me and supposed she was reacting to this second tragedy.

"Where's that photo you took?" she demanded.

I looked at the article again. "You think that's *her*?"

"I'm sure it is."

My hands began shaking again, the way they had at the police station. I reached around to my bag and pulled out the nanny's photo still wrapped in tissue, and put it on the table. Even slightly blurred, even with her head turning away, it looked like it could be the same woman. What I had thought was a smudge was definitely a beauty mark. How many local women would have a mole in that exact same spot?

"Oh, my God," Jane breathed. "She's the one I was talking to when I was hypnotized, I'm sure of it. She didn't have makeup on like that; she was supposed to look plain. But her nose is the same, I know it is!"

"But she died right after. How could she be dead?" What I

meant was, how could she be dead three weeks after she'd kidnapped my child? What had happened to Caitlin?

It was possible we were imagining it was the same woman because we so badly wanted her to be. Maybe this was a common English type. Perhaps this woman was a sister or a cousin of the kidnapper.

I calmed down and reread the story. The woman's name was Priscilla Waters, age thirty-eight. She had been with the Royal Shakespeare Company for two years and had had small parts on the London stage before that. A member of the theater company told the reporter they were shocked and grieved. "Everyone loved Priss. Her Cordelia was to die for."

To die for?

I shook my head to rid it of the travel malaise that was threatening *me* and read the rest of the story. Her death had happened at night, when poor visibility might explain how you could mistake hitting a person for a deer. Priscilla Waters had been knocked into a ditch where she lay undiscovered until the next afternoon when an older couple out walking their dogs noticed the body.

It appeared that the police had stonewalled the newspaper. They would make no comment about their investigation or the search for the driver of the car. Frustrated, the reporter, a James Wattle, had gone to the scene himself and reported on his findings the following week. In one spot he had noticed tire tracks swerving onto the narrow shoulder and back onto the road again and photographed them. Despite his persistence, the police spokesman, a Constable Sampson, would not confirm that the tracks were where the hit-and-run occurred.

"What an idiot!" I said, loud enough that several people at other tables turned around. I pressed my hand against my mouth, then whispered to Jane, "It's like he's trying to do the opposite of investigate. Obfuscate?"

"I know. He probably won't let us see that file either. Don't they have some kind of Freedom of Information Act here?"

"They do, but it would take weeks. We have to know now. Anyway, let's get a photocopy of these stories and her picture. And see if they found out who did it."

But there was nothing more. Though we turned to the next issue and several weeks after that, Priscilla Waters and the investigation into her death never appeared again.

Chapter 19

"WE NEED TO go back to the police station. Now they have to listen to us!" Jane cried.

"I think we need more proof." If DCI Sampson did not agree that the two women were the same, he could refuse to see us a third time no matter what evidence we had amassed by then. "Didn't you want to get coffee?"

"Now? Now I'm psyched."

Out on the sidewalk Stratford-upon-Avon was coming to life. Tourists moved slowly, staring at everything, and a knight in silver armor stood on the corner next to an Anne Hathaway look-alike and a young William Shakespeare. They weren't statues, of course, just actors standing motionless until someone approached to take their photo. Then they would spring to life and offer to pose with them—for a price.

I jumped as a beep sounded from Jane's pocket, indicating a text message. She pulled out her phone and looked at it and then at me. "Hannah."

"What does she say?"

She turned the phone around so I could read it:

Why are u in Stratford?

Busted. Colin must have told her we weren't just in London to buy books and sightsee.

"What should I tell her?"

"That you wanted to see Shakespeare's home?"

"Right. She knows he's my fave."

"Lots of people come here."

"I think she knows what we're doing."

"Probably."

It made me uneasy. I hated to have Hannah upset. And I had the irrational thought that now she knew we were in Stratford, she might come wandering down the street and see a poster of herself taped to a window.

Jane shrugged and went to work with her thumbs, then watched the screen and said, "She says we should have waited." She flipped the phone shut. "For her to finish classes, I guess."

"I thought about that. But then it would have run into Christmas and . . . it doesn't seem like she wants to do this. Find Caitlin."

Jane slipped the phone back in her pocket.

"I want to talk to Celia Banks before we go to the police," I told her.

"Who?"

"The woman in the news story. From the park."

"If she knew anything she'd have told them."

"Maybe they didn't ask the right questions. She might have

known Constable Donnelly or Priscilla Waters. She may have heard what happened with the hit-and-run investigation. It could have taken months. Where's the post office?"

Jane looked mutinous. Still jet-lagged, both of us on edge, we were on the verge of a quarrel. "They're up to their eyeballs in it," she muttered. "I don't know why you won't admit it."

She meant the police and I didn't agree. They were overprotective of their records certainly, reluctant to turn them over to foreigners who were demanding to revisit a twenty-year-old case, but that didn't make them complicit in any crime. While I wouldn't choose DCI Sampson for my prom date, I saw no reason to doubt his integrity. "That's the point. If they are involved, we'll need all the ammunition we can get. Otherwise they'll just blow us off again."

The post office was farther down Henley Street. We quickly found out that Worchester Cottage was not another village or inn, but the name of the Bankses' home. I'd forgotten that so many of the English gave their houses names. Derrick and Celia Banks's house was out on Avenue Road.

"It's just shy of a mile," the clerk warned. "You'll want a cab."

"Oh, that's nothing," Jane assured him. "I walk for miles in Manhattan."

He smiled at her and gave us directions.

As we were leaving, I remembered the newspaper reporter who had gone to the scene of the accident. "Do you know anything about a James Wattle?"

"Jimmy? The newsman? Oh, he's long gone."

Why didn't anyone ever stay in Stratford? "Where did he move to?"

He couldn't help the grin that spread across his cheerful, freckled face. "That great pressroom in the sky."

"Oh." Would they say something similar about me, I wondered, as we moved toward the exit. *She's gone to that everlasting tag sale in the clouds?*

Hopefully not for a while.

As we left the center of town and the shelter of huddled buildings, the wind sprang to life. The sky was the smudged gray of ancient white tennis balls, and there was moisture in the air that heralded snow. The always-present sense that you are in another country far from home grew stronger.

"I'd forgotten it was winter," Jane lamented, pressing her fingers against her face to warm them. "Why didn't I bring gloves? What if we get all the way out here and she's not even home? We'll have to walk all the way back."

"You have your phone, don't you? We'll get a cab."

Worchester Cottage was an impressive redbrick house set back from the road, the upstairs portion clad in white stucco with dark beams. None of the homes on this street was old, but they looked expensive, and several had the same brass nameplates in the yard that the Bankses' did. Because the house had a name, I had been expecting it to be older, with a thatched roof and clinging ivy.

The glossy black door was flanked by two urns filled with holly, a matching wreath circling the brass knocker.

"I don't see any cars," Jane whispered.

"There's a double garage."

I saw us then as the person answering the door would, two foreigners in down ski jackets, noses red from the cold, hair in windblown tangles. Would *I* let us in?

The woman who answered the door didn't, at first. Celia Banks was in her sixties, with a snowy white bob and thick bangs. She was pleasant, but spoke to us through a door opened three inches.

"Can I help you then?"

As the older messy stranger, I spoke up. "Hi, I'm Delhi Laine and this is my daughter Jane. We're looking for Celia Banks."

"Do I know you?"

"Not exactly. It's about something that happened years ago in Bancroft Gardens."

She bit at her underlip, trying to remember. "Where are you from?"

"New York. You were at the park when my little girl went missing. When they thought she drowned."

"Oh." Her head jerked back; a less dignified person might have smacked her forehead. "Come in. You look frozen. A cup of tea will set you right."

Celia Banks sat us down at her wooden kitchen table and moved around deliberately, turning the flame on under a kettle and pulling cups from a glass-fronted cabinet. The kitchen was large and modern, with stainless steel appliances and everything in its place. I marveled at how tidy it was. Amazing that some homes were always ready for unexpected company.

After a minute Mrs. Banks set a dish of Pepperidge Farm Milanos on the table between us.

We eyed the cookies greedily. We hadn't stopped to have lunch. I could have scarfed down the plateful, but delicately took a single cookie. Jane did the same.

"Milk with your tea?"

"Oh—yes, please." I didn't usually take anything in tea, but milk was a food group.

When the table was arranged to Celia Banks's satisfaction, she sat down.

Settling herself to get comfortable, she said, "I do remember that awful day, of course. I had walked down to the park to read by the river, it was so pleasant there. Everything in bloom, you know. I often did that when my boys were away at camp, and I had seen you there before." She smiled at me. "You were such a creative mum."

I laughed.

"Those little girls were always dressed in such interesting clothes!"

"I let them pick out what they wanted to wear." What I remembered were the endless loads of laundry, the constantly dwindling pile that they chose their play clothes from.

"And you've grown up to be so pretty," she told Jane. Then she added to me, "I did wonder how you managed so well with all those little ones and you being in the family way again. I couldn't have done it."

"It was a struggle," I admitted. "We came to ask about something you might have seen that afternoon. I know it was years ago, but did you notice a nanny with a plaid stroller?"

"A nanny." She closed her eyes as if trying to carry herself back. "You know, I might have. But I don't remember anything about her. The police never asked me about the other people in the park. When it happened there was so much confusion, they took our names and said they would get back to us later. I was surprised when they did."

"You were interviewed by Constable Donnelly?"

"Yes, he was the one. A nice boy. Grew up right around here."

"He was a *boy*?" Jane blurted.

"Oh, just a lad then. He couldn't have been more than nineteen. He went off to university soon after, somewhere near London. I was glad to see him making something of himself."

"So he wasn't married?"

"Oh, my goodness, no."

The image of Constable Donnelly and his wife, desperate for a child and dressing her up like a nanny to kidnap one, faded into the cabinetry.

It was time to tell Jane's story.

Chapter 20

When Jane finished explaining what she had remembered in Dr. Lundy's office, Celia Banks sat back and looked at us. "That's quite a tale."

It was okay if she didn't believe it—Colin, Patience, and DCI Sampson didn't either—but I said, "What do you think?"

"I don't know what to think. It would certainly turn everything on its ear."

And that was all she could say. She had nothing to add to the story about Priscilla Waters either; she had never known her personally. "We didn't see many plays in those days with the children so active. I don't think they ever found the car responsible for the hit-and-run. If the police knew why she was out walking in the countryside at night, they didn't say."

"What do you think of DCI Sampson?"

"Gabe Sampson? What should I think? Dedicated to his job, I know. He never married. He lived with his mother until she passed." She lifted her eyes as if consulting an old newspaper. "That was almost four years ago."

"I guess he's been here a long time."

"Came up through the ranks," she agreed.

I pushed back from the table. "We've taken a lot of your time." *And your cookies.* The plate looked pathetic with only one Milano left.

"Where are you staying?"

"The White Swan."

"Brilliant! Did you drive here?"

"No, we walked. It was fine."

Jane looked at me.

"It must have been dreadfully cold, hardly a comfortable day. I have to call in at the chemist's; I'm going right down Rother Street. I'll drop you."

"That would be wonderful." At the memory of the cutting wind, I was beyond protestations.

Driving into town, Celia Banks told us that her husband was a solicitor in Birmingham and her two sons were long-grown, but living nearby. She wished us good luck with our search, then added, "Have you been to Anne Hathaway's Cottage?"

We assured her we would go soon.

"Let's get something to eat," I said as we entered the lobby.

Jane nodded. "Cookies only go so far."

We stopped in the room to leave our coats and wash up. While Jane was using the bathroom, I turned on my iPad and connected with my e-mail. Comments from BookEm.com, my online dealers' group, two book orders, and one odd note.

Signed "Will's Boy," it read: *Neither a borrower nor a meddler be.*

Was this some kind of local advertising? The Internet knew exactly where you were and what you might need. Or had someone noticed our poster? The change of the word "lender" to "meddler" seemed too intrusive for an ad.

WHEN JANE CAME out again, patting down her hair, I showed her the message.

"Did you write back?"

"Not yet." I was trying to think of another quote from *Hamlet* with which to respond, but my memory was failing me.

"Just ask him what he knows."

"Okay." Quickly I typed in, *Do you have information for us?*

The reply was instantaneous. *When shall we three meet again, in thunder, lightning, or in rain? When the hurly-burly's done, when the battle's lost and won.*

"What's he talking about?" Jane demanded. She had no patience for the whimsical.

"It's what the witches say at the opening of *Macbeth*. I don't like that he knows there are two of us though. It's as if we're being watched."

"Maybe he saw us putting up a poster."

"We did those separately."

"Oh—right. What are you going to answer?"

"Nothing."

"*Nothing?* I thought we wanted to find out what he knows!"

"We do, but he's playing with us. Let's see what he suggests."

We waited for several minutes, then were overcome with hunger and went downstairs to the dining room. By now it would serve as an early dinner.

It wasn't until we were halfway through our shepherd's pie that I thought of something else we needed to do and looked at my watch. "Damn! I wanted to get back to the archives, but they closed at four-thirty."

"The place where we were?"

"Same building. We need to look at the playbills from twenty years ago and compare them with current ones. See if there's anyone still with the company who was there when Priscilla Waters was. Someone who can tell us more about her."

If we showed them my photograph could they identify her—or not—all these years later?

"Great idea. Maybe they'll know what really happened to her."

"And maybe what happened to Caitlin afterward." That worry had never left me. Another thought then, so horrifying that the fork slipped out of my fingers. "What if Cate was with her when she was run down? What if they hit her too?" My voice veered into the danger zone. "She was so *little*."

"Easy, Mom. They didn't find her there. They would have said."

"Would they? They don't seem to tell anybody anything."

"Newspapers have other ways of finding things out."

"I guess."

"Now *you're* into the conspiracy theory?"

"No. But if she wasn't with Priscilla, she had to be somewhere."

"Maybe she was with the husband."

"The paper didn't say she was married."

"It didn't say she wasn't."

"That's why we have to find someone who knew her," I said.

"First thing tomorrow morning."

But I hated to wait until then. I thought about going to the stage door and accosting actors as they left after the performance though I knew that was not the right way to do it. And what about Will's Boy? All we'd put on the poster was that we were looking to reunite with family members. Yet he characterized it as "meddling." Didn't that mean he knew something?

"Time here is too precious to waste," I complained.

"Well, the Christmas Market's open late tonight and it's only a couple blocks away. We could do our shopping."

I wasn't sure if she was trying to distract me or was anxious to see the market herself. The idea of wandering around and looking at stalls filled with things I cared nothing about had zero appeal for me. "You go. I want to read."

"Maybe I will later."

WE HAD BEEN back in our room, a fire in the grate, for about an hour. I'd been sitting in one of the comfortable chairs reading *The Cairo Trilogy* and Jane had been lying on the bed, dozing. Now she was in the bathroom getting ready to go out when her phone on the night table beeped with a message.

Was it from Hannah? No reason to think that, except that Jane hadn't mentioned hearing from Hannah since this morning. I knew that looking at someone else's texts was uncomfortably close to reading a diary, but I moved out of my chair, picked up the phone on the bed, and looked down at the screen.

It was from Colin.

U go back to the police yet?

I pressed the suddenly red-hot device back onto the nightstand and was in my chair when Jane returned.

I glanced at her, then back at the book. Naguib Mahfouz's words became unreadable. Jane was reporting everything we found out to Colin. No wonder she kept wanting to go back to the police station, he was pushing her to do so. I tried to rationalize away my feeling of betrayal, but couldn't. Even if I placed her communication in the best possible light, that he was, after all, her father, that maybe she thought by keeping him involved he would come around, I still couldn't stop feeling betrayed.

This was *our* quest.

I put the book facedown in my lap and watched Jane pull on her powder blue jacket.

She caught my gaze and smiled. "Sure you don't want to come? Bet you haven't finished your shopping."

I couldn't say anything.

"Mom? What's wrong?"

"You had a new message."

"Oh." She moved over and picked up her phone, glanced at it, and snapped it shut.

I was beyond coyness. "You're texting Dad everything we're finding out."

She didn't bother with *How dare you look at my phone.* She wasn't even defensive. "So? He wants to know."

"You know he'll block us any way he can."

"Why do you think that? He's just being careful."

"He's afraid it will disrupt his life."

She finished zipping her jacket. "Hers too. But it's not that he's working against us." A stern look. "That's really paranoid—you know?"

I shrugged and turned my book back over, too embarrassed to explain the rest of what I was feeling. Jane had always seemed closer to Colin, partly by temperament and partly because he made it so. This trip to England was the first time she and I had done something alone and I had been relishing our intimacy. But Colin had even managed to be here.

"I won't be long."

"Have fun."

Chapter 21

IT WAS TIME to check my iPad for e-mails again, as I had been doing every twenty minutes. There was another volley of messages from BookEm.com, mostly lists of books other dealers were offering for sale, and a query about mailing books to Russia. Ads from Amazon and L.L. Bean—and an e-mail from Will's Boy.

I went to that first. Nothing else mattered.

Meet me at the Christmas Market. First clue: If music be the food of love, play on.

First clue?

I typed back *What kind of music?*

My kind.

Was there entertainment at the market? It was the time of year for carols. In my mind I saw a stringed group playing "Greensleeves" or "The Holly and the Ivy" on a small platform, shoppers sleepwalking in front of them. I'd wait there until Will's Boy came up to me.

I tried tamping down my excitement, but couldn't help fumbling with my jacket zipper. Could we really be about to find Caitlin? I wasn't sure why he was making it into a game, but I didn't care. Maybe he had grown up with Caitlin right here in Stratford.

Be still, my heart.

Outside the hotel it was even colder but the world was ablaze. Fir trees everywhere were outlined with strings of red and white bulbs, garlands with large stars in the center were strung across the streets. Even if I had not known how to get to Henley Street, I would only have needed to follow the crush of people headed in one direction.

When I stepped onto Henley Street, the Christmas Market seemed to stretch out forever, booths under blue-and-white striped awnings on one side and stands with separate blue-and-yellow umbrellas on the other. I paused, able to see my breath in the freezing air, and tried to hear the music. But though I could smell the burnt meaty odor of roasting chestnuts, and blinked at the lights, which seemed to be in competition as to which could shine brightest, I could pick out nothing but the cries of voices around me.

I was only at the beginning, I told myself. Maybe the music was softer and playing farther down.

The stalls I passed displayed expensive leather purses, hand-knitted scarves, mittens, and gourmet foodstuffs. Keeping to the center of Henley Street, I tried to avoid the clog of serious shoppers eager to fill their bags. I didn't let myself think that maybe this treasure hunt was only a cruel joke, a way for someone to have a bit of fun.

Then I saw a display of antique instruments, mandolins, flutes, and miniature keyboards ahead on my right. Will's kind of music? Dubiously I edged over until I was directly in front of a man in a tweed cap with a pleasant grizzled face.

"Can I interest you in a French lute, ducky?"

It was impossible not to laugh. "Maybe. I'm supposed to be meeting somebody, but I'm not sure who."

"Ah." He reached under the wooden table, pulled out an envelope, and handed it to me. "I think this is what you want."

"Really?" I took out the paper inside and read it aloud. "*Then heigh-ho the holly. This life is most jolly.*"

"*As You Like It,*" he said.

"But what does it mean?"

"Why not go to a booth that sells Christmas wreaths. Down another street."

Was everyone in on this game?

"Who gave this to you?"

"Swore me to secrecy, he did. Said it was to be a surprise."

"Well . . . thanks."

I moved on, stepping around people, looking for Jane as I walked.

The booth in the next block that sold decorations and wreaths had been left in the charge of a teenage girl. She stood shivering and sullen in a red wool coat.

I smiled at her. "Do you have a message for me?"

She gave me a foggy look, as if I had asked for something not in her job description.

"Did someone leave a piece of paper with you for me to pick up?" I prompted.

A shake of the head, then she turned to straighten a boxwood kissing ball.

I stood watching her, uncertain what to do. If the man at the first booth hadn't directed me here, I would have moved on and looked for another stand selling greenery.

"Nobody gave you an envelope," I confirmed.

Her eyes flashed. "You didn't *say* envelope."

I love you too.

Reaching under the counter, she yanked it out by one white corner, nearly throwing it at me. I didn't bother to ask any questions about who had left it with her.

Moving out of reach in case she decided to snatch it back, I extracted the message. *Dost thou think because thou art virtuous there shall be no more cakes and ale?*

Cakes and ale? Every second booth seemed to be selling something to eat or drink. How could I possibly stop and ask at each one if they had a message for me? The crazy American lady looking for signs and portents. *Do you have a message for me? Yes—get a life.* I reminded myself that this was a matter of life and death, that my ego didn't count. *Think.* Not every stand sold alcohol. I could bypass those dedicated to gingerbread castles, gourmet teas, and foods that came in a tin.

There was a jerk on my jacket sleeve. "Mom?"

I turned and saw Jane. She was red-cheeked and breathless and carrying several bags. "You didn't say you were coming!"

"I wasn't. But then I got an e-mail from Will's Boy."

"Really? He wrote back?"

"He gave me some 'clues' to follow."

"Listen, I'm in the midst of getting something, it's for you, so you can't see. I was about to pay for it when I saw you. Go on ahead and I'll catch up."

She hurried away and I kept walking, finally understanding that *none* of the booths was selling beer or ale. Perhaps there was a regulation against it. But up ahead on my left, standing alone beyond the last striped umbrella, was a pub. Was that where Will's Boy meant?

As I approached the weathered wooden door of the Singing Bard wreathed in decorative lights of its own, a high-pitched voice called from the alleyway beyond, "Over here!"

I stopped. Was Will's Boy a *woman*? I had never pictured my correspondent as anything but a young man. *Caitlin?* Could it possibly be Caitlin herself? Breathless, I moved quickly around to the passageway, but couldn't see anyone in the darkness.

There was a laugh. "Don't be afraid. In here."

How long had she been standing in the cold waiting for me? Had she been tracking my progress through the fair, watching me pick up the clues, staying a few feet behind? For all I knew, she had been at my shoulder and darted ahead when I stopped to talk to Jane. It made sense; she *wanted* me to find her. If she saw I was losing the trail, she might decide to confront me directly or change her plan.

In contrast to the lights of the Christmas fair, the tinkle of "Good King Wenceslas" coming from a faraway booth, the alley looked cold and dark. But I stepped into it eagerly. I could finally make out the silhouette of a figure slouched against the building. The excitement, bubbling through my chest and into my throat, was choking me. Would I actually meet Caitlin tonight? Now? *Had she been here in Stratford all along?*

"Mrs. Fitzhugh?"

"Yes!" But why was she or he—now it sounded more like a young man—calling me by that name? In the spirit of the times, I had never taken Colin's name, I had never called myself anything but Delhi Laine. I had put no name at all on the poster. But of course—it was Caitlin's last name too. Whoever this was knew her name.

The figure turned toward me wearing the ubiquitous hoodie, but when I saw the face, I nearly screamed. Where the face *should* have been was a gaudy mask, the visage of Shakespeare, complete with a papier-mâché mustache and ruffed collar.

Will's Boy.

"So you finally came back."

"*Caitlin?* Is that you?"

"Mummy?" The figure moved toward me as if for an embrace, then stepped back with a laugh. "What made you come here now?"

"To find you! What?" The mask muffled a comment I could not make out. "Someone sent a note saying you hadn't drowned." I could barely get the words out. "So I came back and found you'd been kidnapped by a woman named Priscilla Waters."

The figure stumbled back slightly, then recovered. "Who said that?"

"It's a long story. But—"

"Tell me." The voice was suddenly lower, unmistakably male, and I felt a sick disappointment. Not my daughter.

"The police know we're here, but I just found out about Priscilla. She's dead, of course, she got what she deserved, but still— what happened to Caitlin after she died?"

"All you can think about is your daughter?" The high-pitched voice squeaked higher in anger. "You Americans are such pigs."

"Who else should I care about?" My disappointment flared into anger matching his. "Not what happened to some bitch who kidnapped her!"

Suddenly he was moving around behind me and I was terrified he would leave by the back of the alley. "No, wait!"

When I felt the zipper of my jacket press against my throat, I wondered what was wrong. Then I realized the pressure was from his arm, bringing me against him. I started to cough, and then was choking. What was he doing?

Instinctively I bent my knee and jammed my foot against his leg. Too low for his groin, but it caught him off balance and loosened his grip, enough for me to thrust my head forward and then back against his chin. A crack sounded as the papier-mâché shattered in the cold.

He yelped as the material pinched his face. "*You're* the bitch."

I tried banging his leg with my other foot, but this time he was ready, shifting out of the way like a dancer.

His arm tightened more, and spots pulsed in front of my eyes, red, blue, yellow. *Out, out damn spot. I'm going to die.* Leaning forward, I made one desperate thrust with my body, pulling us both to the left.

As we went down, I knew it would hurt.

Chapter 22

THE PRESSURE ON my throat relaxed as his arm hit the ground, just enough to allow me to take a breath. "Help! Somebody help!" I knew it wasn't loud enough for anyone to hear. Yet I thought I heard, "Mom? Mom!" A sudden excruciating pain on my arm as Will extricated himself and pressed down against me to stand up. A scrape of pebbles on cement as he ran from the light.

"Mom! Mom, are you okay?" Someone was pulling at my shoulder, creating a fast- spreading pain throughout my back.

I wanted the pain to stop, but I couldn't say anything. I couldn't even open my eyes.

"Is she breathing? What happened?" A deeper voice, a man's. "Maudie, call the station. Tell them we need the doctor too."

"It's my mother! This guy had her on the ground, choking her. He got up and ran away when I started yelling." Jane sounded frantic.

"Here, let me." A heavier hand, this time on my chest. "Okay now. She's breathing, she's okay. Your mother will be okay. The constable will bring a medic."

Now I did open my eyes and looked up at a ruddy-faced man. Jane was kneeling at my other side, many other people behind them. I wanted to say that I was okay but my throat hurt too much to talk.

"The constable's on his way," someone from the crowd of people called over.

I thought about pushing up on one elbow, but I couldn't make myself move.

"Did he get your purse, love?" An older woman with frameless glasses was holding on to the kneeling man. Kind, so kind, someone who would serve you a cuppa in a tearoom with a warm smile.

He hadn't been interested in my purse. I realized it was the lumpy bulk I was lying on. "No," I whispered.

"That's a blessing." But she was shaking her head. "For such a terrible thing to happen here of all places, and during the fair!"

The man again. "What's keeping that constable?"

As he pushed himself up, I saw that he was wearing a white bar apron and was in his shirtsleeves.

The police, yes. I needed the police.

Constable Bradford, accompanied by a man who must have been the doctor, arrived at the Singing Bard shortly after that. The constable didn't hide his dismay at the attack, stooping down as he watched the doctor examine me and closing his eyes in gratitude when it was ascertained that I was only bruised. By then I had pushed up into a sitting position, Jane supporting my back. But both men insisted I go to the hospital to be checked out.

The drive to Warwick Hospital through the dark countryside

took nearly fifteen minutes. When I shifted, trying to get comfortable in the police cruiser seat the pain was slightly less than at first, but I was dazed, as if I had been dropped from a high building. I had been attacked other times while trying to discover the truth of a situation, but this felt deeply personal, as if he would have *enjoyed* choking the life out of me. Yet he had seemed friendly enough in the beginning . . .

I wasn't allowed to walk into the hospital by myself, an orderly pushed my wheelchair, but I was left in the waiting room with Jane until a doctor could examine me. Constable Bradford, his expressive face etched with concern, once again made sure we had tea. Then he settled himself in the chair next to mine.

"D'you think this has to do with what you were telling DCI Sampson?"

"I know it does." For several minutes I felt too exhausted to explain, too assaulted by the clinically bright lights of the room, but finally I did.

As soon as I began talking, the constable pulled out a small black notebook and started taking notes. "I'll make sure DCI Sampson sees my report," Constable Bradford promised when I was finished and sat back exhausted, eyes closed. Then I reminded him, "Don't forget the man at the antique instruments booth. He seemed to know who he was."

"We'll check with him first thing," he promised.

Given her earlier concern, I might have expected Jane to hover over me, to make sure that answering his questions wasn't too much for me. To keep checking on how I felt and trying to do things for me. Instead she wandered around the waiting area, stopping now and then to text on her phone. Yet I knew Jane. Given how terrified she had been, how frightened she was that I was dying, she *had* to believe that I would be fine, needed to act as if that were true.

And I knew it was true.

A half hour later a doctor confirmed that nothing had been broken, though much was bruised.

Bruised, but not broken. The story of my life.

Chapter 23

Jane and I slept in again the next morning. I finally stirred in the king-sized bed and moved gingerly to look at the travel clock, then snapped my eyes shut. My neck and shoulders screamed when I moved, my throat hurt when I tried to swallow. My relief at being spared to sell books another day had been overcome by a letdown close to despair. Why couldn't it have been Caitlin behind the mask? I had hoped for so much and learned so little. For all I knew, Will's Boy could have seen our flyer and e-mail and simply decided to have some fun.

Some fun? That was ludicrous. He had known who I was, why I was there, and was somehow invested in it. I tried to recreate our conversation. Something about why I had come back. There was nothing on the poster that indicated, in our search to reunite with relatives, that we had ever been in Stratford before. He had used the name Fitzhugh. I had the sense, supported by very little, that he had been angry with Caitlin. Had he known her, had she treated him badly? But he also seemed angry when I insulted Priscilla Waters.

Perhaps he was just an angry young man.

"How do you feel?" The bed jiggled as Jane sat up.

"Ugh. I won't be walking out to anyone's house today."

"First thing, we're going to the police station like Constable Bradford said. What time do you think Sampson gets there?"

"Wednesday he came in around nine."

"So we have time for a real breakfast?"

"Bring it on."

ANOTHER POLICEMAN WAS on duty at the desk when we came in, polite, but without the warmth of Roderick Bradford. The lights on the desktop tree were still blinking out of sync, and I could hear laughter from an interior room. I wondered if they shut the station down for Christmas.

After several minutes DCI Sampson appeared and showed us into what must have been an interrogation room. It was plain with pale green walls, an oak table and chairs. The only wall decoration was an evacuation plan.

When we were sitting facing him, he looked at me as if I were a carton of milk left out all night. "So you had a spot of bother last night."

I rubbed my throat. "I thought you said you only had purse snatchings here," I croaked furiously.

"He tried to kill her!" Jane burst in, indignant, as if he were a salesman trying a bait-and-switch maneuver. "What kind of a place is this, anyway?"

His gray eyes flickered over her face, unperturbed. "One of the safest villages in England. Roddy tells me it had to do with those flyers you've been plastering all over."

That's right, blame the victim.

I shrugged and was sorry as pain rippled through my shoulders.

"Roddy said your assailant addressed you by name."

"He called me by my husband's name. And Caitlin's. It wasn't on the flyer."

Sampson tapped his pen on the table as if he were preparing it to write. "Tell me exactly what he said."

I tried to remember. "It was all so fast, and not what I was expecting. He was wearing that Shakespeare mask, and I had to strain to hear." I couldn't bear to tell Sampson of my hope that it was Caitlin herself. "He said something about being surprised that I came back. He asked me what I knew. Oh, I mentioned Priscilla Waters and he didn't like that. Then I asked about Caitlin again and he got angry. That's when he got behind me and started choking me. I was trying to fight him off when Jane came."

He nodded. "Was he a large man?"

"Taller than me, but not six feet, thin but a muscular build. With the hoodie and the mask, I couldn't even see his hair color."

"Was he wearing gloves?"

"He must have been. It was cold."

Sampson sighed. "Describe the mask again." He was using the pen now, making notes on a lined pad.

"Well, it was obviously Shakespeare. It had that domed bald forehead and hair over his ears, a narrow mustache and white collar."

"Rubber?"

"Papier-mâché. It cracked when I banged against it." I thought of something. "It reminded me of those figures on the street who pretend to be statues. We saw one of Shakespeare yesterday. But I guess the shops sell a lot of those masks."

"Not so many. Considered in bad taste. Not like the States."

I thought of the masks I'd seen around Halloween, every image from Richard Nixon to Bernie Madoff, and decided not to defend my native land.

"You said the mask cracked?"

"Probably around the nose or chin. It really made him angry. Angrier. The other thing I told Constable Bradford was about his voice. It was so high-pitched, it was unusual."

"But a man's."

"I think so. His body felt like a man's. The way he attacked me, that kind of fury. Like someone outside a bar who thinks he's been insulted. I'm not even sure it was something planned. When he e-mailed me it was more like a game."

He jerked back, startled. "He contacted you over the Internet?"

Evidently Constable Bradford had forgotten to tell him that part.

I explained about the treasure hunt and the clues. "The man at the antique instruments seemed to know who he was."

"You have the e-mail address he used?"

I reached in my bag and handed the address I had copied out.

For a moment DCI Sampson looked excited. Then he said, "Probably bounced it off somewhere else, making it untraceable. But we'll check it."

"But the man at the instrument booth seemed to know him." Why not just cut to the chase?

"Roddy interviewed George last night. Your friend was already wearing his mask."

"Is my mom still in danger?" Jane interrupted.

"I don't know." DCI Sampson looked at me directly. "Make

sure you stay close to other people until we figure this out. Don't go wandering off by yourself. If he contacts you again, call me right away. Something else."

I thought he had another safeguard in mind, but he said, "Why did you mention Priscilla Waters?"

"Oh." Jane and I looked at each other, realizing we hadn't yet had a chance to tell him about that connection. I reached into my bag and took out the manila envelope. Pulling out my photo and the newspaper photocopy, I laid them on the table facing him.

He read the news stories carefully. "Where did you get that photograph?"

"I took it. The day my daughter disappeared."

"And you believe them to be the same person."

"It is!" Jane answered before I could. "That's the woman who told me to tell my 'mum' that Caitlin had fallen into the river. She put her in that stroller when I was getting the flower for her."

"We *think* she put Caitlin in the stroller." I hated to correct Jane, but I didn't want him to think it was something Jane had seen.

"Did you mention that to your assailant?"

"No." In the cold light of the interrogation room, I was embarrassed to tell him I had said that Priscilla had gotten what she deserved.

He stood up. "Thank you. We'll take it from here."

That was it?

Chapter 24

FROM THE POLICE station we went back to the Shakespeare Birthplace Trust, this time to look at playbills.

"This could be tedious," I warned, as we sat at a table waiting for the material. "Maybe you'd like to do something else. I hear Anne Hathaway's Cottage is worth a visit."

Jane laughed. "Are you kidding? I'm not letting you out of my sight!"

"I don't think anything else will happen."

"Mom, he tried to *kill* you. If I hadn't been trying to catch up and seen you go in, you wouldn't be here. I'd be trying to have you—what's the word for when they send the bodies home?"

"Repatriated. And we didn't even buy travel insurance to cover it. Dad would be furious."

"It's not funny," she protested. "Imagine if we had come over here to look for Caitlin and you'd been killed instead."

When I saw how upset she still was, I reached over and pressed her hand. Even when she was a little girl, Jane rarely cried. She would get angry instead and stamp her foot, her cheeks flaming, eyes squinched in fury. On the occasions when crying was her only option, she would open her mouth and howl. She wasn't near tears now, but her world had been shaken.

"It was the last thing I was expecting," I admitted. "All those quotes from plays seemed so . . . good-natured."

"I don't get it. I don't get why he'd want to attack you. It makes no sense."

It was a question I had no answer for.

WE FOUND PRISCILLA Waters's name listed in several productions in the early 1990s though she never had large roles. She was usually cast as a lady-in-waiting or someone's mother. We made a long list of everyone who had acted in the plays with her. There seemed to be about forty or fifty actors in the company. I thought about listing the production staff as well, but that was Plan B. If none of the actors was still with the company, we could go back and try to find support staff.

The theater gods were with us. A number of the earlier company remained, and two of the women were in tonight's production of *King Lear*.

"Have you ever seen it?" I asked Jane.

"Are you kidding?"

"Maybe we can still get tickets. We could talk to those actresses afterward."

"Actors, Mom. They call themselves actors now. We don't have to see the play to talk to them."

"I know, but it would be fun. Think how impressed your friends will be when you tell them you saw a Shakespearean play right in Stratford-upon-Avon."

Jane rolled her eyes. "They'll just die."

WHAT CAN YOU say about watching a play in the same theater where it was performed four hundred years earlier? Outside, the lanterns shimmering off cobblestone streets and half-timbered houses helped to create the mood. Inside the theater the excitement was as intense as if the Bard himself were to appear for a curtain call. *King Lear* was one of my favorites, and I took it as a good omen that we could see that rather than having to sit through several hours of tomorrow night's play, *The Merry Wives of Windsor.*

The theater was large, though not as large as the Metropolitan Opera House, with deep-red seats. It had a number of levels like the Met, the tiers protected by wooden spindles. It was not a stretch to imagine the theater looking this way several hundred years ago.

Marian Baycroft, who played Regan, was a black-haired woman with artificially rosy cheeks and a way of giving her head a sarcastic toss. She must have started early with the company, I decided; she looked no older than I was. I hoped she was as friendly as everyone else we'd met. Scratch that; everyone but Will's Boy and DCI Sampson, although the detective wished us no harm. Maybe he was just tired of Americans.

Jane settled in the velvet seat beside me and watched the play thoughtfully. When she was growing up, Colin and I despaired of her resistance to anything not factual. On one dig, when Colin tried to entertain us by reading C.S. Lewis aloud in the evenings, Jane had refused to be engaged. "They can't go through a closet to another country," she declared. "What about customs? Why do they have to go to Narnia anyway? Why can't they stay home and do stuff?"

Colin tried to explain the concept of fantasy, but Jane would have none of it. Being Colin, he kept on reading over her protests until she was drawn into the story.

Thinking about it now, I wondered if it had been related to her own protests against having to travel to so many unfamiliar places while her friends stayed home and built sturdy lives.

My other children had never taken to reading either, not with my passion for books. Hannah loved stories about animals, and was interested in the Sweet Valley High series when it was passed around her classroom. Jason, close to dyslexia, had avoided books altogether. He loved action movies, as violent as possible, and computer games. Would Caitlin have been the child who loved literature, the one to whom I could have introduced the "Shoe" books of Noel Streatfeild and the fantasies of Ray Bradbury? Would *she* have been the one always curled up with a book?

Dangerous thinking. I could not allow myself to give in to imagining a child who filled the gaps left by the others. It was what Hannah had been frightened would happen. My children were my children and I loved them for exactly who they were. Not perfect, but I had never tried to change them into something else.

I shook off my fantasies about Caitlin and watched Jane. The story was intense and her eyes widened in all the right places. No princesses or talking lions here.

I was the restless one. I could not get my sore body comfortable in the seat, and watching the play seemed unbearable. All I could think was, *This is going to end badly*, without distinguishing between the tragedy that would overtake Lear and what would happen to us. Only last night I had been coaxed into an alley and unexpectedly attacked. He had stopped only when Jane appeared and forced him to run off. Was he somewhere nearby waiting to finish what he had started? Did he think I knew a secret he didn't want anyone else to find out? Perhaps he might even attack Jane to get back at me.

Unable to relax in my seat, tense and jumpy at every movement in the aisle, I fantasized that we were safely on a plane home.

I BLINKED—HAD I been dozing?—as the overhead lights flashed on and the applause died away. *Intermission*. People around us were rising from their seats and clogging the aisles.

"Let's go," Jane urged.

"Where?"

"We can get something to drink."

Was it safe? But maybe it wasn't safe sitting alone in our seats either. I got up and followed Jane. Surely in this crush of bodies nothing could happen.

Over a glass of Pinot Grigio, I asked, "Did you tell Dad about the attack on me?"

Jane looked at me for a minute. "No."

"Really?"

"Really."

"Thank you."

"Why? Why wouldn't you want him to know?"

Why wouldn't I? I decided it was because he would either be too worried, especially about Jane, or his attitude would be, *What do you expect? Kick a hornet's nest and you'll get stung.* But there was more to it. What to do about Caitlin had put us on opposing teams. He might see the attack as an advantage for his side. And if I had died? I saw him in a dark suit, hugging the children to comfort them, feeling as if life had dealt him one more blow.

He would also hate being identified as the man whose wife had been murdered in Shakespeare's picturesque town. I knew he would mourn my dying so young, perhaps agonize over what might have been in our future. But I was a book he had already read. I couldn't make him break down and throw himself on the flames.

I had to be careful not to demonize Colin though. He and Hannah had a right to their reservations.

"How are we going to approach this actress?" Jane said. "Just walk up to her?"

"I don't know. Go backstage and see if she'll talk to us, I guess. Why wouldn't she?"

"Maybe we could send her a note asking to have a drink with us. Say that we're New York theater lovers. Invite her back to the hotel."

"You think she'd come?"

"For a free drink and admiration? You don't know theater people, Mom."

Shrugging, I pulled out the notebook I always carried to keep book information in, removed a page, and waited for Jane to dictate.

She thought. "Okay. 'Dear Ms. Baycroft.' " She paused. "Uh— 'We're visiting from New York and a friend suggested we get in touch with you. We'd be pleased if you would join us for a drink at the White Swan after the performance, where we are staying. Sincerely, Jane Fitzhugh and Delhi Laine.' She'll be impressed that we're staying there. Celia Banks was."

"*I'm* impressed that we're staying there. But—'a friend'?"

"Well . . . we don't want to frighten her."

"Fine. You handle it."

"Lighten up, Mom. It's going to be fine." Jane took the paper, folded it, and approached an usher with a smile that could charm the stripes off his dress pants.

"He's going to take it to her right now," she reported.

"Let's hope she shows." I still thought that ambushing her at the stage door was the better plan.

Chapter 25

WHEN WE GOT back to the White Swan, we found that our seats on the couch by the fireplace had been usurped, so we positioned ourselves at a small wooden table where we could watch the door. I ordered my usual cider and Jane, white wine. She saw Marian Baycroft before I did and waved.

When she came closer to us, smiling expectantly, I saw that with her stage makeup scrubbed off she was at least fifty. Marian had not done a great job cleaning off her greasepaint, though. It stuck in the lines of her forehead, accentuating the creases, and made the crow's feet around her large brown eyes more noticeable.

Jane, smiling too, pushed back the third chair.

"I'm intrigued," Marian said, unbuttoning her black cloth cape and giving her hair a shake. "Did Leo send you?"

"I don't remember who it was exactly," Jane said smoothly. "We know so many theater folk. Whoever it was got excited when we said we were coming to Stratford, and told us we had to look you up."

"Are you in—"

"Actually," I interrupted, "We wanted to ask you about an actress you used to work with. But first things first. What can we get you to drink?"

She laughed. "A half pint of Guinness would be grand."

I raised my hand for the waiter.

"Your Regan was wonderful," Jane told her. "I was captivated. It's not easy to make her as sympathetic as you did."

"Why, thank you. Do you act?"

"No, I'm in finance. But I live in Manhattan and spend my life in the theater. My mother"—she indicated me—"lives out on Long Island."

This was the girl who scorned anything "not real"?

Time to get this horse back into its stall.

But Marian did it for me. "This actress you mentioned—is she in some kind of trouble?"

Worse than that. "Her name was Priscilla Waters."

"Priscilla? But she died ages ago! How could—"

"I know. We're trying to trace members of her family. For the American branch."

I didn't want to tell her the whole story but didn't want to lie either. Trying to find her family was not untrue.

The waiter set down a cardboard coaster with the White Swan logo and placed her beer on it expertly. She reached for the glass. "Have you talked to Nick?"

Jane and I looked at each other. I took a stab. "Her husband?"

"Ex-husband. I don't even know where he is these days. They were already divorced when she joined the company. Actually I don't know what his first name is. I meant her son Nick. He's Nick Clancy."

"He's here in Stratford? Really?"

"Oh, he's around. Does odd jobs for the company, props and

box office, and does some street theater. Her older boy, I can't remember his name either, he went off to university and didn't come back. Nick was the one most affected by the accident."

I hadn't envisioned Priscilla having children. "How old was he when it happened?"

"Around eleven, I think. Certainly no more than twelve. It hit him badly. He went to live with his father but had a rocky go of it."

"We'd love to meet him," Jane said eagerly. "To let him know he has cousins in the States. They'll be excited to hear about him too."

"Well, he's always around the theater. Or on Henley Street, dressed as Shakespeare." The humorous turn-up of her mouth indicated what she thought of that. "He must be thirty now, but you'd never know it."

Oh, my God. Priscilla Waters's son in a Shakespearean mask? And I had told him she got what she deserved. And called her a bitch.

"Is he an actor too?" Jane was asking.

Marian looked heavenward. "Everyone in Stratford is an actor. Every last resident has secret hopes and dreams. But no, Nick will never be any more than a would-be."

I struggled to think of what else we needed to know. "Did they ever find out what happened to Priscilla?"

"Not as far as I know. They blamed it on wild youngsters who didn't even know they'd hit someone. Those country roads have no lights at all. But no one knew why she was out in the countryside at night."

"Was she a good actor?" Jane asked.

"She'd only joined the company the year before. She was older than I was and did character bits. It was only my third year; I didn't have large parts myself."

She had nearly finished her beer and flicked her wrist to see her watch.

"So she had two sons," I said quickly. "Did she ever say she wanted a daughter?"

"She may have. People always want what they don't have, don't you know. My sister had five girls before the boy came along. She said afterward she needn't have bothered."

I laughed. "Would Priscilla have adopted a girl, do you think?"

"A daughter? Why? She had a hard enough time getting on as it was. There was never enough money for her. She complained about her ex-husband not paying his fair share. The last thing she would have wanted was another responsibility." Marian finished her Guinness. "It was all so long ago, but I don't remember her as a happy person. She was sure she would be happy *if only*. If only she had better parts, if only she'd meet the perfect man." She pushed up from the table. "Sorry, I have to run. Say hi to the New York chaps."

Then she stopped in the middle of fastening her cape. "I'll tell you who knows more about Priscilla. Marjory Kingsley. She was her closest friend in the company and I know she's kept up with the boys. She's retired, but she volunteers at Anne Hathaway's Cottage. What's tomorrow, Saturday? She should definitely be there. If you go, tell her cheerio from me."

When we were alone again, Jane said, "Are you thinking what I'm thinking?"

"Nick Clancy."

"It all makes sense!" She signaled the waiter to bring her another Chardonnay.

I finished my cider quickly though I didn't want another. "Except for Priscilla Waters. There's no reason why she would have taken Caitlin. According to Marian, she was an ambitious actress with two kids to support already. And divorced. Why would she want the extra burden of a two-year-old, especially one she'd have to explain? It was too risky, especially with Caitlin's photo in the papers."

"I know. When you put it that way . . ."

"Priscilla might not be the woman in the photo at all. And—damn!"

"What?"

"We didn't show Marian my photograph. We should have showed her the photograph."

We both looked at the door as if she might miraculously still be there.

"But look at it from another way," Jane argued. "Her son Nick has a Shakespeare mask. That's huge. He might even be that Shakespeare we saw standing on the corner yesterday posing for photos."

I nodded. "He didn't deny she had taken Caitlin. He just got angry."

The waiter set down Jane's wine but she didn't look at it. "And he sought us out for a reason. Maybe the woman who kidnapped Caitlin was his aunt. Or something."

We went on fantasizing—what else was there to do? "Suppose Pricilla's husband had always wanted a daughter, and she thought this would bring him back. But instead she dies mysteriously."

"And the husband takes Caitlin when he takes Nick," I suggested.

"That's why Nick was so angry with you. His father loved Caitlin and gave *him* a hard time."

"And he wanted to kill me because?"

"You're her mother."

We had reached the end of the yellow brick road. "But wouldn't Nick and his brother have told their father where she came from? He probably would have just handed her over to the authorities. Why would he want the responsibility of a strange child?"

"Yeah."

A leaden disappointment fell over the table. It didn't matter if Priscilla Waters or someone else took Caitlin, or even if we were horribly wrong and my little girl had drowned. She was still lost to us and finding her was as improbable as it had ever been. What we needed to do now was keep out of harm's way until we left for home Sunday and went back to the way our lives had been. My bruises would heal and we'd be none the worse for our adventure. Jane and I might even stay close. Our family would limp along as before. "Maybe we can leave a little earlier. Tomorrow instead of Sunday."

Jane's head jerked up from studying the coaster. "What are you talking about? We have to call the police and let them know about Nick!"

"At almost midnight? I don't think so."

"First thing in the morning then. Come on, let's get to bed. We have a lot to do."

"Aren't you going to finish your wine?"

"I need sleep more."

Chapter 26

AND THEN IT snowed. Detouring over to the window on my way back from the bathroom at dawn, I saw that the world had been outlined in white by a fine pen—tree limbs, the curves of wrought-iron gates, the tops of shop signs. The snow had left a white line along the edges of half-timbered buildings. Yet it did not plunge me into any fantasy about the world looking this way in Shakespeare's time. I fretted that the snow would not stop falling, and we would never be able to get home.

"DCI Sampson probably doesn't even work on Saturdays," I grumbled to Jane an hour later. She had leaped out of bed and was doing morning stretches.

"You know what? You're suffering from post-traumatic stress. How are you feeling anyway? Physically, I mean."

"Oh, I'm okay." I moved my neck experimentally, and felt an unwelcome twinge that radiated down my back. When I swallowed I found that some soreness lingered. "I guess I'll live."

"You need coffee. And oatmeal. Wouldn't oatmeal with brown sugar taste good on a snowy day?"

"I *said* I'll live."

"Good. Then get dressed. We have a lot to do and the police station opens early."

"WE KNOW WHO attacked my mother." Jane had picked up the reins of the investigation, rescued them from my lifeless hands, and gotten us through breakfast and back to the police station.

We were sitting in DCI Sampson's own office, a comfortingly efficient space with no Christmas decorations, a relief after the blinking colors and artificial garlands everywhere else. The prints on the walls were of fine-textured fish, so detailed that they might have come from an old zoology text. With each successive visit, Sampson let us a little further into his world, like a shy furry animal gradually inviting us into his lair. Next he would be taking us home for tea.

"He contacted you again?"

"No. We talked to an actress last night who knew Priscilla Waters. She said Priscilla had a son, Nick Clancy."

"She said he does street theater and has a Shakespeare mask," I added.

Sampson looked as surprised as he probably ever did. "I'd forgotten about the boys. Different last name, of course."

"Do you know Nick Clancy?"

"Let's just say he's no stranger to the Stratford constabulary. I remember the hit-and-run too. No one ever came forward, and it was closed as an accident by persons unknown."

I leaned forward. "Marian Baycroft—the actress—thought Nick had been very affected by his mother's death."

"Perhaps he was. But that was years ago." His pursed lips under the small mustache indicated that holding on to grief for so long was unseemly, that Nick should have manned up long ago and gotten on with his life.

"How can we find him? We need to talk to him."

"Mom!"

"I wouldn't advise that, Ms. Laine."

"And what would you advise?" Perhaps I was too used to making demands of Long Island policemen, but I was not letting this drop. "I need to know why he attacked me and what he knows. If I promise not to press charges, do you think he'd talk to me?"

Sampson sat back in his chair regarding us. "I'll bring him in. You can talk to him here. We were going to question him anyway." I must have looked skeptical, because he added, "The vendors at the fair couldn't identify him because he was wearing the mask. But we're familiar with the high-pitched voice you mentioned."

In America they would have already had him in a cell. I wondered how the British could afford to be so leisurely and still solve any crimes.

"You won't leave us alone with him, will you?" Jane worried.

"Jane, he's not Hannibal Lecter."

"He tried to kill you!"

"Nick's a wildcard," Sampson said. "I want to hear what he has to say and have a look at that mask. If you damaged it the way you say you did—"

"Maybe he's already left town." Jane sounded as if he had fled to South America.

"Nick? Your original bad penny? He has nowhere else to go and he's too arrogant to think he'd ever get caught." He pushed back from his desk. "Come back in an hour. We'll have him here."

"I DON'T THINK he's taking the attack on you seriously enough," Jane complained, as we sat in a shop on the main street, having coffee. "If he knew who did it, why hadn't he arrested Nick already?"

The Merrie Tea Cosy was fully given over to the holidays, with ropes of fragrant evergreens stretching from corner to corner, Santas and felt elves on every shelf. A topiary ball near the fireplace was covered with tiny scarlet bows. Even the shortbread bars we ordered were dusted with red and green sprinkles.

"Well, he didn't see me right after it happened. I guess I don't look that bruised now."

"But still. And what was all that about not pressing charges?"

"If it's like it is at home, if you don't press charges, it doesn't stick. Unless there's serious damage maybe. But if there's a dust-up and a victim refuses to testify, there's not much they can do."

"But why wouldn't you?"

Once again I felt Will's forearm cruelly crushing my throat, my fight to take a breath. "I want to know what he knows. If he won't talk to me, I will press charges."

"He's a monster! He needs to be locked up for a long time. And Sampson is right. He should have gotten a life years ago."

DCI SAMPSON LED us into the interrogation room where we had met with him—was it just yesterday? Even though we were at a police station, even though a detective was with us, I couldn't tamp down my apprehension. What if Nick leaped up from the chair and thrust a knife into my chest? He'd be arrested, but I'd be dead. I had said he was no Hannibal Lecter, but that didn't mean he couldn't move fast. Two months ago a friend of mine had almost died from such a knife wound.

"Just here, Ms. Laine."

And then I was sitting across from a slight figure in a sweat-shirt who glared at me but stayed rooted to his chair. When he was viciously pressing me against him, trying to choke away my breath, he had felt immense, unstoppable.

Now I wondered if it was the same person. Splayed across a straight wooden chair, wearing a leather jacket with the hood of a gray sweatshirt sticking out the back, he looked more like a super-market bagger than a killer. He was good-looking enough without his mask, his black hair in loose curls, cheeks still rosy from the cold. Only the resentful twist of his mouth and eyes half closed as if in boredom, spoiled the image.

Still, the air around us crackled. It was like being put in a cage with a lion that was supposedly trained not to attack humans. But the only human he had had contact with was his trainer—so who knew? I thought I could feel Jane's tension as she stood behind me clutching my chair back.

DCI Sampson spoke to us over Nick's head. "I've explained to Mr. Clancy that you may decline to press charges if he gives you proper answers and never approaches you again. This interview is not being recorded."

Nick sprang to life. "Who the hell says I did anything to her," he flared. "I wasn't even at the market Thursday night."

I jumped. It was the same nasal voice, a high-pitched whine that would have been fatal to an actor aspiring to play Shakespear-ean drama.

"Ah, but we know different, laddie. George of Musica Anciens identified your voice. He's got a good ear, though you were wear-ing that mask and tried to fool him."

Nick pressed his hands against the table. "You believe that fucking pouf?"

"I'm sure we'll find that broken mask in your digs," DCI Sampson went on.

"I'm sure you won't. I—" He stopped, giving his head a furious shake.

"Why did you attack me?" I asked.

"I didn't *attack* you. Just gave you a hug." He smirked like a junior high felon in the principal's office. "It was all in fun. I saw your poster and thought I'd wind you up a bit."

"I don't believe that. You knew exactly who I was. You're Priscilla Waters's son."

His head gave a small, shocked jerk, and he pressed his lips in a stubborn line.

"Your mother kidnapped my child. I'm the one who should have attacked *you*." I'd decided on an offensive approach, treating the assumption as a fact. If he denied it, he might still say something damaging. "She dressed up like a nanny and stole my daughter from the park."

"You know what? You're daft. That's why I was playing wit' you. I saw your broadsheet and thought, *That's one crazy lady!*"

In a move as efficient as any other he had made, DCI Sampson reached out and grasped his hoodie, tightening it until Nick gagged. His arms jerked upward like marionettes, flailing around to free himself. "You're wasting my time."

Although I watched my share of BBC mysteries and saw physical persuasion often enough when no tape recorder was running, I was surprised.

Sampson loosened his grip and nodded at me to go on.

"I have a photo of your mother in the park on the day she took my daughter," I said. "I never knew who she was until I came back and saw the story about the accident. I'm sorry she was killed—I shouldn't have said what I did—but why blame me?"

Nick jerked his head back at Sampson. "I want a solicitor!"

"Right you are. I'll have one delivered to your cell." He made it sound as if Nick had ordered a fish and chips dinner. "Right after Ms. Laine signs the complaint forms and we formally charge you."

"What do you call attempted murder here?" Jane asked him over my head.

"Just that. Or attempt to cause grievous bodily injury. When the victim and the attacker are strangers, it's a more serious charge. The perpetrator can be put away for years."

Nick started.

"Okay, laddie, come along."

"No! Are you going to believe her lies? It's her word over mine."

"Ah, but the publican saw you running away," Sampson told him. "His wife and other people. You're no kiddie either. Thirty-one, are you?"

"Thirty."

"Thirty." DCI Sampson considered that. "You'll be a lot older than that when you're on your own again. But maybe they can teach you a useful trade inside so you won't have to stand around on street corners bothering tourists." He reached out and yanked on the shoulder of Nick's leather jacket. "On your feet."

I wanted to protest. I didn't want to press charges if it meant I would learn nothing from Nick. Surely we could wear him down if we stayed in that room long enough.

Nick glared at me with enough hate to put us back in the alley. "My mother didn't kidnap your brat."

"I have the photos," I said. "And an eyewitness." No need to tell him the eyewitness was Jane. "I just didn't know who your mother was."

"She wasn't a kidnapper. It was only supposed to teach you a lesson." He looked up at Sampson. "I'm talking to her, okay?"

Sampson released the leather jacket. "Start at the beginning."

It was a command impossible to resist if you were afraid of spending the next few years in jail.

I SAT IN the overheated room, a windowless pale green chamber with nothing on the walls but the fire evacuation plan, and listened to a story I could not have imagined.

Priscilla Waters had been approached one night after a performance of *A Midsummer Night's Dream* and offered a role in a very exclusive production: She would be playing a nanny and would be coached on exactly what to say and do.

"How much did they offer her?" DCI Sampson asked.

"Who cares? It doesn't matter."

"It matters."

"I don't know exactly. *She* thought it was a lot. All she had to do was take this kid, to teach this mum a lesson, to make her watch her kids better."

"So it was a prank?"

"Yeah. She thought it was."

My heart began banging around my chest so crazily that I pressed my hands against it to keep it from exploding into the room. I ordered myself to breathe. Had I had been such a terrible mother that someone felt compelled to teach me a lesson? Had one of the English people I thought were so friendly despised me all along? I felt washed by a deep, dark red shame—the kind I had felt only once in my life when my father had come upon me sprawled on my bed doing something Christian girls weren't supposed to know about.

How could I have been so unaware that people around me were staring and pointing fingers? I'd blithely gone my own way, toting a jumble of picture books, diapers, juice boxes, and extra binkies. I hadn't bothered with damp washcloths for cleanup, or carrot and celery sticks for healthy snacks. The ice cream wagon had been the highlight of the afternoon. We headed for the same bench every day and set up tribal headquarters. Jane always reminded me to bring the bread to feed the ducks and swans. I remembered warning the girls that swans could be mean and to not get too close.

But that didn't make you a good mother. No. Some days I would get so absorbed in the book I was reading that too long would go by before I checked on what the girls were up to. Other days I would be busy taking photos, the way I had been on that last day.

Indicted. I hated to imagine what DCI Sampson was thinking of me now as well as Jane. A colossally bad mother. The worst the English had ever seen.

Except—it didn't make sense. Why would someone pay so much money just to scare me into being more responsible? Why not confront me directly—yell and lecture, and read me the British version of the riot act? Besides, Celia Banks had said I was a good mother. Well, at least she hadn't scolded me for being a bad one.

"You're admitting your mum snatched this little girl," DCI Sampson said. "What happened next?"

Nick slumped in his chair as if he had been tricked into the revelation. "She brought her back to our flat and waited for the people to pick her up. They said that after they had scared the mum enough, they would give the baby back. But the kid was there all night. In the morning my mother got a call and took her somewhere."

"Where?"

"How should I know? I wasn't even up. Micah told me."

"Wait," Jane demanded from behind me. She sounded out of breath. "She was at your *house*? My sister stayed at your house that night? What did she look like?"

Nick seemed impatient at this intrusion, as if talking to her had not been part of the deal. "I dunno. Like a kid. Like your flyer. She was cute—at first—my mum gave her stuff to play with, but then she started screaming and crying for her 'mama.' " He glared at me as if it were my fault. "Wouldn't shut it and Mum was afraid people would hear. Summer and all, the windows were open. So she gave her some sleeping powder to knock her out." He seemed to be remembering something he had not thought of in a long time. "Yeah, she was afraid she'd given her too much. She sat up all night to make sure the kid kept breathing." He raised his head then and gave me another scornful look. "See? She wouldn't have worried like that if she was such a bad person."

From behind I felt Jane put her arms around my neck and hug me hard. My still-aching muscles screamed, but I reached up and stroked her arm. I couldn't take it in. The image of Caitlin screaming for me was the only thing that made it real. I made myself spell it out. Here was proof that Caitlin had never been near the water that day. My little girl had *not* drowned in the Avon River. If they had dredged every bit of river and hung it out to dry, they would not have found her body.

That—or Nick was playing with me again, this time in the cruelest way possible.

"When did your mother realize it was no prank?" Sampson asked.

"There was all this stuff in the paper about the kid drowning. *We* knew she hadn't drowned. My mother finally figured out they never planned to give her back. She'd been gulled."

"So your mum realized she had been tricked," DCI Sampson said.

"Yeah."

"Did she go to the police then?" I asked. I knew she hadn't. I said it to point out that it was what she should have done.

"She did. She wrote a note saying that she saw a woman walking out of the park that day with a kid that looked like the Fitzhugh kid."

The shocks just kept coming. I stared up at DCI Sampson, openmouthed.

"We get a lot of anonymous tips," he said evenly. "Most of them come to nothing."

"You mean you didn't even follow up?"

He moved a hand impatiently above Nick's head. "If she didn't sign her name how could we? We'd already interviewed everyone who came forward to say they'd been in the park. No one told us they'd seen anything like that." He peered down at Nick. "I can guess what happened next. She hit them up for more money, didn't she?"

"Blackmail," Jane said censoriously.

"They owed her big-time! They'd used her to kidnap a kid. It wasn't just some silly prank, they'd made her part of a *crime*. She could have gotten in big trouble."

Either Priscilla Waters had been dimmer than a night-light or fundamentally twisted. You didn't abduct a toddler from a park and hide her in your apartment overnight while her parents went out of their heads thinking she had drowned. How many hours did it take you to realize it was no "prank"? So she had sent the police a vague note without any real details for them to follow up on—Nick thought that made her St. Teresa?

He might have been reading my thoughts, because he added, "You don't know what it was like, we needed the money. They didn't pay her squat at the company, they told her she had to 'work her way up.' My dad didn't pay what he was supposed to. We could have lost the flat."

It was too warm in the room. I stared at the dots of sweat on Nick's forehead and realized he was still wearing his sweatshirt and leather jacket. The stale odor I had been smelling was a mixture of alcohol and lack of a good shower. Just how marginal was his life now?

Soon I would have to take off my own jacket. "How much more money did she get?"

"None!" He was furious again. "They promised her more, they knew she'd go to the police if they didn't. But this time they wouldn't send it through the post, they said she had to meet them." He lowered his head and pressed his fists into his eyes. "Micah wanted to go with her, but she wouldn't let him. She should have! It was out in the country; they sent a cab to bring her. We waited all night for her to get back, but she didn't come. Then next day some constable banged on the door and said that she was *dead*. He told me my mother was dead!"

"That was me," Sampson said. "I came to your flat."

"That was you? Jesus! You said it was an accident." Now Nick was the accuser. He craned his neck to try and meet Sampson's eyes.

"Why would I think anything else? You wouldn't tell us what

she was doing out there. If you had, it would have changed everything. We could have found her killers and Ms. Laine would have been reunited with her daughter."

Don't think about that. Don't think about it now. The idea of what had almost happened, how different the past twenty years would have been, threatened to swamp me. *Don't think.*

"Who were these people she was going to meet?" Sampson demanded.

"You think I know? You think they'd be alive if I knew?"

Hands grabbed Nick's shoulders roughly. "What did she *say* about them?"

Nick jerked away. "Nothing! Why would she tell me anything? I was eleven-fucking-years old."

"She must have said something."

"Well, she didn't. You can throw me in the hole for twenty years and I still won't know."

"Stop watching American cinema. We don't have 'holes' in Britain."

I pressed my fingers against the table until the tips glowed white. "Did she say it was a couple? Or a single woman?"

"Yeah, there were two of them. She said them."

"A man and a woman?"

"*Them.*"

"Why did you want to hurt my mother?" Jane demanded. "She didn't do anything to you."

Nick glanced at me with a hate that made me feel his arm crushing my throat. "Because if she hadn't come here with her brats in the first place, none of this would have happened. My mother would still be alive. I was curious to see who she was. Then she started insulting my mum, and I wanted her to shut up."

DCI Sampson motioned to me not to answer.

Nick pushed against his chair. "Can I go now?"

In your dreams. "Where's Micah?"

"Leave him out of this! I don't know anyway." He lowered his eyes sullenly to the table. "We lost touch ages ago. He thinks I'm just a bum. Someone told me he emigrated to Australia."

He started to rise, but Sampson clamped his hand on his shoulder again. "Not so fast, laddie. Stick around. Ms. Laine may have more questions later on."

"No! You said I could go." Nick reached across the table to me, thrusting his body forward as I jerked back. "You gonna press charges or what?"

I shook my head. He had done what we had agreed on. "Not if you promise to e-mail me if you remember anything else. Anything at *all.*"

"I won't," he assured me. "Remember anything." Then he seemed to think about who I was, where we were. "Yeah, okay. If I think of something, I will. Whatever."

I sensed that DCI Sampson didn't approve of such contact without his involvement. "If you ever approach Ms. Laine or her daughter again, it will be a long time before you're out bothering tourists on Henley Street."

Close to his chest where Sampson couldn't see but I could, Nick raised a menacing middle finger, then spat.

Chapter 27

I HAD TO be alone. It was too overwhelming, there was too much to think about before I could talk about it with Jane or anyone else.

Outside the police station the snow had stopped falling, leaving a pale slushy gleam on the cobblestones. Water dripped in slow motion from the signs and street lamps. People moved briskly as if it had all been a false alarm.

"I still can't believe it. I heard it but I still can't believe it," Jane marveled. "She was actually in his apartment. Wait until we tell Dad! And Hannah."

"Umm."

"It's okay to tell them, isn't it? I mean, this changes everything."

"It's fine." I couldn't think about them now. "I need you to do something. Go to Anne Hathaway's Cottage and interview that retired actress. See if she can tell us how to get in touch with Micah Clancy."

"You don't think he's in Australia?"

"No. "

"What are you going to do?"

"I need to think."

"Okay, let's get coffee or something."

"I mean by myself."

"I won't say anything. It's not safe; what if Nick comes after you again?"

"He won't. He's shot his wad." Now that DCI Sampson knew the story, there was no reason to try and keep me from exposing his mother as a criminal—if that had ever been his intention.

"Sampson called him a 'wildcard.' Even his voice gives me the creeps."

"I'll see you back at the room."

The details of the interview were already fading. I had to get away.

WHEN I REACHED the Avon River, I was able to find the bench we had camped out on so long ago. It was farther from the river than I remembered. Seeing the distance between the bench and where I had been standing by the river that day made me realize just how foolhardy I had been. Someone could as easily have come along and scooped up the sleeping Hannah. But because it had been England, because nothing tragic had ever happened to me before, I had felt invulnerable. Until I wasn't.

The water was the smooth, dark gray of a well-tailored suit. Summer's ducks had flown away and nothing moved except for a woman in a yellow jacket walking a black Scottish terrier. If the snow had continued to fall it would have been a Christmas card. Now the scene looked unfinished, as if the artist had packed up his brushes and gone home.

I sat down and the slats of the bench felt like strips of ice through my jeans. But I needed to come here and revise that final memory, discarding the old pages and replacing them with the truth. I stared at the spot where I had plunged into the water, screaming Caitlin's name, thrashing around wildly to try and feel where she was.

All I had managed to do that afternoon was roil the water further, adding to the murk stirred up by oars and paddleboat wheels. Even while I was thinking, *This can't be happening*, and groping like someone blindfolded, I could hear voices from over the water, laughter and music from someone's radio, the endless chirping and calling of birds. Life had not stopped even for that moment.

And all the time I was panicking and looking for her, my daughter was being wheeled into a different life. We had started the day together as a family, me dressing Caitlin in her well-loved shirt and pants and feeding her Cheerios and a banana—the only breakfast she would eat. But remembering her breakfast plunged me into despair. From that afternoon on, *nothing* was the way she expected it to be. They had dressed in unfamiliar clothes, given her strange food to eat, made her play with toys she had never seen before. They were strangers too. Her cries for "Mama" had brought her nothing.

I pressed my fists against my thighs. I couldn't stand it. I couldn't stand how terrible it must have been for her. The devastation of her mommy and daddy never coming to rescue her. The kidnappers had not been as cruel to us, but cruel enough. Besides stealing my daughter they had, with a few misleading words sentenced me to years of guilt and regret. There was something deliberate about this punishment, something *personal*. Something about the way I was with the children had created the desire to lash out. If I could figure that out . . .

Yet if they had not misdirected us to the water, the search would have gone in a whole other direction. There would have been a manhunt, a careful searching of Stratford. The water would have been a possibility, but since no one had seen her fall in, it would not have been assumed. I hugged myself against the wind that had risen. We were just as far from finding Caitlin as before. I had expected it would end when we found Priscilla Waters. Instead it was just beginning.

For the first time I could understand Colin's objection. Caitlin would have finally adjusted to the trauma of being uprooted from everything she once knew and settled into what I hoped had been a good life. Assuming she had been loved and been raised with tenderness, was it fair to destroy that world and force her to face yet another reality? And if she had been treated badly? That was the darker side Colin feared, that she was fatally damaged. If we found her would she cling to us like someone drowning and pull us under water too? I pushed that thought away immediately. No matter what had happened or would happen, she was my *daughter*.

I sat frozen under the choppy gray sky, unable to leave the bench. It was impossible to imagine the last day I had spent here, the dense green grass of August, the beds of red and orange flowers, knots of excited tourists.

Out of the corner of my eye I saw something white move on the water. Who would be sailing a toy boat on such a raw day? I turned to look and saw that it was not a triangle of sail, but a swan. Not a baby wrapped in downy fluff, but not full-grown either. Perhaps it had been born last spring. I remembered from some child's nature book that not all swans migrated, that if they found a sheltered cove they would winter there. Soon there might be ice patches on the Avon, but right now the bird glided unimpeded.

As I watched the young swan, there was a honking from the direction she had come. For a moment she stopped, as if considering what it meant. Ahead lay opportunity and adventure. A new world to explore. Yet with a jerking motion she turned around and glided back to the call.

Was this a message? I had been raised by a clergyman father in a household familiar with biblical signs and portents. No one around me found it strange that a young man blew a trumpet and a city's walls crumbled like toy blocks. Or that a leader raised a hand and the Red Sea parted and stood at attention to let the Israelites pass. Doves were a favorite symbol at floods and baptisms, and even a rooster had its moment. Did a winter swan, responding to her mother's signal, mean that Caitlin would want me to find her too?

The trouble with religion is that you have to believe it all the time to have it work for you. Why would God bother to give reassurances to lapsed Methodists? Maybe it was a signal from my parents instead, or a benevolent universe trying to tell me not to give up.

Whatever it was, it freed me from the bench and gave me the impetus to walk back into town.

Chapter 28

WALKING UP SHEEP Street, I knew I wasn't ready to go back to the hotel, though I wasn't sure what else to do. Christmas was bearing down like the Polar Express, but I was in no mood to think about shopping. Then up ahead I saw a hanging sign, "Garnet Hill Books," the name painted around a bucolic meadow. I gave the sigh of someone dropping into an easy chair after an all-day hike. A bookstore was the one thing I needed.

The shop had a brick facade with deep blue trim, its windows filled attractively with books, though not with a Christmas theme. I looked at the titles to make sure the shop sold secondhand books, and went inside.

In many used and rare bookstores, the proprietor does not acknowledge you when you walk in, does not look up from the counter or the computer or whatever else he is busy with. Sometimes people take this for arrogance, as if their presence is an imposition. In most cases it is to allow customers the freedom to explore, so that they will not have to say defensively that they are "just looking" or feel that the gloom in the atmosphere will lighten only when they buy a book.

It was no different in Garnet Hill Books. A man in his early fifties with a head of gray curls and a red plaid shirt kept placidly pricing books until I went over to him.

"Are you on BookEm?" I asked.

Now he did look up at me, his brown eyes friendly behind gold-rimmed glasses. "The Internet dealers' group? I used to be. I've fallen by the wayside lately, I'm afraid."

"I'm Delhi Laine from Secondhand Prose. I think I've seen your postings."

"Ah. Likewise. What brings you to Stratford?"

"You wouldn't believe it."

"Try me."

BACK AT HOME, Marty would be attending the odd sale and Susie just unlocking the shop. I had forgotten it was the Saturday of the Dickens Festival and the streets would be filling up with visitors and residents in Victorian costume. I had always wanted the children to dress up as old-fashioned urchins and even offered to make costumes for them, but they never would. *Caitlin would have.*

I reminded myself not to do that.

Stratford was quiet by comparison. The bookshop owner, Thad Daniels, produced a young woman Jane's age to stand behind the counter and ring up sales, then led me to a stiff brocaded settee in front of the fireplace. He handed me a cup of Earl Grey tea.

The first time I ever drank milk in tea was one afternoon when I was at an auction and a chair hanging on a barn rail above me came loose and grazed my head. I wasn't seriously hurt, but one of the helpers rushed to get me tea and handed me a cup heavy with milk and sugar. At first I hadn't wanted to drink it. And then I had.

That's the way I drink tea now when I need comfort.

I told Thad the story of what had happened here nineteen years ago, gave him a summary of my life since, and explained why I was in Stratford now. He was a good listener, smiling once or twice, nodding with understanding, filtering everything through a sharp intelligence.

"Do you have a copy of your flyer?"

"Sure." I reached in my bag and unfolded a sheet for him.

He studied it for a long time, then shook his head. "No, I've never seen her. Beautiful child. I would have remembered." He turned around to the counter. "Susan? Come here a minute. My daughter might have met her in school or at some sporting event."

But Susan didn't recognize Caitlin either.

It was to be expected, though I was disappointed. It would have been an enormous risk to keep Caitlin in Stratford, the place where she had disappeared. Still, Susan might have seen her at some regional teenage event or even university—but she hadn't.

"Have you spoken with the older Clancy boy? His mother might have confided in him the way she wouldn't with a younger lad."

"We're trying to reach him. My daughter's at the Hathaway Cottage talking to someone who's kept in touch with the family."

"Good. And you'll have the police investigating now."

I hoped we would. "This is going to change our lives," I said. "Even if we don't find Caitlin. My husband has always blamed me for letting her drown, and now it turns out I didn't. I'm not blameless, but I was set up. It's just—if only. If only Nick and his brother had told the police the truth, our lives would have been entirely different."

"How so?"

I ran my finger over the silky pattern on the settee arm, trying to find the words. "We were so carefree before. Colin wanted six or seven children, he envisioned a whole tribe. His only sister lived on the West Coast—she's dead now—and he was in love with the idea of a big family. We assumed we could pack them up and take them anywhere, that it would be good for them to see the world."

Thad set down his mug of tea, his third, and watched me.

"When we came home without Caitlin, we didn't feel that way anymore. Jason was born a month later and Colin insisted I go on the pill. The pill! He never changed his mind about that, and I never got pregnant again. Three children was okay with me, but it wasn't the life we had planned." I leaned back against the carved wood top of the settee and closed my eyes. "We still traveled to archeological digs and universities, of course, but he never seemed to take me seriously. It was as if I hadn't turned out to be the woman he thought. He was okay with the kids, but they weren't the family he'd envisioned." I thought of something else. "Except for my oldest daughter, *they* never lived up to his expectations either."

Suddenly teary, I stopped. Why would Thad want to know my life story?

"It's Delhi, isn't it, Delhi like the city? Delhi, why would either of you expect life to turn out the way you'd planned? It never does, you know."

"It must for some people."

"Maybe one or two out of a hundred. But there are always complications—illness or death, divorce, unemployment, even war. That doesn't include people maturing and wanting some-thing different. *My* wife wanted a whole tribe of children too, but she found morning sickness so unbearable we only managed Susan. Instead, she fell in love with interior design and now she creates sets for the BBC."

I laughed.

"My point is that even without this tragedy, your husband might have changed."

I looked into the fire and thought about that. Were we just people after all?

"What are you going to do?" Thad brought me back to the bookshop, the cozy room we were settled in.

"I don't know."

"Why haven't you posted the photos online? The Internet is a wondrous thing."

"My other daughter, her twin, doesn't want us to find her. I'll ask her now, but—"

"Knowing her sister is alive may change her mind."

Would it? And was it really true? I couldn't help myself, I reached across and grasped his hands. "What if this story is an-other lie? Nick Clancy is a little crazy. Maybe a lot crazy. What if this is just some sick fantasy he's dreamed up to explain why his mother died? What if he made it up for the attention?"

Thad squeezed my hands back. "But you know that his mother did dress up as a nanny and play a role. You have the photo that proves it. Your daughter remembers her too. Nick may be as cracked as the queen's china, but the story isn't just his."

"No."

We sat, hands linked by goodwill and our love of books, not caring that we would never see each other again.

Chapter 29

By the time I went back to the White Swan, the sky, which had been the creamy white of old pearls, had darkened. *Too little, too late.* But that didn't apply to our situation, did it? Still, it was hard to keep the other ifs from swamping the boat. If only I had turned around unexpectedly and seen the nanny with my girls. If only Jane had insisted on looking inside the stroller for her promised rabbit and seen Caitlin instead. If only the police had investigated Priscilla Waters's note and found her. *If, if, if.*

Trust no one. I should have heeded that. If I had, we might have headed in a different direction. But I didn't.

I did think about Constable Donnelly, a young man focused on getting his education. Where had he suddenly gotten the money to head off to university? If we found him, would he admit he had been paid to look the other way? Frantic, I reminded myself that we had less than a day left. Without DCI Sampson's cooperation, there was no way to find Donnelly. If I asked now, would Sampson tell me where he was?

Jane was waiting in the lobby, rosy-cheeked and lovely. She stood up as I came over to her. "Guess who's coming to dinner?"

"The retired actress?"

"Nope."

"DCI Sampson?"

She grinned, grasping me by the arm and steering me toward the bar. "Micah Clancy."

"No! Really? He's really around?"

"Actually, he's not coming for dinner. He's meeting us for a drink."

"Not at the Singing Bard, I hope." A bad joke.

"Nope, he said outside it in the alley." She laughed at my shock. "Here at seven."

"Well done, Jane!"

She checked her watch. "Do you want to call Daddy first?"

"You didn't tell him?"

"I texted him that we had some news. That you'd call later."

"Really? That's so—" It took me a moment to find the word. "Thoughtful of you. Really thoughtful."

"I figured you're the one he should hear it from."

"Thank you. Let's go upstairs."

She looked longingly toward the bar. "We could get a drink."

"No, I need somewhere private."

When we were settled in the two chairs near the window, Jane retrieved her phone from her purse and pressed a number on speed dial, then handed it to me.

"Hey-lo, kid," Colin answered jovially.

"It's me," I said. "We found some things out."

"So Janie said."

Thad Daniels had warned me not to spring it on Colin.

"You remember the nanny that Jane said tricked her? She's dead now but we found her son. He said she was an actress, paid to dress up that way and take Caitlin. Supposedly as a joke. But Caitlin was in his apartment all that night, then his mother turned her over to the people who paid her."

"What are you telling me?"

"That someone *kidnapped* Caitlin. This boy's mother. She didn't drown."

"Do the police know about this?"

"That's where we talked to him, at the police station."

"And they believe that's what happened."

"As far as I know."

"And who were these kidnappers?"

"That's what we need to find out."

Silence. Sitting across from me, Jane was biting her lip between her teeth.

"I know it's a lot to take in. We're meeting with the older brother tonight to see if he knows any more." And then, stupidly, I began to cry. I rarely cry. "We should have paid more attention to what Jane was trying to tell us. We should have insisted that the police investigate more. The nanny, Priscilla Waters, even sent the police an anonymous note saying someone had taken Caitlin. They didn't listen to *her* either. It's all such a mess!"

"We did our best."

"I know. But where do we go from here?"

"We hope Caitlin has a good life."

Incredulous, I broke the connection.

Chapter 30

"Think he'll be wearing a mask?"

I smiled at Jane. "Did he sound like he would be over the phone?"

"No, he sounded nice. He was the one who suggested meeting. Like he was anxious to talk to us." Jane shifted her elbows on the white cloth and sat up a little. Her cap of light hair shone in the candlelight. "When Marjory called him and told who we were, he didn't seem that surprised."

"Maybe Nick called him."

"Maybe. But he said they weren't in touch. Wait—is that him?"

We both looked at the tall, black-haired man who had spotted us and was moving quickly toward our table. A flash of paranoia: Was *he* coming to avenge his mother's memory and finish what his brother had started? But he didn't look crazed. Unlike Nick in his hoodie, he had on a suede jacket and a deep blue dress shirt that accentuated his eyes. He was even handsomer than Nick.

When he reached us, he held out his hand to me and smiled at Jane. "I'm Micah Clancy."

Smooth.

We introduced ourselves as he sat down in the vacant chair. "Are you enjoying Stratford?" he asked pleasantly.

"Not so much. But we're not here on vacation."

"Ah. Why did you come?"

I looked into those striking blue eyes. "The note." At that moment I had no doubt that he was the one who had sent it. His lack of surprise at our being here and his desire to meet with us made me sure. And if I was wrong, no damage done.

But he nodded. "I hoped it would make you come here."

We didn't talk more about it until he was holding a glass of Jack Daniel's, which he insisted on paying for himself.

"It was a terrible thing my mother did. I didn't realize how bad until my daughter turned two a few months ago. Then it all came rushing at me. I knew if anything like that happened to Angelique, I'd kill myself."

The kidnapping . . . or something worse? I suddenly felt too frightened to hear what he had to say.

He took a sip of whiskey. "I should have let you know years earlier. But it was all such a muddle, my mother dying suddenly, us leaving Stratford. I spent the next few years trying to get away from my crazy father."

"How old were you?" I asked.

"Fourteen. I knew university was my only hope. But trying to do that and support myself, it took a long time." Then suddenly he turned up his palms dramatically; maybe he was an actor. "There's no excuse. I'm sorry."

Jane caught her breath.

"People do what they have to do," I said. "When they can. Your note changed everything. Nick told us what your mother did. But he didn't know anything about the people who paid her."

Nick sighed. "I wish I did. All I know is that they had a lot of money and they weren't English. My mother said that at least English people wouldn't be such rotters."

"She didn't say what they were?" Jane's first question.

He drank more Jack Daniel's, looking regretful. "No. I think it was a married couple."

"Do you know anything about the—car?" A sensitive question.

"The car? Oh."

Perhaps Priscilla had never seen their car until she heard it behind her and turned. And then it was too late to tell anyone.

Micah moved restlessly in his chair. He might have been thinking of leaving. But he sighed and sat back. "My mother did something else. Something there was no excuse for . . ."

I couldn't stop the flashes of alarm bursting over me. Something to *Caitlin*?

"What was it?" I whispered.

He finished the drink and set it down. "She told them that if they didn't give her more money she was going to the police."

Oh. He didn't know that we had already heard that from Nick.

"They agreed, and she was meeting them to get the money the night she—the night she never came home."

"What did you think had happened?"

"I was so *dumb*. The way the constable explained it, it just sounded like another sorry accident."

"But if it were just an accident, wouldn't they have found the money on her? If she had already met with them."

And the penny dropped. "My God. I never thought of that. They never even gave it to her."

"Either that—or they took it back."

It was a picture you didn't want to think about.

Chapter 31

"WE CAN'T GO home yet," Jane protested when we got back to our room and started gathering our things in little piles. "We don't know enough!"

We were flying home Sunday so that she could be back at work Monday morning, ready to start the week. I had thought four days would give us plenty of time to look at the newspaper archives, talk to the police, and post Caitlin's picture. We hadn't counted on Priscilla Waters and having to go a layer deeper—like archeologists who had discovered that the burial chamber they were excavating was only a sham and that the real tomb was somewhere underneath.

"We can always come back." But I knew we wouldn't. We hadn't exactly wrung Stratford dry, but Caitlin would not be found here. The search had opened up, not narrowed. Even if we could eliminate people not interested in a Caucasian child, that left the rest of the world. Caitlin could have seemed perfect to a German or Swedish couple who had driven across the continent. I had never been to Scandinavia but it felt remote, unforthcoming. A child like Caitlin could be lost among other children just like her and never be seen again.

I pictured Caitlin in Norway or Denmark happily finishing her studies and preparing for a career. How would we ever find her there? We wouldn't find her there.

"It went too fast," I said ruefully. We had to leave for Birmingham Airport at seven tomorrow morning to get down to London for our international flight home. The same cabby who brought us to Stratford was taking us down. No doubt he would want to know all about how we enjoyed the Christmas Market.

Lots of fun until Shakespeare attacked me.

"And we found out the most important thing." Something occurred to me then. "We have to talk to DCI Sampson!"

Jane looked up from the floor where she was trying to fit the gifts she had bought into her carry-on. "He won't be there now."

"I know. But someone will be and they can patch me through. Or give me his number."

"What if he's gone out somewhere?"

"Jane, he's the head of everything! He has to be on call."

"Maybe they do things differently here."

Why was she giving me such a hard time? "I'm only going to call him, not go over there. It's not even that late. We have to tell him what Micah said."

"My phone's in my bag."

"Well I don't have the number." It seemed insurmountable, a pyramid with no visible entrance. "Never mind, I'll just go." I moved toward my jacket on the bed.

"Don't be so touchy, Mom. Siri will find him for you. What do you need to tell him, anyway?"

"You'll hear."

To my relief, Constable Bradford was on duty. I explained to him that I needed to talk to DCI Sampson. "We're leaving first thing tomorrow morning," I pleaded.

"How are you feeling? That was some spill you took."

"Much better, thanks."

Yesterday's news.

"So sorry it happened and I hope you'll come back again anyway! Here's his number."

Sampson did not sound as happy to hear from me as his constable had. I imagined he had been listening to music or watching the telly, a glass of whiskey at his elbow. "What is it, Ms. Laine?"

"We talked to Micah Clancy, Nick's brother? He remembered his mother saying that the kidnappers weren't English. Which leaves—"

"The rest of the world."

"Okay. Yes. But I was thinking, if they were from somewhere else, unless they drove all the way from Europe, they must have rented a car. So you could check on cars rented during that time period, especially if they were returned with damage after the hit-and-run."

"The car could have been leased in London. We're talking in the thousands."

"But not all with damage."

"This was nineteen years ago."

"Don't you have a cold case unit? Like *New Tricks* where those retired policemen—"

"I know the program. And no, we have nothing like that here.

There's no backlog of unsolved crime. We'll be revisiting the hit-and-run now that we have new information, but it was thoroughly examined when everything was fresh."

I felt deflated. "Can I call you sometimes to see if you've found out anything?"

"You may do that. Just not every day."

I said good-bye and consigned him to his calm and pleasant life in England's green and pleasant land.

Chapter 32

DECEMBER RACED ON. Unlike the years when the children were younger—the years of Christmas concerts, letters to Santa, and gingerbread houses—this holiday was a minimalist's dream. I was so busy filling book orders and helping out at the shop that I didn't notice the sparseness until Hannah came home and insisted we have a Christmas tree. It stood alone in the living room like a paid mourner at a funeral. Yet every time I came in the house, its piney scent gave off the promise that next year had to be better.

Jason had decided not to come home. He begged me to give him the fare money to buy a laptop instead. He reminded me of how isolated he was without a computer.

"But we want you here," I pleaded. "We'll work something else out about the computer. Dad—"

"Dad doesn't want me home. And I don't want to see him."

"This is the first Christmas you won't be with us. What will you *do*?"

"Mom, it's just another day. I have friends who've invited me over."

"But I haven't seen you in ages."

"So come out. You love the Southwest."

"I will. When things calm down." Yet who knew when that would be?

"Ma, I've gotta run."

"No, *wait*. I have to tell you something."

He waited.

"Long ago—before you were born, I mean—Hannah had a twin sister. We were in England and she disappeared. We thought she had drowned, but—"

"I know. About the twin."

"You . . . know?"

"One time Grandma slipped and said you'd had *four* children. And I was looking at your portfolio of photos a few years ago and I saw Hannah with another little girl just like her. I thought it was trick photography, but I asked Dad."

"What did he say?"

Denied it, of course.

"He told me about the little girl who had drowned, but said I wasn't to ask you about it, that it would only make you depressed. So I didn't."

I could not have been more surprised if Santa and his reindeer had pushed their way into the barn and started unloading gifts.

"The thing is, she didn't drown. That's why Jane and I went to Stratford, to try and find out what really happened. Do you have time to hear this?"

"I do now."

So I told him everything. I had planned to talk to him at Christmas face-to-face, but I couldn't put it off if he wasn't coming home.

"Holy shit." He sounded awed. "This girl is alive?"

"It seems that way. But Dad and Hannah don't think we should pursue it."

"They're crazy. Always were."

"I can't believe you knew about it and never said anything."

"In this family? Sorry, Mom," he added.

"You think we're *that* bad?" I thought with longing of my own family, the perfect home I had grown up in.

"Naw. Artists need to come from crazy homes. Anyway, I'm late."

"Okay. Bye, sweetheart."

After he hung up I stood holding the phone for a long moment, thinking about what he'd said. If we ever found Caitlin, would she think we were crazy too?

THE GIRLS WANTED gift cards, but I needed them to have a few presents to open, so I went to Macy's and spent more than I should have on sweaters, gloves, and Godiva. I always gave them books, of course. It was a family tradition that no doubt made me happier than it did them. Colin was impossible to buy for. Finally I picked out a deep red cashmere scarf and, from my stock, a signed copy of William Carlos Williams, whose poetry Colin admired.

There were friends I could have invited for Christmas, and I even thought about having Bruce Adair. I had kept him updated by e-mail and phone and he knew as much about the search for Caitlin as Colin did. There were Patience and Ben and the girls, of course—though I was still cross with Pat—but cooking a large holiday meal seemed as feasible as swimming Long Island Sound to Connecticut. Even if I could do it, I wouldn't enjoy myself. Instead I suggested that we celebrate on Christmas Eve with supper, gifts, and a midnight walk on the beach. If Colin wanted to take the girls out for dinner on Christmas Day, he could.

We had a plan.

The thing about starting with few expectations is that you can end up pleasantly surprised. Since Hannah now ate fish, I made oyster stew, a favorite shrimp and pasta recipe, and served a chocolate Yule log (not crafted by me). We sat around the living room fireplace and drank bottles of white wine. I was surprised and pleased by my gifts: a new red Cornell sweatshirt from Hannah, a leather bag with many secret compartments from Jane courtesy of the Christmas Market, and a black cashmere turtleneck sweater from Colin. He also gave me an iPhone.

"You're on the road so much you need something reliable."

It meant I could also check book rarity in situations where I was not sure.

"Wow. Thanks!" I went over and kissed him.

"The subscription's covered under my plan."

"You'll have to show me how to use it."

"Janie can."

Before we left for our walk, Colin raised his hand for attention. "I have something to say." He knew how to command an audience. "I know I haven't been supportive of your plans to find Caitlin. At first it seemed like wishful thinking, with the potential of getting hurt all over again. I still have mixed feelings about what to do if we find her. But we're a family and we'll work together. All I'm asking is that if we find her, we don't spring it on her. That we take it very slowly."

"Of course," I told him. No matter how delicately we approached Caitlin, it would be an enormous shock.

"Daddy, that's so great!" Jane was beaming at him from where she was snuggled into a corner of the striped sofa. "I *hate* fighting with you."

"I know." He was smiling now. "One other thing. We don't go to the media with the story, either before or after. I don't want it made public."

"I understand." Then I turned to see Hannah's reaction. Wide-awake now, she was looking at her father in bewilderment, the expression of someone who has just been handed a final exam for a subject she was never enrolled in. "But you said . . ."

"Hani, I'm not making light of your feelings," Colin soothed. "A lot has to happen before we even get to the point of having to make a decision. If we ever do. And we'll make sure you're comfortable with it first."

"But you *said*." I suddenly realized that what Jane had said about Hannah's gaining weight was true. Her pretty face looked pudgy and confused.

"I know what I said before." He leaned forward earnestly in his wing chair. "But now it looks as if your sister didn't drown. Your mother won't be satisfied until she knows what really happened."

"I *know* what really happened. I won't be satisfied until we find her." I appealed to Hannah. "What if Priscilla Waters had taken you instead? You know I wouldn't rest until I found you. And I would hope that Caitlin would have wanted you found too."

But Hannah could not stop looking at Colin. "Does this mean you won't help me get into vet school?"

"Hannah, what are you talking about?" I asked.

My daughter finally looked at me. "Dad told me that if I said I didn't want to find Caitlin, he would make sure I got accepted into a good vet school. He would talk to some people he knew. But now that he's changed his mind, I don't know if he will."

There went Christmas.

Chapter 33

It would take a lot of talking to get *that* cow back in the barn. I didn't want to attack Colin in front of the girls, but I was furious. How dare he try to bribe Hannah by using something so important as her dream of being a veterinarian. Was that what their private dinner at Thanksgiving had been about?

Colin leaned forward earnestly, his voice gentle. "Hani, you misunderstood me. I was only trying to show my support for you as a person. That no matter how you felt about it I'd still try to help you."

"That's not what you said."

"Well, it's what I meant. Did I ever once try to change your mind about looking for your sister?"

"No, but—"

He held up one finger. "All I said was that I agreed with how you felt. It makes no difference what I feel about it now. Of course I'll help you get into graduate school. Okay?"

"Okay." Her voice was as small as if she were eight years old again, agreeing to wash the dishes when it wasn't her turn.

I believed Hannah's version. Colin was a smooth talker, a tour guide who could make you believe that your trip to the guillotine would be an adventure. But I pushed down my anger. It was Christmas. Sitting there, listening to the crackle of wood settling in the fireplace and mellowed by the wine I had been drinking, I made myself look ahead to next year when Jason and Caitlin would be with us. At that moment I was sure it would happen.

THE NEXT EVENING we went downtown to Slices, which had enough varieties of pizza to satisfy everyone. The restaurant was a large plain room with wooden tables and chairs and a bar at one end. If there had been peanut shells or sawdust on the floor, I would not have been surprised. What did surprise me was the number of people here on Christmas night. We had to wait fifteen minutes for a table.

Jane and I split a small Cajun pie, Colin ordered the same for himself, and Hannah selected a four-cheese pizza. Except for Colin, a legendary beer drinker, the rest of us had Diet Coke. It all seemed very familiar: Colin expansive, Hannah sulky, Jane eager to move forward and make plans. And I was feeling, once again, as if I had been hogtied by my husband.

I'd expected to wake up feeling grateful that Colin's opposition had melted away. Instead, bracing myself Christmas morning to throw off the covers and go down to the kitchen and make blueberry pancakes, I realized that what he had actually done was put a fence around the investigation. By stipulating no media involvement—and my agreeing—he had cut off a major way of finding Caitlin. The easiest thing would have been to go to a commentator like Nancy Grace who specialized in cold cases and publicize the story nationally. Yes, the press could be obnoxious and going public might send her kidnappers into deeper hiding. But still . . .

That was the point I attacked now in Slices. "I know what you said about not alerting her kidnappers, but she's not a baby anymore. She might see the story and realize it was about her."

"And that wouldn't be a terrible shock?"

"Maybe at first. But—"

"And once the press learned the whole story, they'd never leave us in peace. To say nothing of the social media backlash. No, Delhi. No publicity."

"Aren't there Web sites for missing persons?" Jane asked.

"Yes, but she's not missing. At least she doesn't know she is," Hannah said. With the family lined up against her, she seemed to have stopped objecting out loud. Although I wanted her acquiescence, I didn't want her bullied.

"But if someone who knows her sees her photo—your photo— they might point it out to her," argued Jane.

"It's a long shot but we should at least do that," I said. "If it's over the Internet, it won't cost us anything."

"You should be checking foreign sites," Colin said. "I still think England's our best bet."

I didn't agree, but didn't contradict him. "She's Hannah's age, so she's probably in college. At least I hope she is."

"Wait." Jane pulled out her iPhone. "Siri, how many four-year colleges are there in the United States?"

"Checking for you," said the prim voice.

"Do I have Siri too?" I asked Colin.

"You do."

"There are approximately 2,774 four-year colleges granting degrees," Jane's Siri said.

We thought about that.

"They probably all have school newspapers," Jane explained. "We could ask them to run a photo and a caption, 'Have you seen this woman?' without explaining too much. Just give our e-mail for responses. Daddy, you can't object to that. There'd be nothing to connect it with you. Or us."

"Do you know how long it would take to get all those e-mail addresses?" he asked.

"Weeks," I agreed. "But there has to be some kind of association of college papers that has their addresses in one place. I'll look for it."

"We could send blanket e-mails under bcc," Jane said. "Not too many at once or the computer will think it's spam. It will take time though. Hannah, when do you go back?"

We looked across the table at my other daughter, who stared back defiantly. She was the only one who had finished her pizza. "What do you plan to do when you find this new, improved version of me?"

It was the kind of comment that could make me crazy. I held up a hand to keep Colin and Jane from rushing in to answer her. "Why do you think we want to replace you?"

She took a sip of Coke. "Jane thinks I'm fat and stupid. Dad loves me, but like a little pet dog. He doesn't respect me as a person. You . . ."

I held my breath, imagining the things she could accuse me of, going back to when I first pushed her to read the books I'd loved.

"All you can think about is finding this girl. You didn't even want to bother doing Christmas. It's like the rest of us don't really matter. And don't tell me you'd look for me just as hard. I don't believe it!"

"Hannah." Colin was the first to respond, pushing back his wooden chair and standing up. "Come with me." It was a command she had heard all her life. She pushed back her chair slowly and stood up. Colin put his hand on her shoulder and guided her to the back of the restaurant near the bar and restrooms.

"I never said she was stupid," Jane protested.

"I know, but—try not to talk about her weight, okay?"

"Mom, it's only temporary. Dorm food and stress. It's not like she's missing a leg or something."

"Still, *don't*."

Yet who was I to correct Jane? I thought I'd simply been too busy with book sales and the shop to put much effort into Christmas this year. But maybe I had been preoccupied with something else. That without Jason and Caitlin there for the holiday, I just hadn't cared enough.

Jane turned in her chair to look at the back of the restaurant. "I wonder what he's telling her. Maybe I'll go to the ladies' room."

"Maybe you won't." But I was curious about what Colin was saying to Hannah too. Assuring her he had never tried to bribe her? Saying how much he admired her as an adult woman? How proud he was that she was his daughter? I had no doubt that she would feel better when they returned.

"Okay, I'll do it," Hannah said when they came back to the table and sat down again.

"Do what?" I asked.

"Anything you want."

"Look, I'm sorry about Christmas. It won't happen again."

"S'okay."

"And you're not stupid," Jane said firmly. "Why would you ever think that? You go to Cornell, for God's sake."

Hannah shrugged. She reached for the last of her Diet Coke, and with a quick look at Colin said, "Dad thinks he can get a list of newspaper e-mails from the *Statesman* office, that they have to have them to exchange copies. Maybe they even have a mailing list in one file. He said I could use his computer at school."

"That's okay," I said. "I'd rather you use mine and keep it all in one place. But that would be a huge help." Even as I said it, I could feel Jane's eyes on me.

Do you trust her to do it right?

Chapter 34

SUSIE PEVNEY CALLED me the next day from the bookstore.

I glanced at the clock. She must have just opened up.

"Delhi, can you come in? Something terrible's happened!"

My heart lurched. Was that bookshop forever cursed? Ever since the previous owner, Margaret, and her assistant had been savagely attacked inside, ever since I had unraveled the knotted threads that led to murder, what had once felt like a home-away-from-home had lost its charm.

"Did Marty—is somebody . . ." I couldn't put my fears into words.

"No, nothing like that." But her voice shook. "It's Marty's books! And your windows."

"What *happened*?"

"Just come," she begged.

I picked up the books I had wrapped to mail to customers, grabbed my bag, and headed downtown. I went right to the book-shop, finding a parking space on Harbor Street.

I saw the windows first. It was as if a furious child had grabbed the toys and thrown them in the air, not caring where they landed. The china doll's face was cracked.

Inside Susie was cowering behind the counter, head down. Marty was sitting on the leather sofa making calculations on a pad. A customer in the next room wandered into view and disappeared again.

I went right to Susie. "What happened?"

"Merry Christmas, Delhi. How was your holiday?"

"Never mind that shit." Marty jumped up and crossed the room to me. He was wearing a navy sweatshirt with a white image of a cartoon chef nearly hidden by a handlebar mustache, flipping a pizza under the name "Goodfella's." "We've got a *problem*."

"So I see. Did they hurt the books?"

"No, just stole them." Marty turned and glared at Susie.

Her mouth turned down in a stricken mask. "I swear, I was behind the counter all the time. I *never* leave the good books alone!"

"I believe you," I told Susie.

"Who cares what you believe?" Marty interrupted. "They're not *your* books."

"Why are you lashing out at *me*?" I demanded."Or Susie? You think she stood here and watched someone destroy the windows? Or maybe helped? Obviously it happened when the shop was closed. What did they take, anyway?"

He consulted a list in his mind. "A Flannery O'Connor first, *Art, Magic, Spiritism*—from 1876—and *The Old Man and the Sea*. A first in dust jacket."

I winced. "Who else has a key? The cleaner?"

"No, nobody. Just you and Susie Sunface and, oh, shit"—he

knocked the heel of his hand against his head. "I bet Howard Riggs still does."

Howard Riggs had the bookstore up the street, a no-frills barracks that would have been at home on a military outpost. It had dusty wooden floors and books on metal shelves like a Pentagon office, with a few held prisoner in glass cases. He had been friends with Margaret Weller, the former owner of the Old Frigate, and they'd had each other's keys. She had also left him her book stock.

"You mean you never changed the locks?" I hadn't liked his Susie Sunface comment.

"I meant to. That stupid little turd." He turned toward the door. "I'm going to kill him."

"Wait. If you go barging in now, he'll only deny it. Check on AbeBooks and eBay first. Does Jen know about her stuff?"

Marty looked grim. "Susie Q. just came in and found it. And called me. And you. You better check and see what's broken."

"You have insurance, don't you?"

"That's not the point."

I turned and went over to the front windows, dreading what I would find. It looked like the aftermath of a temper tantrum. A tiny tea set cup had broken and the hinge of *A Christmas Carol* had come loose. And there was the doll. Yet these tin toys had served generations of active children. When I set the Ferris wheel back up and turned the key, miraculously it still worked.

"At least he waited until after Christmas," I said.

Neither of them smiled, but I hadn't been trying to be funny.

LATER ON, AFTER I had taken the toys back to Dock Street Antiques and Jen had confessed that the china doll was actually a replica, Marty, Susie, and I sat by the fireplace and talked more calmly about what to do. Marty had called a locksmith, who promised to be there tomorrow morning.

"I can't picture Howard vandalizing the windows," I said. "But maybe we could have someone go to his shop and look around. Or ask for one of the missing books specifically."

Marty hooted. "You could wear ones of those Groucho Marx disguises, blondie, those glasses and fake nose. He'd never know it was you."

"I wasn't thinking of me. But my daughter's home from college. He doesn't know her."

Poor Hannah, being volunteered for tasks she never would have undertaken herself.

"You think it's safe to send her there?" Susie asked.

Marty turned to me. "She can run fast?"

He and I found his comment amusing but Susie wasn't smiling.

IT TOOK COLIN almost a week to bring us the flash drive with the college newspaper e-mails. "Don't tell anyone where you got this. I'm not sure it's legal to use it this way." Lately he had been showing up around dinnertime and eating the healthy meals I was cooking for Hannah, a lot of vegetable dishes or fish.

"How did you get this?"

"You don't want to know. Having it isn't the problem anyway. It's what you're going to do with it. What are you going to say?"

I grinned at him. "You don't want to know."

He sighed. "I have to."

"Then let's figure something out."

It took the three of us forty minutes to agree on anything. We didn't want to tell the story, but what we said had to be compelling enough for the editors to pay attention and run it in the newspaper.

"My friends will know it's me," Hannah fretted.

"We won't send it to Cornell," I said. "If she were there you would have seen her by now."

How to be compelling and not say too much was a challenge. Not having a name we could use was another complication. We decided to go with an attachment with a photo of Hannah at nineteen and the following:

HAVE YOU SEEN THIS GIRL?

We lost touch with her several years ago and need to contact her for medical reasons. Confidentiality precludes further details. If you know of her or have any questions, please contact lstgrl@gmail.com.

The account was one I had created solely for this purpose.

"What if it goes viral?" Hannah said.

Having the story picked up and sent around the Internet, around the world, would be an answer to my prayers. But I couldn't tell Colin and Hannah that. "It's not going to be that sensational," I reassured her.

Still, I could dream.

Chapter 35

"HOW ARE YOU feeling?" I asked Hannah. She had finished the last batch of e-mails a few minutes earlier and was slumped across from me at my worktable in the barn.

"Scared." She looked at me directly and I saw that her eyes, pure blue in childhood, had taken on subtle green and brown flecks. Her beautiful dark gold hair was pulled carelessly back onto her neck.

"Scared how?"

"Oh, scared that we'll find her. Scared of what she'll be like when we do."

"But it could be exciting to meet the one person on earth who has exactly the same DNA as you."

"That's the stupidest thing I ever heard."

"Okay . . ."

"I never *wanted* another me. One is too much."

My heart dropped. "Are you that unhappy?"

"No!" Her eyes flashed. "Who said anything about being unhappy? All I want is to do what I've planned, without any complications."

"Why would this stop you from being a vet?"

"She might have other ideas. I want to live upstate and have a practice. And a big house where I can have lots of my own animals." *And be left in peace.*

"And kids?"

"No. I don't want to get married. Animals are good. Animals love you no matter what."

When had my daughter become so insecure? "*I* love you no matter what."

Now she laughed. "You have to. You're my mother."

"I'd love you anyway. I love the way you care about animals. I love the way you say what's on your mind. I'm just not sure you trust me."

"Trust you? Trust you how?"

How could I put it into words? "Trust that I'm not going to betray you. That I'm not going to love anybody else more than you. Let's say you had a litter of kittens in your upstate farmhouse, and you loved them all. But one accidentally got outside and you couldn't find her. Would you decide since you had three anyway you didn't really need another and just let her fend for herself? Maybe die of hunger or exposure? Or would you go outside and try to find her no matter what?"

I didn't need to say more. Tears had already started to fill Hannah's eyes, and in a moment I was hugging her hard.

HANNAH FELT NO ambivalence at all about approaching Howard Riggs. She brushed her hair down around her face and wore her light blue parka. She even put on some coral lipstick she found on my dresser. I didn't have the heart to tell her that Howard seemed immune to feminine charms—masculine charms too, come to think of it. I had no idea what got Howard up in the morning.

Marty, Susie, and I waited in the bookshop for Hannah to come back from her mission, joking nervously. We had promised to come and rescue her if she was not back in a half hour.

I first met Howard long before I became a bookseller, when I brought down several cartons of books to sell to him. His shop had "Fine First Editions and Rare Art Titles" painted in gold on the window and the books were attractively displayed. But as soon as you stepped inside, you were in front of a rickety sale table of mistakes labeled "Future Treasures." The experience went downhill from there.

Howard Riggs had been in his thirties in those days, a wire-taut man with sandy hair and gold-rimmed glasses through which he surveyed the world sourly.

I'd entered the shop and asked if he bought books.

He sighed and threw out an arm. "Show me what you've got."

After I set the carton on the floor, he slipped on a pair of thin white vinyl gloves, then poked at the books like a proctologist. Would he tell me they had hemorrhoids? His diagnosis was worse. Straightening up and peeling off the gloves, he gave me an outraged look. "Don't ever waste my time like this again." He looked like he was about to kick the carton. "And take this dreck with you!"

As if I would try to sneak a few onto his "Future Treasures" table.

In hindsight I'd learned how bad the books really were: outdated textbooks of Colin's, a children's paperback series, cookbooks my mother had given me that I'd never used. Books that no self-respecting dealer would make shelf room for.

Perhaps that was the moment I had decided to learn everything I could about book values.

I knew that Howard treated Susie like something he picked up on his shoe, and Howard and Marty had a history that went back years. Unlike me, Marty had the financial means to keep Howard in his place.

Hannah was back in fifteen minutes.

"You're in one piece," I said.

She looked around, but spoke to me. "Mom, he was so nice! He didn't have a good first edition of *Kon-Tiki*, so he went online to this book site and showed me how I could find one."

"You're sure you went to Howard Riggs Books?"

"Uh-huh. It looked just like you said."

"What did he say about the Harper Lee book?"

Hannah rubbed the bridge of her nose, embarrassed. "I didn't ask him. He was so nice that I didn't want to try and *trap* him. I didn't buy anything, and he still said to stop back anytime."

"Do you think he knew who she was?" Susie asked me.

I shook my head. "How could he?"

Marty sighed. "Well, I've changed the locks and paid Jen for the damage. Any more books missing, someone *else* is going to pay."

He glared at us to make sure we knew who we were.

Chapter 36

HANNAH WENT BACK to Cornell the next morning. Her vacation wasn't over yet, but she said she could get more studying done at school, and I didn't try to stop her. What was there for her to do at home anyway? In the three days after she left, I received several responses to the e-mail about Caitlin, editors trying to find out the details. One assured me that he would print it on the front page only if we "came clean." Another demanded to know if she was wanted by the police.

The best thing about the e-mails was that they confirmed ours had been received.

Then late Thursday morning, I received another:

Hi,

The girl you're looking for was Betsy Cavanaugh. Unfortunately she died in a skiing accident when she was fifteen. I'm sending you a photo of her so you can see if it's her. Sorry to be the bearer of bad news.

There was no signature. I looked to see which college the e-mail had come from, but I saw only a Hotmail address.

My heart banged like the drum in a funeral march. I scrolled down to the photo of a smiling, red-cheeked girl in a dark green parka. It could have been Hannah in high school.

No, it can't be. We can't have come this far to find this.

The girl could only be Caitlin. She could have been Hannah except for a small white scar at the base of her chin.

I couldn't move.

A mad rush of images: Stratford-upon-Avon, Nick Clancy, DCI Sampson, the White Swan. Trees outlined in snow, Garnet Hill Books, Micah's confession. All for nothing. All the effort to persuade Colin and Hannah had been for nothing. We might as well have left the tragedy buried, spared ourselves this fresh pain. Patience had been right, although she hadn't known why.

How could Caitlin be dead? How could she be dead?

There were people who didn't seem any different from me who went through life protected. It was as if they were living under a clear plastic dome where nothing tragic could reach them. Until what happened to Caitlin, I had thought I was under there too. But I wasn't. I hadn't been saved from losing my little girl or from Colin deciding the marriage was over. Not from Jason's difficulties and family estrangement or close friends dying young. I was just the kind of person who *could* lose a daughter in a skiing accident.

But to come so close to actually finding her . . . This was un-bearable. I couldn't stand it. Something inside me was about to explode, scattering my body all over the room. When they finally came to search for me in the barn, they would find only traces. I pounded my fists on the worktable. No, no, no! It couldn't be hap-pening to us again.

I couldn't stay there, I had to move, find someone to talk to before this pressure destroyed me. Not someone from my family; that would only make it worse. Friends . . . but I hadn't seen my college roommate, Gail, since September, and Bianca Erikson was over an hour away in Springs. I doubted I could drive that far. I thought of Bruce Adair then. He could calm me down if anyone could and I wouldn't have to explain anything. Bruce—I had to talk to Bruce!

Of all the times I had called and found him in his office, this time his phone rang six times and went to voice mail. I didn't have his cell phone number, I didn't know if he had a cell phone. He was just contrary enough not to own one.

I can't stand it, I can't stand it.

Maybe he was teaching a seminar. No, second semester hadn't started. What if he were away on vacation? *Please God, no—he never goes on vacation!* But what if he had? What if he were in the Caribbean with some star-struck young poetess? Or teaching an intersession course in Colorado or Illinois?

It didn't matter. I had to find him. Grabbing my parka from the chair, I didn't even bother to zip it. My van started immediately despite the cold, and I raced to the university. These days, with e-mail and cell phones, people were rarely out of touch. Even if Bruce were in Tahiti, the division secretary would know how to reach him, I promised myself as I pulled into the parking garage. It made no sense if he didn't have a cell, but I clung to the fantasy anyway.

What if the whole department closed in January?

But I couldn't think that, I had to focus on finding Bruce. Otherwise I would have to think about my poor lost child. *Doomed.* She was doomed right from the beginning, fated like a princess in a fairy tale to be stolen, fated to be sold into slavery or die young. Far from being protected under the dome, she had been born under an evil star. Unlike most fairy-tale heroines, she hadn't survived it.

THE DEPARTMENTAL SECRETARY was just returning from lunch, removing the headscarf from her salt-and-pepper curls and starting to unbutton her tweed coat. I wasn't sure if she knew who I was but I forced myself to smile.

"Is Bruce Adair around?"

"He's not in his office?"

Ah. I hadn't known how heavy my apprehension had been until it slipped away, a yoke being lifted from my shoulders. "When I called him before there was no answer."

"He may still be at lunch. But check."

Thank God, thank God.

I let go of one last image, Bruce sunning himself on a beach in Martinique.

Just then we both turned as we heard Bruce's voice. He was laughing up at a skinny young woman, probably a teaching assistant, who towered gawkily over him. One thing I loved about Bruce was his self-confidence regardless of his scoliosis or his height.

He stopped laughing when he saw me. "Delhi! You have news?"

I nodded mutely. He knew I was waiting for responses from the college newspapers.

Motioning me along, he unlocked the door and I stepped into the familiar office with its waist-high bookshelves and my tinted photographs of England. Something about the room seemed to wrap its arms around me. *You're no worse off than you were a year ago*, it chided.

But I was.

Bruce moved to the specially designed chair behind his desk, and I stumbled into the student seat across from him.

"It must be good news or you wouldn't have come in person." He tilted his head, watching me. "Is it?"

I couldn't say anything.

"Well, it's early for you to get a response. There hasn't been much time for your appeal to be published. It's intersession and—"

"She's dead. She died at fifteen in a skiing accident. I got an e-mail." My horror was too deep for tears. "I'll pay your money back. I didn't—"

"Delhi. Where is this e-mail?" He sounded much too calm for the news.

"On my laptop. At home."

"Show me." He gestured at me to bring my chair around, then turned to his computer, and motioned at the keyboard. "Get your mail."

I did as he asked, my fingers slipping as I tried to type. With only a handful of responses on this new account, the last e-mail was easy to find.

Bruce read it, looked at the attached photo, and studied it again.

Then he turned and looked at me, his Scottish features relieved. "It's bogus."

"Bogus?" I felt as if I had never heard the word before.

"Bogus. A hoax. Not real."

"But how do you know?"

"Why do I think that? A few reasons. Hotmail accounts are suspect in my book. Second, when people get an e-mail they want to respond to, they press reply to make sure the address is correct. That way the message they're answering is also shown. It's definitely more work to send a new message entirely. It's unusual.

More than that, this message is unsigned. An anonymous message from a suspect account . . ."

"Are you just trying to make me feel better?"

"Watch this."

He opened the Google screen and typed in "Betsy Cavanaugh, skiing accident."

Nothing pertinent came up. He tried "Elizabeth Cavanaugh" and added "Obituary" to the name. A number of genealogical entries appeared, but no one who had died later than 1980.

"I bet if you go to Facebook you'll find a lot of Elizabeth Cavanaughs. But none will be the right one. Because she doesn't exist."

"You're saying that Caitlin didn't die?"

"I'm saying that someone wants you to think she did. You're supposed to read this 'friendly' e-mail, feel devastated, and call off your search." He eyed me sternly. "That's what you were going to do, isn't it?"

"No! That's why I came to you. I had the feeling you would know what to do."

He smiled, then looked at me soberly. "Now whoever it is knows you're actively looking for her. And they know where you live."

"But I didn't put my address in the e-mail. Or my name."

"Delhi, think. They know whose child they took. Colin has a high profile. Anyone who sent this message knows how to find him. And you."

"You think it's from her kidnappers?"

"Probably. Someone could have recognized the photo you sent and told her. Or her parents. What makes me think it isn't just a prank is the photo of her they sent of her at fifteen. Who else would have that?"

I nodded mutely.

"How many colleges did you send your appeal to?"

"Thousands. Can't we find out from Hotmail who opened the account?"

"With a court order, maybe. But there's nothing criminal in this e-mail."

"It's not criminal to send an e-mail saying someone's dead?" I felt outraged.   "Cruel, maybe. But not a crime. You do think it's Caitlin in the photo?"

"She looks exactly like Hannah at that age. She has a little scar on her chin that Hannah doesn't, but otherwise . . . yes."

"Let's try something. Send a message back to them and see how they respond."

"What—what should I say?"

"That they've made a mistake and this isn't the same girl. Thanks, but you'll have to keep looking. Something like that." He turned the keyboard toward me.

I moved closer to Bruce so I could see the screen, then hit reply and typed shakily, *Thanks for the information, but this isn't the girl we're looking for. We'll need to keep looking.* I didn't sign my name either.

"Is that okay?"

Bruce read it over and hit send. "Now we wait."

Nothing happened.

"So they know about you, but you're ahead of the game too. You have a more recent photo of her." He smiled at me. "So get back to work."

I leaned over and kissed his cheek.

"And watch your back, Delhi. I mean it."

I kept checking my e-mail. There was no response until the next day.

COLIN CALLED THAT night. Since Hannah had gone back to Cornell, he hadn't stopped by for dinner. I found that disappointing.

"Any news?"

"Not really."

"*Nothing?*"

What was he expecting in less than a week? He was the most impatient man I knew.

"Well—a couple of school editors want more information. They say they won't print the notice until they know more."

"That's it?"

"There was another e-mail saying she was—not alive anymore." I was reluctant to give the words any power by saying them aloud. "But it was a hoax."

"What are you talking about?"

"I got an e-mail saying that the girl in our notice died in a skiing accident at fifteen. They used another name, of course, and sent a photo. But it wasn't true."

"How do you know it's not true?"

"It sounded fishy. So I had an expert look at the e-mail and they said it was bogus."

"An expert? Who?"

I wasn't going to tell him it was Bruce Adair. They had been colleagues for a long time, but more like coworkers in a labor camp than friends. If Colin heard I had told Bruce before him . . .

"Just a computer nerd I know."

"And you showed it to some stranger first?"

"Colin, I had to know! I was beside myself. I needed to talk to someone who would know." I felt as if he were pushing me into a lie, the same way he had when I changed my story in Stratford.

The mythical computer nerd was turning into someone so real he would soon come walking through the Book Barn door.

And it was Colin's fault because? He was *forcing* me to lie? I was the one afraid to face his anger. Instead of telling the truth, I was taking the easy way out as I was used to doing.

I started again. "This is what happened. I got an e-mail today saying that a Betsy Cavanaugh had died in a skiing accident, and that they thought she was the girl we were looking for. But the message wasn't from any of the colleges. It wasn't a *reply* to anything, just something sent from an anonymous Hotmail account and not even signed. So I went—"

"I want to see that e-mail."

"I'll forward it to you. But—"

"If I hadn't called you, I still wouldn't know."

"Well, I got used to your stopping by. I would have shown you then."

A silence. "Do you want me to? Stop by?"

"Sure. If I know ahead of time, I'll cook something."

I was probably as surprised at my offer to cook dinner for him as he was.

Chapter 37

THE NEXT MORNING it snowed. Not the blizzard the newscasters were hoping for, not a record for Long Island, but twenty-three inches in Port Lewis. It was enough to cover my van to the tops of its tires and keep me housebound, since I hadn't remembered to park at the end of the driveway. There was enough snow to make me sit at my kitchen window looking out at where my yard had been and think of graves under winter's blanket and the dying of hope. I had once seen a photograph of Arlington Cemetery in winter, rows of markers in the snow, each punctuated by a wreath. *Gone, forever gone.*

If Colin came now, he would have to eat comfort food, all that I had in the house: saltines crushed into tomato soup, crackers and peanut butter, Kraft macaroni and cheese, and canned corn beef. At least I had bags of dried food for the cats and wine left over from Christmas. But when Colin called he announced that the university was closed, the roads impassable. The condo where he was staying had been plowed out, but he didn't trust the rest of the island.

I did what I always did when I was snowed in: made a fire in the living room, wrapped myself in a blanket with a cup of peppermint tea nearby, and read from the stacks of books I had set aside. I would run out of food long before books. Lately I had been fascinated by art theft and the novels of Jane Gardam, and was soon lost in those worlds. Just for once, just for a few hours, I let myself escape from mine.

After a lunch of tomato soup and crackers, I turned on my laptop and found that colleges in Kentucky, California, and North Carolina were planning to run Hannah's photo and description. I wrote back and thanked them and asked them to let me know if anyone responded to them directly. I wasn't good at math, but three out of 2,774 seemed the tiniest fraction of one percent. There were also two book orders and e-mails from Hannah and Jane. Hannah in Ithaca was blasé about the snow, but Jane worried that I had lost power and urged me to keep warm. I responded to everything though I didn't plan to battle my way out to the Book Barn to fill the orders until tomorrow morning.

Yet this contact with the world outside made it hard to become reabsorbed by books. It didn't matter now if more colleges ran our appeal. If the e-mail about Betsy Cavanaugh was a ruse to make us abandon our search, then we had already reached the right people. Or the wrong ones.

Something about being trapped inside the house, not knowing what to do next to find Caitlin, made me cranky. I sat on the green-and-gold couch and created a mental done-me-wrong list. At the top was Jason, who had never called again to find out about his missing sister. My sister, Patience, who had called Christmas Day in a conciliatory mood, wanting to hear all about England, but skirting the issue of Caitlin.

DCI Sampson had promised to keep me updated on anything new he learned, but I had never heard from him. Okay, I had said I would call him, but still . . . . Even Jane and Hannah had gone back to their lives. They cared about their mythical sister, but not in the way I did.

Colin was the only one I could not accuse of indifference.

I added wood to the fire and picked up *The Gardner Heist* again.

LOST IN THE book finally, I was back at the Isabella Stewart Gardner Museum in Boston when there was a soft thud against the front door. If I had not been in the living room I would not have heard it. I waited for someone to knock—probably Colin, though he usually barged right in—but there was no other sound. It could have been snow sliding off the roof, except that it would have fallen beyond the front porch, and this noise was much closer. Besides, it was still too cold and sunless for melting to have started.

I waited for another thud, but heard nothing.

Getting up meant disturbing Raj who had settled in next to me on the blanket and purred whenever I reached down to stroke his head, but now I was curious. Lifting him to one side I stood up and went to the front door. When I looked out I saw nothing but swirling white for a moment. Then I screamed.

There was a trail of blood, red as holly berries against the white snow, leading to the front door. On the worn sisal mat lay a ragged bundle.

Chapter 38

I DIDN'T WANT to touch it. I kept staring down at the squeezed-together rags until I was sure it was nothing alive—nothing that had ever *been* alive—though it was bloodstained too. Something about the white-and-yellow striped knit fabric haunted me. I kept looking until I knew what it was.

I still didn't want to touch it, but I knelt down and picked the bundle up. Quickly I closed the front door, locked it, and set whatever it was on the coffee table, next to the cup of tea I had recently drained and the pile of waiting books. I couldn't feel my fingers as I reached down, untangled the bunched-up cloth, and saw a familiar smiling goldfish. *Oh my God oh my God oh my God.*

Safety-pinned to the shirt Caitlin had been wearing the last time I saw her in Stratford was a white folded piece of paper. It took me much too long to unfasten the tiny gold pin and open the paper. Printed in block letters:

YOU'RE WASTING YOUR TIME.

If I'd lived in Jane Austen's day I might have crumpled to the floor. But I was part of the twenty-first century, so I pushed up from the couch and staggered into the kitchen to call Colin.

"Hey-lo!" His cheerful voice carried into the room.

"You have to come over. Something's happened."

"To one of the kids?"

"No. Yes. It's horrible!"

"Tell me."

"You'll see."

"Okay, Delhi, calm down. Is the driveway plowed?"

"No, but—"

"How are the roads?"

"I don't *know*. But—"

"I know, I know. I have to come. Just tell me what happened."

"I can't!"

"Okay. I'll be right there."

I went back to the couch and stared at the tiny blood-soaked shirt, at the note, until I heard Colin's boots on the front porch steps. Then I jumped up and unlocked the door.

He came in breathing hard, stomping the snow off his feet and looking at me.

We didn't even embrace.

"Where did the blood outside come from?"

"I don't know! I looked out and it was there."

"There are no footprints around it. Not even animal tracks."

"Really? You looked at it closely?"

"I could see it from the path." Then he added, "Someone probably reached out from the path and dripped it. But why?"

"Do you—do you remember the shirt Caitlin had that she loved so much? With the goldfish?"

He winced as if a strong light had been shone in his face.

Mutely I pointed to the coffee table.

Colin had no qualms about picking up the little striped top and shaking it out. "This is what she was wearing? But this isn't *her* blood. It's still fresh."

"Thank God."

Then he saw the note and his face changed. The color in his cheeks deepened, not into red but into something darker. A dusky rage. When he looked at me his blue eyes were colder than I had ever seen them.

If I had been sickened and terrified, he was possessed by a fury that made him capable of anything. "Wrong. We *will* find her. And when we do there'll be more bloodshed."

I HAD WANTED Colin on our side but he was frightening me. Neither of us knew what the police could do, but we called them anyway. "For the future," Colin said grimly.

The young patrolman who came didn't have many ideas. "There's a lot of footprints on the path," he pointed out. "Even mine. But it could have been a dying bird who dripped as he flew away."

"What about the shirt and the note?"

"I don't know. Why does it say you're wasting your time?"

There was no use telling him the whole story. "We don't know," I said.

COLIN DID NOT want macaroni and cheese for dinner—it had been our fallback meal, served with cut-up hot dogs when the children were younger—so we drove downtown, back to Slices. He was calmer now, but still grim. "From now on, I'll handle this. It's too dangerous for you."

"What are you talking about?" We were both drinking beer, and I set my glass down.

"These are dangerous people, Delhi. They'll do anything they can to keep us from finding her."

I nodded. "And we have no idea who they are."

"But they know who we are. They can't be that far away, to do something like that in a snowstorm."

"That means Caitlin's close too!"

"Not necessarily." His fingers played with his napkin. "She's probably away at college."

"What I don't understand is—why would you even keep a shirt you kidnapped a child in?"

He shrugged. "People hold on to things. Things have power."

That was true. But if it had been me, I would have destroyed the evidence right away. "What do we do now?"

"We wait. And think."

Thinking, I could do that. But I had never been one to wait.

Chapter 39

WHEN I GOT back from the restaurant there was a frantic message from Susie. She was sobbing.

Before I even took my jacket off, I called her back.

"Delhi?"

"Susie, what happened?"

"Marty stopped by the shop just now. Three more books are gone!"

"You opened up today?"

"No, not with the snow. The shop was all locked up, with the new locks. He went to pick up two books people had ordered privately. Then he checked the shelves."

"What books are gone?"

"*The Emerald City of Oz*, a Steinbeck, and this pamphlet on the assassination of Abraham Lincoln. It was in a special holder."

I knew the one she meant. One of the most valuable things in the shop. I wasn't sure why Marty even left it there.

"He's going to fire me! After I earn out what the books were worth." Her voice trembled.

"He's just upset. He can't blame you for what happens when the shop's locked and you're not there. That's crazy."

"He's threatening to shut it down completely. To go back to just selling to collectors."

Maybe that's what he really wanted to do. Could Marty himself be hiding the books so he would have a valid reason for not keeping the shop open?

It made as much sense as anything else.

I KNEW I had to stay alert to any danger, but I couldn't stop my life. Two days later I got up early and drove into Whitestone, over the Nassau County border into Queens, to attend a book sale. As usual the selection at this temple sale was good, particularly in the area of art catalogs and vintage children's picture books, though the prices were higher than I liked to pay. But in winter you took what you could get and were grateful for it. I was pleased with a first edition *Stuart Little* in a beautiful dust jacket that would pay for my trip there.

I saw a number of dealers I knew, but was most surprised to encounter Paul Pevney, Susie's husband. Instead of his usual modus operandi of coming late to carry off the dregs, he was standing in front of me in line to pay. For once he did not seem excited to see me.

"You're far from home," I said. "Not working today?"

His lanky frame straightened up from arranging the books in his cartons. "I took the day off." He gave me an accusing look through his rimless glasses. "Susie should be here with me. If she wasn't working at that bookstore, she would be." His look conveyed his feeling that it was my fault.

I started to point out that the money had to be coming in

handy, then remembered Susie telling me she was squirreling it away. That would be for nothing, of course, if Marty insisted she reimburse him.

"You find anything good?" I asked.

"I like her with me at sales, then going home and listing the books. That's what she's good at."

We were almost to the cashier, and I pushed my vinyl boat bag along with my foot.

Belatedly he answered my question. "I found some good books. No Ernest Hemingways, but I did okay."

And then his books were on the table, the amounts being totaled. By the time I had finished with my own books, Paul was gone.

I GOT HOME in the early afternoon and carried my bag to the Book Barn, stopping every few minutes to flex my arm and look behind me. Would I be able to schlep books this way when I was sixty? Seventy? Would I reach old age without mishap? Before I stepped into the barn I checked around it carefully to make sure the snow had not been trampled near the windows or door. It did not look as if anyone had been here though, so I unlocked the door and went inside, switching on the heat immediately. It would take nearly an hour for the cavern to warm up enough to take my jacket off, and I sat down at my worktable still rubbing my hands.

Perhaps it was the snow outside, or the ski slope updates they'd given when I turned on the news in the van, but the hoax e-mail suddenly stirred a memory. The writer claimed Betsy Cavanaugh had died in a skiing accident. Years earlier my friend Diane was sure she had seen Hannah on the slopes in Colorado. Was skiing a common denominator?

A tenuous thread, but it was all I had.

If Caitlin was a good skier, she might have belonged to a ski club or junior association. Sending the photo I had received to organizations within driving distance of Long Island would be the longest shot yet. But what else was there? I could even get a list of young women who were ranked as accomplished skiers and see if their names matched up with—what? I had read somewhere that when people chose false names they tended to pick names with the same initials as their own. If the hoax e-mail had been an attempt to make us abandon the search for Caitlin, that could be significant. What if I concentrated on last names that began with C, first names starting with B or E? I decided it couldn't hurt.

On the computer I found a few organizations that were devoted to national champions, and many more regional youth ski clubs, from New England to Minnesota. I hadn't thought about amateur clubs, but those might be a better way to go. Even if Caitlin wasn't a national champion, a local group might recognize her as one of their own.

This time there was no flash drive of e-mail addresses to plug in. I scrolled through lists of organizations, laboriously cutting and pasting individual information. The longer I worked, the more apprehensive I grew. Suppose the club contacted her parents first to make sure it was all right to release the information? What if that pushed them deeper into hiding and made them lash out at us again? And the blackest possibility of all: What if an organization confirmed that it was Betsy Cavanaugh in the photograph and that she had indeed died?

Doomed.

It took several hours but I sent individual e-mails hinting at an award, explaining that her photo had been submitted by someone who had seen her skiing and admired her expertise, but did not know who she was. I attached the new photo. It was not a message you could overthink. There were holes large enough for a Nordic village to schuss through. But it was all I had.

At first I sent the e-mail only to New York and New England, then expanded the search as far as Chicago and down to Virginia.

And then, as Colin had suggested, I waited.

Our opponents evidently knew how to wait too. Colin stopped by for dinner and took me to a seafood restaurant in town. He was skeptical of the skiing connection but saw no harm in trying it. Slumped across from me, a weary Santa, he admitted he had no better ideas himself.

"But look how much we've narrowed it down," I said. "We know she's in this country, probably in the Northeast. We've eliminated the rest of the world. That's *huge*." I thought of something else. "DCI Sampson can concentrate on car rental records for Americans now. I'll call him tomorrow morning and tell him."

"How much longer are we going to grasp at threads?"

His words made me cold. But I said, "Threads? I thought it was straws. I guess as long as it takes. But we are getting closer."

Exactly how much closer I could not guess.

Chapter 40

It was barely 7 a.m. the next morning when I finished my coffee and headed for the Book Barn. The last remnants of the snowstorm had retreated, crouching under the bushes like a defeated army. The exposed ground was muddy, the sky still sunless overhead. Worse than snow, worse than frigid temperatures with bright blue skies, were these overcast days when the world seemed small and without interest.

Since Christmas, book orders had been slow. I dragged myself to the barn and kept listing more anyway. Sometimes even the act of uploading books to the Internet sparked interest, though not necessarily in the new books.

Looking around cautiously as usual, I unlocked the barn door, then downloaded my mail from the night before. Besides the Abe-Books notification of orders, the usual BookEm.com messages, Hannah's daily dose of cute animals, and advertisements from Amazon and B&N, there was an e-mail from the New England Youth Ski Club.

They identified the girl in the photograph as Elisa Crosley. They wrote that she was now a student at St. Brennan's College outside Boston and that they would forward the e-mail about the award to the family as soon as they could locate their address.

Elisa Crosley. It sounded rude and intrusive that anyone would dare to call my child by that strange name. That she would grow up thinking her name was Elisa, not Caitlin. Colin's words that she'd had a life all this time came rushing back. Though I hadn't admitted it to myself, I had imagined her in a kind of suspended animation, waiting for us to rescue her so that her real life could begin—as if she had been granted only one, her life as our daughter.

Instead, all this time, she had been having her own experiences as someone named Elisa. Perhaps, since they were twins, her experiences had even intersected with Hannah's: dressing up as the same fairy princess for Halloween, loving Care Bears, learning Spanish as her foreign language in school. The skiing was what was different; why had she done that? But why shouldn't she? She had not been on an extended vacation, waiting to come back to us and tell us what she had found. She had been living the only life she knew. A life that she might not want to leave.

That thought was so bitter that I sat back in my chair, barely able to take the next breath. That day in Stratford, she had died to us as surely as if she *had* slipped into the river. Why would she want to know us after all this time? We weren't the family of anyone's dreams. Perhaps she would feel like Hannah, that her life was settled and she did not need any further complications.

In a lifetime of reading I had come across stories about people who had gone through life feeling incomplete, as if they had a twin somewhere from whom they had been separated. Sometimes they found out that there had been another baby in the pregnancy, a baby miscarried or not fully formed in the womb. But if that were true, then why didn't Hannah feel any lack? She had lived with her twin for two and a half years. Would Caitlin feel the same way?

I was so focused on Caitlin growing up as someone called Elisa that I didn't at first think of her last name, Crosley.

And then I did. Suddenly I was hot and cold at the same moment, my face frozen and then burning up with fever. As if I had been picked up and thrown back into another time, I was in Stratford, on the back patio with the other young archeological families, the cries of our children mingling with the plinking chirps of crickets and evening insects. We adults were deep into our own conversations. The children were there but it was *our* time.

Ethan and Sheila Crosley, Colin's best friends, were not part of this group. Because they had so much money and no children, they were staying at a nearby inn instead of being crammed into "family rooms" at the residence like everyone else. They went out to dinner in Stratford or Warwick or Birmingham and skipped the hostel food the rest of us complained about. Colin sometimes went out with them to eat, though I was never invited. As he pointed out, he and Ethan had a lot to talk about.

I hadn't like Sheila very much anyway. Nobody had. In contrast to our cotton summer clothes, she was usually turned out in expensive jeans, black blazer and chunky real gold jewelry. The other wives had speculated that the reason that Sheila with her artfully cut black bangs and model's face was always unsmiling, always aggrieved, was because she hadn't been able to get pregnant.

That was the accepted wisdom: *They have the money, but we have the kids.*

Sheila must have known how we felt about her, but she acted indifferent. Yet inside she must have been burning. How obsessed was she with wanting a child? Enough to steal their best friend's? *Impossible*. I couldn't get my head around it. No wonder they had dropped us as soon as the tragedy happened. Not, as Colin had speculated, because we were unforgivably careless. They had to stay far away if they had Caitlin.

I sat at my worktable, chin in hands, the enormity of it breaking over me. Still, there were parts that did not fit. Ethan Crosley was a respected archeologist, not a kidnapper and killer. If it *had* been them, how had they gotten Caitlin back into this country without a passport? Priscilla Waters had been run down in September, long after Ethan's teaching responsibilities in California had started up. He could not have been driving the hit-and-run car and standing in front of a class of students at the same time. I had a foggy memory of Sheila refusing to drive on the "wrong" side of the road. Cross with the English, as if they had changed their driving habits to annoy her.

She would never have stayed on alone in England and handled it all by herself.

Call someone. Colin. Jane. Bruce.

Find Caitlin before they get the message from the ski club and spirit her away forever.

Chapter 41

SOMEHOW I MANAGED to answer two book order e-mails, lock the barn, and get back to the house in less than five minutes. Out of breath, I changed into my most conservative clothes: my black velvet blazer, a classic white shirt I had found discarded in Jane's closet, and dark pants. A silk scarf for color, and my hair pulled back in a twist. It would look incongruous with my dark green winter parka, but that was the warmest jacket I had.

All I cared about was seeing Caitlin. I couldn't be in the same world with my child and not see her. I wouldn't approach her. I wouldn't spring any terrible surprises on her: *Before you go to your history class, let me introduce myself.* I would look at Caitlin/Elisa from a distance, take her picture, then discuss it with the others. We would figure out the best way to approach her and do it the right way.

With this plan firmly in mind, I couldn't explain to myself why I stopped in the living room where the Del Monte cartons of mementos had been stored since Thanksgiving and took out Sheepie, Caitlin's favorite toy. Why I sifted frantically through the secretary drawer and found the latest photograph of all five of us at Jason's high school graduation and slipped it inside a manila envelope and into my bag with the lamb. Another thought: Back to the carton of photo albums for the snapshot of Hannah and Caitlin at the top of the slide.

The ferry dock was only five minutes away. When I drove down Harbor Street, the large maw of the boat was up in the air and the last of the cars were driving on. The man by the guardhouse with the clipboard, a veteran ferryman I knew by sight, waved me on and I drove into the dark metal bowels of the 8 a.m. ferry. Behind me I heard the start-up of the gears to retract the gangplank. And then they stopped.

As I climbed out of the van, I turned to look. A man in a black Ford sedan was leaning out of the driver's window, arguing vehemently with the clipboard holder, who was shaking his head no. Suddenly the driver pulled himself in and the car skidded toward the ferry as if he would force himself on. The ferryman swept up his arm in a signal to *go* and the wide metal plate started to lift again. As if realizing he would be driving into the water, the man in the Ford wheeled abruptly and squealed onto Harbor Street.

I watched him go. He could have been anybody who needed to catch that ferry and was angry when he did not get on. I was surprised that they hadn't let him; the vehicle area was less than half full. The driver could have been an innocent commuter—or he could have been the man who left Caitlin's shirt on the doorstep. Perhaps he had had me under surveillance and been caught off-guard when I left the house so suddenly.

Was I being cautious—or paranoid? I didn't know, but I couldn't shake the image of him driving around to Connecticut instead, taking the long way to Boston but getting there nonetheless. Yet he wouldn't have to do that. He could notify the Crosleys where I was headed and they could whisk Caitlin away.

Was this the race of my life?

I climbed the metal stairs to the main cabin, a large room with booths and vinyl benches, and realized I had had nothing so far but espresso. I wasn't hungry, but I needed food as fuel. Going through the small cafeteria line, I picked up a small crumb cake, a carton of orange juice, and more coffee.

The cabin was sparsely populated on this weekday morning and I was able to find an empty booth. I ate my breakfast and stared out the window at Long Island Sound, watching the small whitecaps beat against the gray water like tiny protests. I needed to call everyone, but I wasn't sure I'd get reception out here, even with the iPhone. Instead I planned my strategy.

Three hours to Boston. Siri would help me find the college. I would go first to the admissions office. They would surely have Caitlin's class schedule and I'd try to get them to tell me where she was living. I hoped fervently that Ethan was still teaching in California, that even if the ski club mailed the Crosleys this morning they would not have time to get her.

Another person I needed to speak to urgently was DCI Sampson. Again I doubted that I could get through, but while I was sitting here I needed to try.

After a few false starts trying to find the right code sequence, the phone was miraculously ringing in the Stratford police station. I calculated the time difference. DCI Sampson should be just having his tea.

I had hoped to speak to Constable Bradford, but didn't recognize the voice that answered the phone. When he asked who was calling, I told him, "Delhi Laine from New York. It's important."

And then Sampson himself was on the line.

"Good afternoon, Ms. Laine."

No time for small talk. "Did you have a chance to get a list of car rental names?"

"A very long list." Reproof in his voice.

He actually had the names! "Do you have dates too?"

"I have dates." Now he sounded amused. No doubt I was easier to take an ocean away.

"Is there an Ethan Crosley?"

"It will take a minute to check. If you can hold on."

"As long as it takes."

The sound of the phone being laid on the desk and the rustling of papers.

If the records showed that Ethan and Sheila had turned in the car at the end of August, the last name would be just a coincidence. It would mean that Priscilla Waters had demanded more money from someone else named Crosley, some other people who were responsible for her death. Ethan and Sheila could have had confederates, but I doubted it. They were strangers in the country: Where would a law-abiding American academic find someone to commit murder for him? Just how much money did he have? I knew Ethan's father had owned a farm machinery company in Pennsylvania that had done well. I just didn't know how well.

And there was still the issue of the passport. They would have had no birth certificate to apply for a new one. At home they could have gotten forged documents more easily. That had to be harder to do in England. Harder, but not impossible. If you had enough money, you could get convincing forgeries of anything.

I realized I was still hoping that it was not them, that I would not have to tell Colin his best friend had betrayed him, when DCI Sampson came back on the line.

"Are you talking about Ethan L. and Sheila M. Crosley? They rented a Mercedes from July 12, 1995, to September 27, 1995. Are you going to tell me why you picked out those names?"

The news was so chilling that for a moment I assumed that the ferry was unheated.

Colin's best friend. Colin's best friend stole his little girl.

Chapter 42

St. Brennan's College was outside the city in Chestnut Hill and, thanks to Siri, I found the campus with no trouble. I had driven like the wind. I parked in the Beacon Street Garage and ran past the stadium. There was more snow on the ground here than at home though the walkways were clear. Even the majestic bronze eagle I passed looked cold. The students going in and out of the tan brick buildings were dressed for the weather.

Somehow I convinced the young woman in the records office that I was Elisa's West Coast aunt, passing through Boston with a few hours' layover. I saw her look at the ID photo in the folder and then at me. There must have been enough of a family resemblance to convince her to photocopy a class schedule for Elisa Crosley and explain that she was living in a residence hall half a mile from campus. I wrote down the directions.

Elisa was in an advanced literature seminar until noon. The fact that she was majoring in English was reassuring. *This was my girl.* If the paper in my hand had declared her major to be applied mathematics, I would have accepted it but had a moment of doubt.

This was her last class of the day. Would she go back to her room now or to the library to study? I had no idea, but decided to station myself in front of her classroom and hope that she did not slip out a back exit.

Even so, there were complications. Her seminar met in a tan stone building with a beautiful steeple—and a door at each end. For a while, I stood on the paving between doors, unable to get a close enough look at either. As I stood there, the open-work iron clock moving slowly toward noon, the sun passed behind the clouds, making the day even colder and bleaker. I wished I had Jane there to guard one of the exits. She would have also helped to calm the anxiety bubbling through me and threatening to run over.

Caitlin. My daughter. After nineteen years I was going to see my precious girl again.

Or not. I did not know if she was even attending class today, although it was still the beginning of the semester. Reluctantly I moved to the door on my right where I had a clear view of whoever came out. There was an equal chance that I would miss her, but I couldn't think what else to do. If I didn't see her I would drive straight to her residence and wait for her to come home.

A little before twelve, students in sweatpants and ski jackets began pushing through the doors in search of lunch. They moved into the gusty wind, a wind that brought more doubts. Even if I had picked the right door, would I be able to recognize Caitlin? Suppose her hair and face were shielded by a parka hood? Would she have gained weight the way Hannah had? Would someone see me taking photos with my iPhone and have me arrested?

I reminded myself that these students were already considered adults. They could vote, drive cars, and kill people in foreign countries. I was no predator lurking outside a playground at dismissal time, but I shivered inside my jacket anyway.

And then I thought I saw her. She was wearing a navy parka with a white insignia on one pocket. Her hair was the dark golden blond of Hannah's, but her head was turned away from me, and she was laughing up at two young men. I took the photo anyway. I was about to click the button a second time when she turned and looked directly into my face. Quizzical, as if someone had asked her to do something she wasn't sure about, such as, "Why don't you give your sister a turn?" A look of hers I would know anywhere.

I smiled and quickly refocused the camera phone on the statue of a holy man, hand outstretched, declaiming a theological point. I was just an innocent tourist, just the parent of a prospective student documenting the scene.

She moved past me.

I lowered the iPhone, the hand that was holding it trembling. I made myself stand like the statues in the quad around me, though every cell was screaming at me to run after her, to grab her and hold her forever. Surely, from some deep place within, she would know who I was.

I let her go.

Although it was lunchtime, my stomach was clenching and unclenching too painfully to consider food. Yet what if she'd gone into Magdalene Hall where I had seen a cafeteria? I circled around, searching for a girl in a navy parka and bought a tuna salad wrap and bottled water that I might need later. No Caitlin. I ran all the way to my van, then pushed inside and turned on the heater to get warm. I couldn't keep from looking at the photos any longer. The first was a blur that could have been any blond college student. The second picture, Caitlin gazing startled into the camera, was perfect. She and Hannah didn't look exactly alike, I realized. Caitlin's face was narrower and she had the white scar on her chin like a comma.

The scar didn't surprise me. Even at two she had been a daredevil, anxious to try everything new. She had been widely admired among other parents for her outgoing charm. Had that been her downfall, the tipping point that made the Crosleys decide they *had* to have her?

Now I had to get to Caitlin's residence before she did. Wishing that I were driving an anonymous dark sedan instead of a dented white van with "Got Books?" on the side, I gave Siri the address and listened to her guide me to Gin Factory Street. I turned onto it and found a parking space four cars back on the same side.

I just have to see her one more time. I had promised Colin I would not spring anything on Caitlin and I wouldn't, but things felt too unfinished now to drive home. I couldn't turn my back on Caitlin, not after all these years. But as soon as I saw her again, I would leave.

Meanwhile there were things I had to do. From the iPhone I sent the better photo to Colin, to Jane, to Hannah, and as an e-mail to Bruce, with a simple caption: "I Found Her." Then, exhausted, I leaned back into the driver's seat, unwrapped the sandwich, and unscrewed the water. My stomach felt hollowed out, still unsettled from the ferry crossing. I took a bite anyway, and my phone beeped, indicating a text. And then a second. And a third.

> Jane: OMG she looks just like I imagined! I cant believe it. What did she say?

Colin: Delhi, where R you?

Bruce: She looks like you. And Colin. Well done!

Hannah was probably in a class or lab.

I made myself eat more before I answered any of them. Then I sent the same message to everyone: "She's at St. Brennan's College, I found out this morning and took the ferry as soon as I knew. I wasn't going to lose her again, but I won't approach her now."

I just need one more look.

Chapter 43

I DIDN'T CARE how long I had to wait. Even if the ferries stopped running from Bridgeport for the night, I could continue to drive down Route 95 and cross over to Long Island.

Except for texting briefly, I hadn't taken my eyes off the street. A dry-cleaning van delivered clothes on hangers to a building across the way. A young mother passed pushing a double stroller, the kind a friend had lent me for the twins. A stooped grandmother tugged her shopping cart over the uneven sidewalk as if it were a balky puppy, her gray hair frizzing out of a red babushka. Two young women in identical yellow parkas entered the residence.

I was still watching when I saw a car slide in and park right in front of the building in a space that had just become free. Not just any car, but a dark blue Mercedes-Benz. An odd car for this neighborhood, I thought, then realized whose it must be. I straightened up in my seat and craned to look, but no one got out. Finally the driver's door opened and a dark-haired woman in a three-quarter length loden coat emerged. After looking up and down the street, she pressed something in her hand, probably a remote lock, then headed for the entrance to the building.

My stomach churned and I was sure I would throw up. I was shaken by nausea, a sickness more violent than any flu I had ever suffered. A splash of tuna fish rose, burning, into my throat. I gasped and made myself sit still, careful not to close my eyes and make it worse. This was no motion sickness left over from the ferry. I took a deep breath that ended in a spasm of coughing.

Sheila Crosley disappeared into the building.

I opened my window and begged the frigid air to save me. *You're not going to be sick. You're going to get through this.*

Sheila. How she must have prayed this day would never come.

She came back out a minute later, pressed something in her hand, and got back in the Mercedes. She did not drive away.

Seeing her the second time, I felt less nauseated though still dizzy. Did she know how close I was? I hadn't thought to look for the man in the black car, but he could have warned her. He might even be lurking close by as well. Voices only I could hear started shouting orders as if we were evacuating the *Titanic*. Go and confront her, tell her how she's ruined your life. *Kill* her. Don't do anything now. Drive away and let the police handle it. No, wait and see why she's here.

I paid attention to the last voice. Perhaps Sheila's being here was only coincidence. Maybe she drove into the city to see her daughter—*my* daughter—every Thursday.

And maybe Sheila would wave at me and invite me to go with them.

The next sequence felt as unreal as watching a movie being filmed. The Mercedes' door was flung open again, and Sheila Crosley moved around to the sidewalk. Caitlin was coming toward her in a hurry. They reached out to each other, hugged intensely for what seemed much too long, then turned and went into the residence.

The way they held each other . . . Not just like family members happy to see each other, again, but as if they were meeting after learning of a crisis. Was I the crisis? But that was hard to believe. Why would Sheila ever want Caitlin to find out about me? She had tried twice to make sure it didn't happen. Yet why was Sheila going inside with her? She could be warning Caitlin about me in another way completely.

This crazy lady who thinks she's your mother is trying to get in touch with you. We don't know what she'll try.

Nothing moved on the street now, no shoppers, no mothers pushing strollers. As the minutes dragged, I wondered what they could be doing in there. I fantasized them slipping out of a back exit, leaving the car to be picked up later. But finally the heavy glass door opened and Sheila and Caitlin came out carrying things. An overnight bag and an armload of books. A black laptop case and printer. My worst nightmare was unfolding before my eyes. Sheila was stealing my daughter from me again.

This time Sheila stayed in the car, but Caitlin went back inside the building. As soon as she had disappeared, I grabbed my woven bag and pushed out of the van. I had no idea what I planned to do now, only that I knew I could not lose Caitlin again. I pulled up my parka hood to cover my hair. If Sheila was not expecting me to be there, I doubted she'd recognize me after all this time. And if she was, I was ready for her.

When I reached the glass double doors I could see into a lobby area with couches.

The inner door was locked.

I was moving my hand toward the row of buttons on the wall when one of the two girls in yellow parkas appeared again, backpack in hand. She smiled politely and held the door open for me.

The area was meant to be a living room with couches and coffee tables, and porcelain lamps with tarnished brass bases. The room looked as if it had hosted generations of girls. I moved over to a faded flowered couch and sat down facing the elevator beyond, not letting the top of my head show. If Sheila came in, I would have the advantage. If Sheila came in . . . Even then I considered returning to my van and following the Mercedes when they left. But what if I lost them in traffic? I didn't know my way around Boston the way they must. And once they disappeared, everything was lost.

This might be the only chance I would ever be given. I extracted one of my Secondhand Prose business cards from my wallet, and slipped it into the manila folder with the photos.

Waiting gave rise to a new emotion, a deep, deep hate, a feeling so unfamiliar I couldn't identify it at first. I couldn't remember if I had ever felt this burn that started in my chest and then reached everywhere. In childhood, when emotions ran hot, I had yelled, "I hate you!" many times and felt its fury. Yet within hours the emotion had dissolved back into friendship or at least indifference. What I knew now was that if Sheila climbed out of her car and was hit by a speeding van, I would never turn the driver in.

Then the elevator door opened and Caitlin was stepping out, a navy backpack dangling from one arm. She looked serious, as if listening to some inner dialogue she had never heard before.

When she had almost reached me, I said, "Elisa, can I talk to you?"

"Oh!" She looked down at the couch, startled. "Well, I'm kind of in a hurry. My father had another heart attack and I'm going home for the weekend."

"This will only take a minute."

"Okay." She came and sat down next to me, our knees nearly touching, then looked at me more closely. "Weren't you taking pictures on campus today?" And then, "You look so familiar. Are you . . . my birth mother?"

Of everything I had ever imagined her saying to me, this was a complete shock. "Well, yes. But—"

Then I stopped. Her face was taking on the look of Hannah when she was told that something she always believed in wasn't true. It was a furrowing of the brow, a quiver to her full upper lip. "My parents told me you died in a car accident."

"Dead? They said I was dead? They must have wished I was dead after they stole you from us. Your father is alive too."

"I guess adoption must seem like theft, but—"

"Adoption? Cait— Elisa, listen to me. There wasn't any *adoption*. You have a twin sister, Hannah, and a wonderful family. We were in England the summer you disappeared." I knew I sounded frantic, incoherent, but I had to make her understand. "You were kidnapped from a park. All these years, we thought you had drowned. We just found out recently that you hadn't." I put out my hand to grasp her arm, to hold her there, just to touch her. The urge to reach out and put my arms around her was overwhelming. Yet I held back. I was a stranger to her.

She moved away from me to stand up. "I'm sorry, but I think you have the wrong girl."

As she straightened, I saw that the insignia on her jacket was for snowboarding.

"Wait." Desperately I fished in my bag and brought out Sheepie.

Shaking the tissue away, I said, "This was your favorite toy. You wouldn't go to sleep without him."

She stared at the tattered lamb. Something moved across her face then, a touch of memory, insubstantial as the brush of silk on skin. She put out her hand halfway, but didn't touch him.

"You called him Sheepie."

There was a rattling at the door and we both looked around, startled. Sheila was gesturing to get in.

"Take this!" I pulled out the manila envelope and handed it to her, then pressed Sheepie against her arm. "It's a picture of you and Hannah, and one of our family. *Your* family. And how to reach me. We never stopped missing you. *Never.*"

The pounding on the glass was louder.

"I forgot to lock my room." Caitlin jumped to her feet and fled toward the elevator, taking Sheepie and the envelope.

I turned to face Sheila Crosley.

Chapter 44

WE STARED AT each other through the black iron bars and slightly wavy glass, combatants in an arena I could never have imagined. Then she stepped back and I slipped into the tiny lobby, pulling the door rapidly closed before she could push in to Caitlin.

"How could you?" I gasped. "How could you steal my baby?"

She eyed me coolly, as if I were the old lady with the shopping cart and babushka. "What are you talking about? Who *are* you?"

"Come on, Sheila. You know exactly who I am. You just didn't think this day would come. How could you do it? Colin was supposed to be your friend!"

Her face turned to porcelain. She was still slender, still beautiful, her face only slightly lined. "Whoever you are, if you're talking about my daughter, we have adoption papers. Yes, I know who you are. It was too much of a struggle for you. All those children at once and your cocaine habit."

"My *what*?"

"I hope you've gotten clean." She eyed me. "I understand you have. But that doesn't undo what you were in the past."

The words clogged my throat—what to say first? "Any—any 'papers' you have are forgeries. All they need to do is check my handwriting. The British police know all about you anyway. They know you paid Priscilla Waters to steal Caitlin and tell Jane that she drowned. And they know you killed her when she demanded more money. I don't know what the extradition laws are, Sheila, but you're in big trouble."

Her expression gave nothing away, but the lid over one deep blue eye started to twitch. It was like seeing a statue move.

A voice cautioned me not to tell her everything, but it felt too good to stop.

"The police have the car rental records and how it was returned damaged."

"It *wasn't* returned damaged. We . . ."

"Had it repaired. I know. There are records for that too."

She didn't seem to notice that what I was saying no longer made sense.

"If you don't leave my daughter alone *I'm* calling the police. You were always so complacent, you and your little tribe, thinking you were superior to everyone else. You never appreciated what an amazing child she was. You could never have given her the life we have."

"You could have adopted any child." I was still trying to understand what had happened.

"You mean the child of some drug addict or crazy person? You don't get it, do you? Why would we adopt some stray when we could afford the best?" She was backing away from me as she talked, feeling around for the outer door handle. "Elisa was the child we would have had if we could have—I knew it the moment I saw her. You had so many children, grubby little brats, you didn't notice how special she was."

"Oh, you're so wrong. Just wait till I tell Colin what his 'best friends' did to us."

She turned away and opened the door, then looked back at me with an expression close to a smirk. "You think he doesn't know?" And then she escaped to the shelter of her expensive car.

Chapter 45

You think he doesn't know?

I made it back to the van, switched on the ignition, and watched as Caitlin, carrying a red backpack, came out and got in the passenger seat. For a moment the light caught the gold of her hair, a flash of sun on a cloudy day. Then it was extinguished and the Mercedes pulled away from the curb.

I had to go after them. I could not let Sheila steal her again. I was backing up, preparing to move out of the parking space, when a black Ford sedan pulled up alongside me. I thought the driver wanted my space and motioned him to back up so I could get out. He did not move. Ahead of me, I saw the Mercedes signal and turn left. Furiously I beeped my horn and motioned him back again.

It was another minute before the car pulled quickly forward and I caught a flash of a New York license plate. I would never find Sheila now. And I had other things, terrible things, to think about. How could Colin have known? Had he signed some kind of papers back in Stratford, after all? Was that why he had been so opposed to looking for Caitlin?

No, that was ridiculous. Caitlin had been his favorite, at least of the twins, the child he took sheer pleasure in. He'd loved her pert responses. When he heard the news, he had first been disbelieving, then crazy with grief. When Jane changed her story, he had gone immediately to the police, demanding that they try to find this "bad lady." When he had to return home to teach, he had supported my staying on in Stratford to work with the private detective.

And he had never acted the same toward me again.

Could Sheila have meant that he had found out later and decided that Caitlin was better off where she was, in the privileged life they were providing? Was it possible that he had even met her from time to time, not as her father but as one of Ethan's colleagues?

As soon as I had texted that I was at St. Brennan's College, had he called Sheila to warn her? She would have had to be in Boston already to get here so fast. She would have had to call Caitlin immediately, make up a story about Ethan's "heart attack," and arrange to pick her up. I hoped my showing up would give Ethan one now.

I sat in the driver's seat with the heat turned high, unable to get warm. I wanted to call Colin immediately and scream at him, demand answers. Yet I knew it was better to talk face-to-face.

It might not even be true. What if Sheila were being spiteful, trying to plant doubt? Making sure, despite Colin's protestations, that I never completely believed him?

Go home. But I just sat there with my head back, eyes closed, replaying my conversation with Caitlin, straining to tell if she'd believed me at all.

My phone rang then, jarring me, making me fumble frantically in my bag. As it rang for the fourth time, I looked to see who was calling. Jane. *No.* I couldn't talk to her now, I couldn't talk to anyone before I had seen Colin. I listened to her cheerful, excited voice mail wanting more details. If Colin had betrayed us, how could I ever let her know?

While I had my phone in my hand I pressed his number. I didn't know what I was going to say, how I was going to say it. The number rang and went to voice mail.

"Colin, it's Delhi. I have to see you. Don't meet me at the house, come to the Whaler's Arms at seven. If you can't meet me, let me know. Otherwise I'll see you then."

I laid the phone on the seat beside me, then picked it up again. "Siri? I need the best way back to Route 95."

When I had the directions, I left. There was nothing more for me here.

I MANAGED TO make the five-thirty ferry from Bridgeport with fifteen minutes to spare, and though I was tempted to sit in the bar with a glass of white wine, I stayed in the main cabin and read a memoir by a woman who was fighting breast cancer. I needed a clear head more than Dutch courage to confront Colin. Memoirs were my refuge. They have little resale value, so I buy them at book sales for myself. This one reminded me that there were worse things than what I was going through.

The Whaler's Arms was next to Port Lewis Books. It was also the restaurant where my friend who owned the Old Frigate, Margaret Weller, and I used to go for cappuccino and conversation, and where I get my coffee now if I'm opening up the shop. Otherwise it is a dive with a nautical theme; pirate's treasure map placemats on dark heavy tables and portholes for windows. It has the greasy smell of fish and chips fried in oil that should have been tossed the day before.

I chose it because I doubted we'd run into anyone we knew. With the noise level around the bar, no one would be able to hear what we were talking about.

Colin was already sitting in the back at a table for two, a Corona Extra in front of him.

I slid into the chair across from him. "I barely made the ferry. I need a drink."

"Delhi, what the hell do you think you're doing, running off to Boston like that? I told you I would handle it."

I wondered if he noticed I hadn't leaned over to kiss him. "But I found *Caitlin*—isn't that the thing that matters?"

He opened his mouth and closed it again, then said, "What do you want to drink?"

"I'll have a Corona too."

As soon as I ordered it, I was sorry. Drinking beer with Colin reminded me too much of the early happy days on digs when we would sit and watch the sunset streak the sand orange and crimson, discussing what had happened that day while the children played around us. This was the brand we'd always drunk in the Southwest.

"But how did you know she was there?" He leaned across the table. "And is it really her?"

"You saw the photo. And there are—other things." I told him about getting the ski club e-mail, my fears that the kidnappers would get the information, my rush to St. Brennan's.

"But how did you find her? Did they give you her name?"

I gave him a steady look.

"What?"

And then, looking at this man I had lived with for twenty-five years, longer than my parents, my sister, or anyone else, looking into his blue eyes wrinkled around the edges by life, his wide, still-handsome face, I knew he could not have been involved. His integrity was something I should never have doubted. I was glad he didn't know that I had. "You won't like it," I warned.

"Delhi, just tell me."

"It was Sheila and Ethan Crosley. They took her."

"What are you talking about?"

"Back in Stratford. They arranged everything."

"That can't be. Ethan? How do you *know*?"

"She grew up as Elisa Crosley. I saw Sheila today."

"You saw Sheila? Did you talk to her?" I saw how hard he was fighting not to believe it. Could not believe it.

My Corona sat untouched in front of me. "Where is Ethan teaching now?"

"As far as I know, he's still at Brown."

"In Rhode Island?" No more than an hour's drive from Boston.

Colin took a frantic gulp of beer, leaving a streak of foam on his upper lip. I had never seen him unable to speak before.

"Are you in touch with Ethan at all?" I asked.

He gave his head a sleepwalker's shake. "I e-mailed him last year about a dig I thought he'd be interested in. The bastard never even wrote me back."

"I wonder why."

"But how did they do it?"

I finally reached for my beer. I'd never known what to do with the chunk of lime stuck in the neck of the bottle. Now I just pulled it out and took a long swallow. Then I told him everything I knew, even about my call to Sampson and the rental car. "Sheila admitted it. She said I had signed adoption papers because of my 'cocaine habit'! She intimated you knew all about it."

"About what? Their kidnapping Caitlin?"

He looked so disbelieving that I said quickly, "I knew you didn't know. It was like my taking drugs."

He thought of something he must have forgotten in his shock. "Did you talk to Caitlin?"

Even one swig of beer was too potent on an empty stomach. Dizzily I signaled our waitress. "Could you bring me a bag of potato chips or something?"

"And I'll have another," Colin added, tilting his empty bottle.

"I didn't plan to. But then Sheila was at her dorm to take her away and I couldn't let that happen, without Caitlin even—so yes, I did."

"You actually talked to her." I expected his reproaches but his voice was wondering. "Is she still so bright?"

"Colin, it was horrible. She thought Ethan and Sheila adopted her because I died in a car accident in Stratford. Then she thought I was her 'birth mother' wanting a reunion. I gave her Sheepie and my card to contact us, but I don't know if she will."

Colin put his face in his hands. I knew his mind was racing, reinterpreting everything that had happened since Stratford in light of this new knowledge.

Then he covered his face completely and groaned.

"Colin?" I felt a flash of terror. I had no idea what was coming.

The waitress set Colin's beer and my chips down on the table, but I couldn't move.

He finally took his hands away and stared at me. "Sheila's right. I did know. But I didn't know I knew."

I put my hand over my mouth.

He leaned close to me, forearms on the table. "I visited them, I guess about 1999, when I was at a conference in Berkeley. I dropped by the house uninvited to try and reestablish the friendship. I missed it. They had a little girl and a boy, both adopted, he was from Nicaragua,. They said she was five and in kindergarten. The boy was just a toddler. Sheila whisked them out of the room before I could really get a look at them, but something about the girl reminded me of Hannah. Except that Hannah was six."

"They lied about her age to you to throw you off. You showing up like that must have been terrifying. What if Caitlin had recognized you?"

We stared at each other.

"Damn! Why didn't I recognize her? My own child." He looked as anguished as I had ever seen him.

I reached across the table and held his arm. I couldn't let myself think about the years we had lost.

"I knew Caitlin was dead so I didn't consider it."

I nodded. "What are we going to do now?"

"After I kill Ethan?"

"Right. I was hoping Sheila would be hit by a car today."

"Don't worry, they're going to pay." He placed his hands on the table as if getting ready to stand. "Let's get something to eat."

I turned to look for our waitress.

"Not here."

"The clam chowder won't kill you. I'm too wiped out to go anywhere else."

He looked reluctant, but settled back down and we ordered two bowls.

"I CHECKED SOME things out this afternoon," Colin said when we were eating our soup. The oyster crackers floating on top of mine looked like little life jackets. "After you sent the photo, I did some research. But it's a complicated situation legally."

"Why?"

"It happened in another country, not here. So the FBI can't initiate an investigation. The statute of limitations on kidnapping runs out in most states once the child turns sixteen."

"But they investigated the Lindbergh kidnapping for years!"

"Because the baby died. That made it a capital crime with no limitations."

Everything that had happened in this endless day, the beer, Colin's words, conspired to make me feel dizzy, as insubstantial as the paper placemat. I stared down at the maze printed in blue with a treasure chest in its center.

"The Brits have to extradite them to stand trial there."

"We can't do anything?"

"File a civil suit, maybe. But we aren't going to do that."

"Why not?"

"Delhi, think. Do you want to drag Caitlin through the notoriety of a trial and see her 'parents,' her whole life exposed? Do you think that will endear us to her? If anything, it will polarize the situation and force her to choose."

"You don't know that."

"You said they had papers?"

"*Forgeries.* We don't even know whose name was on the papers, mine or someone else's entirely. If you have enough money, you can get phony passports, birth certificates, everything. We have to get those papers!"

Colin gave me a fond, indulgent look as if I were a child proposing to fly to the moon for a picnic. "And you plan to burgle their safety deposit box?"

"I don't know. Maybe they keep them in the house." But I was crashing, moving beyond rational thought. "If the authorities get involved, Ethan will *have* to produce the papers."

"You're fading." Colin looked around, as if for the waitress. "We'll talk about it tomorrow."

"Just one more thing. The records say they rented the car until September 27. But didn't Ethan have to be back to teach before then?"

Colin shook his head. "He took a leave of absence that fall. He told them he had discovered something in England he had to research further. I remember because I was pissed that he hasn't told me about it. We'd been to the same sites, after all, and whatever he'd found would have stayed his discovery. But he didn't come home until January, and never published anything about what he thought he'd found."

So he'd had plenty of time to run down Priscilla Waters. Time enough to work out the paperwork to bring Caitlin home.

Chapter 46

I DIDN'T BOTHER getting undressed and going to bed. When I got home I dropped my jacket and bag on the kitchen table, grabbed the alpaca throw from Colin's wing chair, and lay down on the couch. I planned to only sleep for a few hours, enough to clear my head, then call DCI Sampson and get things started.

It was just before 6 a.m. when I woke up, After putting water on to boil for French press coffee, I went upstairs and changed into my usual jeans and a thrift-shop sweatshirt. This one was red and advertised a dude ranch in upstate New York.

Downstairs I waited impatiently for the coffee to finish. I had put DCI Sampson on automatic dial. I expected we would be having a lot of future conversations.

"Ms. Laine." He sounded resigned.

"You know my missing daughter, the one who was supposed to have drowned? She didn't drown, she's *alive*. I met her yesterday!"

"Oh, yes? Well, congratulations. I'm impressed. You're a true force of nature."

"The Crosleys, her kidnappers, live in Rhode Island. I'm calling to give you their address."

A pause. "And why would I want their address?"

"So you can arrest them. Have them extradited, I mean."

"For what?"

"For kidnapping my daughter in Stratford! And killing Priscilla Waters. They're murderers." I heard my voice, too high-pitched, too loud, and told myself to calm down. I took a breath. "The FBI can't do anything until there's an extradition order."

"Ms. Laine, the only evidence of anything I have on this case is a car rental record along with several thousand others from the same time period. The vehicle was returned without damage and no—"

"They had it repaired! Can't you check repair records?" But as I said it I knew how hopeless that was. Of the thousands of shops all over England, how many of them kept records nearly twenty years old or would be willing to go through their files?

"In the unlikely event that we did find repair information on that car, they could say that they went into a ditch or a grazed a tree and there would be no way to prove otherwise. We worked diligently to try and solve that case when it happened. We canvassed that road for any witnesses. We found the cabdriver who had dropped Priscilla off at an intersection a half mile away. But he saw nothing and did not wait. Now we have even less."

"You have a name." It was so clear to me. Why couldn't he see it?

"And you have your daughter back."

"But Nick Clancy doesn't have his mother."

"Nor will he."

"He could have the satisfaction of seeing justice done. Of seeing her killers in jail."

"He won't be seeing them in any English jail unless those people fly over here and confess. Perhaps in America you can file a civil suit about your daughter. She must be a young lady by now."

"Wait a minute! I don't want a civil suit. I want these people punished! I want them to admit what they did. We can never get that lost time back—but I want them in jail for the rest of their lives."

"Extradition is a serious matter. Even if we had evidence linking them and the car to what happened—which we don't, and we investigated it thoroughly—a twenty-year-old hit-and-run would not be given priority."

"But what about the kidnapping? That's what I'm talking about."

"Evidence, Ms. Laine. We need some tangible evidence that these were the people involved."

"Caitlin's the evidence. Her DNA matches ours. You heard Nick Clancy tell you that his mother took her from the park for money."

"I did."

"Would it help if I contacted Scotland Yard?"

"No. They don't have jurisdiction here. I'll look into it further."

"Thank you."

I sat back down at the kitchen table.

When I was growing up with my minister father, parishioners would come to him with their troubles at all hours. The phone would ring, sobbing people would arrive and be hurried into the study. The door would be shut tightly. I would overhear bits, but

I was always on the edge, not old enough or important enough to know the story.

Patience and David Livingstone hadn't cared. But I couldn't wait to grow up, God help me, so I could be in the middle of important adult dramas.

Be careful what you wish for.

Chapter 47

WINTER WAS HANGING on.

After another cup of coffee, I trudged out to the barn to get to work. There was no snow in the forecast, which at least would have made the homes and meadows around me look picturesque. It wasn't even March, which meant at least another month of overcast skies.

Colin was teaching until noon so I couldn't report DCI Sampson's response. I had talked to Jane on the ferry, omitting Sheila's insinuations about Colin, and answering her questions about Caitlin. Perhaps she would see more hope in DCI Sampson's response than I did.

I was sitting at my worktable listing some books I had bought at a library sale last August, when there was a knock on the barn door and it was pushed back. "Hi?"

At first I thought it was Hannah. But then I recognized the navy snowboarding jacket. "Caitlin—I mean, Elisa!"

"Can I come in?"

"Of course you can." I stood up quickly.

If this had been one of the Harlequin romances that my friends passed around in high school, we would have embraced and lived happily ever after.

But I don't live in that book.

I brought her around to the shabby chocolate brown velour couch that I had brought from my parents' house. No matter where you sat, it sank down unevenly, tipping you to one side or the other.

"Take off your coat. I think it's warm enough in here."

"Oh—I can't stay." She unzipped her jacket though. Underneath she was wearing a red ski sweater with white reindeer. Today her hair was pulled back in a ponytail the way Hannah wore hers.

I smiled at her, but my hands were icy and my heart was beating much too fast. *What do you mean you can't stay? I found you after nineteen years and you can't stay?*

"Did you drive down here by yourself?" I knew it was a loaded question.

"Not exactly." She tilted her head and gave me an apologetic smile. "Someone who works for my father brought me."

In a black Ford sedan?

She looked around. "You have a lot of books."

"I sell them."

"I saw that on your card."

I nodded. "Your father—Colin Fitzhugh—is an archeologist and poet. Hannah is a senior at Cornell, she wants to be a vet. Jane's in finance in Manhattan, and Jason's in Santa Fe finding himself."

A rueful grin. "I know that feeling."

"Really? You're a literature major?"

"I love books and sports. Winter sports," she amended. "But I'm not sure how to make them into a life. Anyway . . ."

"Anyway, I'm glad you came." I didn't want to ask her why; I was afraid what the answer would be. Instead I got up from the couch and went to my worktable. "I want to show you something."

I came back with a clutch of papers and handed her a photograph I had removed from one of the albums at Thanksgiving. It showed three little girls in navy coats and straw hats with flowers, smiling up at a younger me and clutching their new Easter rabbits.

Caitlin took it in both hands and studied it. "Is that *me*?"

"That's you next to Jane. Your grandmother gave you the bunny. I have albums with photos of you."

"Thanks, but I can't—"

"Another time then." I felt like Scheherazade. *Keep talking.* I told her about going to Stratford-upon-Avon for the summer and how we used to go to the park every day. "Your—'adoptive' father, Ethan Crosley, was part of the group of archeologists."

I watched her face, but couldn't tell what she was thinking.

Then she moved restlessly, and I said, "I know you have to go, but this is what happened." Rapidly I told her about Priscilla Waters and how she had deceived Jane, then handed her several photocopies. "These are the stories that were in the papers."

She read them, wide-eyed.

"I went back to Stratford last month and talked to Priscilla Waters's sons. They remember you being in their apartment overnight. Before she gave you to the people who paid her to take you."

"This is so different from anything I've heard! Except that my parents adopted me after you died in an accident in England.

That's all they said, they never told me about a *twin*. Why didn't they adopt her too?"

I sighed. "Priscilla Waters was the one who died. She demanded more money for kidnapping you and was hit by a car on her way to collect it."

"How awful!"

I looked into her eyes, blue with green flecks, so much like Hannah's. "It was deliberate, a hit-and-run. What did your mother say when you saw that I was alive?"

She looked at her lap. "That she hadn't wanted to tell me the truth, that you were a terrible mother. You—took drugs and neglected me. That's why you were forced to sign the papers."

There was no end to their treachery. "For the record, I've never even smoked anything. I was too busy having babies to get drunk. And how did she explain why your father, Colin, signed papers—was he a drug addict too?"

"She said he thought it was the best thing for me." She looked past me to the books on the shelves.

"I'd like to see those papers. I'll bet any handwriting expert would say they were forged. And if we'd signed any papers—which we never would have—why did Priscilla Waters steal you from the park and say you drowned? You saw the newspapers." I told myself to calm down, that getting angry would only push her away. In a softer voice I said, "You must have had a reason for coming."

I pressed my hands together in my lap to keep them from shaking. This was the part I didn't want to know. This was the part I had to know. Would she tell me she never wanted to see me again?

She nodded sadly, like a woman about to fire someone who couldn't do the work. "I came to tell you to leave me alone, to just forget the whole thing."

"Is that what *you* want?"

"I don't know!" She turned on me as if I were deliberately trying to confuse her. "I didn't know anything about the drowning. Or having a twin! I don't know anything about being stolen. But I trust my parents."

Perhaps I should have tried to woo her then. I could have told her that her "parents" lied because they loved her, that we loved her too and we could all work something out.

Instead I heard myself say, "What they did was *unconscionable*. They paid someone to kidnap you, and killed her when they were afraid she'd go to the police. They bought forged court papers to pretend they'd adopted you. And that's just for starters."

She pulled back from me. "That's crazy. They'd never do something like that. They *aren't* criminals. Even if this woman took me, they probably didn't know that when they adopted me." She reached out her arm to me as if their safety were the only thing important to her. "Please don't get them into trouble."

The easiest thing in the world: Just promise her you won't. *If you do that, maybe they'll let you see her again.*

But I couldn't. I breathed in the drafty air of the barn and looked at her. "I know you don't know me the way you do the Crosleys. How could you? But I remember you very well. My whole life was changed when I thought you'd drowned. I loved you then and I love you now." I reached out and grasped her hand before she could pull her arm back. The top felt winter-rough, but her fingers underneath were soft. "I'm not your 'birth mother.' I'm your only mother. I wanted you to know the true story. What happens now is up to you."

"But you promise not to—report them or anything?"

"You know I can't promise that."

I let go of her hand then and stood up. She stood up too and fumbled with her jacket zipper.

I couldn't help myself. I reached over and grasped it firmly, zipping it almost to her neck. We were standing very close for a moment.

Then she pulled away, turned, and walked toward the door. Grasping the knob, she went through and pulled the door shut hard.

Chapter 48

I WENT BACK to my desk chair and sat down, propping up my head that felt too weak to stay upright on its own. I replayed the clear bright notes, the snatches of melody, the whole unfinished symphony. Had I given her enough information? I'd thought I had until she wondered why the Crosleys hadn't adopted her twin too. Didn't she understand that she had been stolen from us, that because they already knew us, the Crosleys couldn't be thought of as an innocent third party who'd arrived late on the scene? Would she ever realize that they were the ones who had nearly destroyed my family? *Her* family?

I let my eyes close. When I started looking for Caitlin in December I had been as determined as a crusader pushing through the woods brandishing a torch, not caring what got burned along the way. I had been on a mission that could have destroyed the whole forest. Luckily I hadn't. Even Caitlin, whose life Colin had been so worried about upsetting, seemed more intrigued, if confused, than devastated. Of course, knowing she was adopted all along had cushioned the shock, though they had lied to her about a few little things.

Colin had stressed that her well-being was paramount. And it was. If I never saw her again—and I might not unless it was across a courtroom—I had to accept that she was satisfied with the life she had. But that didn't mean I had to give Ethan and Sheila a free ticket to ride.

Then I thought of something else. Today was Friday. Bruce Adair was coming to dinner tonight and I had completely forgotten. That meant a trip to the supermarket. *Now.*

First though, I called Colin and Jane to tell them about Caitlin's visit. Colin answered his phone as he was heading into a classroom and had time only to absorb the basic facts. Jane was more expressive.

"You saw her again? How come she only appears to you? Couldn't you make her stay around so we could meet her?"

"Re-kidnap her? I don't think so."

"But does she want to meet us?"

"I don't think she knows what she wants right now."

HAVING BRUCE FOR dinner meant cleaning the downstairs of the farmhouse and buying chicken to fry. Despite his protestations, I owed him big-time. I made Spanish rice, cornbread, and green beans with almonds to round off the meal, and then, my creativity exhausted, bought a small cheesecake for dessert. I set the dining room table with my mother's Limoges china and red candles.

All the time I worked I was obsessed by the thought that Colin might drop by as he often did these days. How would I explain

Bruce? I couldn't. I thought about calling Colin and warning him off, telling him I was not feeling well. But I was done lying to protect myself. What happened happened from now on.

Bruce had promised to bring wine and I knew it would be better than anything I could afford. He arrived at seven, suitably dapper in a tweed jacket and argyle vest, his cheeks rosy from the cold. He'd brought two bottles of wine, a white Viognier and a red Côtes du Rhône.

I took the bottles from him and laughed. "You're planning for a long night."

"I wasn't sure which we'd want. Wine is the gift that keeps indefinitely."

While we ate I filled him in on everything that had happened.

"Bruce, I don't know what to do."

"What do you want to do?"

I sighed and drank more red wine. "Colin doesn't want a civil suit. Caitlin wants me to drop it completely. It won't go well for me, whatever I do. She'll either hate me for getting them in trouble, or she'll listen to them and refuse to see me anyway. I can't believe she believes them instead of me."

Bruce lowered his chin and gave me a considering look over his wineglass.

"Oh, okay, I can believe it. She's listened to them most of her life. But what about the facts?"

"Well, she knows she didn't drown. And you've told her that she was kidnapped from the park and that you never signed any papers. But do you have any physical evidence that they ran that actress down?"

"No. But it makes sense."

Bruce looked thoughtful in the candlelight. "I don't know British law, but in this country you wouldn't have much of a case. There were no witnesses to the hit-and-run. No one even knew about it till the next day. A car was rented to the Crosleys, but there's no proof either of them were driving it anywhere near there. I doubt the car itself exists any longer.

"There are no witnesses to the abduction either, Jane, but she only implicates Priscilla, not the Crosleys. You have no evidence that they even knew each other."

"But Sheila admitted it to me!"

"Did anyone else hear her?"

I played with my glass. "No."

"I'm talking about what can be proved in law. What you have is conjecture. If you and your next-door neighbor had a fight and you came out the next day and found your front tire flat, you might be sure he did it. But unless there were any eyewitnesses, the only people you could call are AAA."

He leaned back in his chair and smiled. "A few years ago I came out of the bank and found a note under my windshield giving me the license plate number of a car that had backed into mine. I looked and sure enough there was a dent in my fender. So I called the police. But the person who left the note hadn't given any contact information, and without an eyewitness—the cop said whoever left the note could be trying to frame someone he didn't like. So that went nowhere."

"I get it." But I couldn't accept it. I'd supposed that as soon as I told DCI Sampson where the Crosleys were they would be whisked off to England, put on trial, and jailed forever. Caitlin would renounce them, turn to us, and we would—not live happily ever after, maybe, but we would work things out. She would be part of our family again.

"Your best hope is for Caitlin to come to believe what actually happened and renounce them. Join your family and forget them."

Good luck with that.

Chapter 49

Colin called very early the next morning. "Guess where I was last night?"

Not here, thank God. "Where?"

"Providence." He sounded pleased with himself.

"Really? You saw Ethan? What did *he say*?"

"I went to the college first. I figured they wouldn't tell me anything over the phone, but they know who I am."

"Doesn't everyone?"

He ignored my teasing. "They told me Ethan had had to take an emergency leave of absence. They wouldn't say why or when he'd be back. John Eliot—you remember him?—gave me his home address."

"Did you see him?"

"So I drove to the house. It was locked up tighter than— anyway, there was obviously no one there. I talked to a neighbor. He thought they'd left for somewhere yesterday morning. They have a home in the Caribbean somewhere."

"Oh, my God. Do you think they took Caitlin with them?"

"Isn't she supposed to be in college? Whatever you said to Sheila must have scared the hell out of her. When you wouldn't agree to drop it yesterday, they apparently decided it was dangerous to stick around. They may never come back."

"We'll never see Caitlin again!" It was close to a wail. "What was all this for then?"

"Easy, Del. She's not eight years old. She wouldn't drop out of college now. That's not something Ethan would want her to do anyway."

"If Ethan had been there, what would you have done?"

"You don't want to know."

IT WAS TIME to focus on the books again. The next morning I was heading out to the barn, thinking about the ones I had bought at the temple sale in Queens, when I remembered something Paul Pevney had said to me. If I hadn't been distracted, I might have thought about it earlier. As soon as I unlocked the Book Barn, I headed for the phone on the table.

"Delhi?" Susie sounded groggy though it was after eight o'clock.

"I need to see you."

"Now? I can meet you at the bookstore later."

"No, I'll come there."

"Delhi, what's happened?"

"Are you still in the same house?"

"Of course. It's ours. Our humble home. But tell me what's going on."

"I'll see you in a few minutes."

THE PEVNEYS LIVED in a converted bungalow in a beach community that had flourished in the 1940s. Most of the modest cottages had been winterized and a few expanded, though not Paul and Susie's dark green box.

"Hi, Delhi. Sorry for the mess." Susie indicated a Dumpster explosion of books and newspapers, and a computer set up in one corner of the small living room. "But I do have coffee."

"Great." I followed her into the kitchen and sat down at a Formica-topped table. The kitchen looked as if it had been purchased furnished from the original owner. Patterned oilcloth on the shelves, dented silver canisters, even a yellow metal bread box.

"I just have skim milk," she apologized.

"That's fine."

Then I looked at Susie again. Her wholesome face looked rounder than usual and her skin had a glow I hadn't noticed before. "You're pregnant!"

She beamed. "Just. Even Paul doesn't know yet. How could you tell?"

"Women know."

It made me even more reluctant to tell her what I had to. "Did you tell Paul which books were missing from the shop?"

She sat down opposite me. "No. He doesn't like to hear about the store."

Interesting. "Do you have a basement?"

"No. This is built on a slab."

"Okay. I need you to do something. Where would Paul hide stuff?"

"Hide stuff? Paul? Why would he hide anything? He wouldn't keep anything from me."

"Just think where a good hiding place would be."

"I don't know, but—Delhi, wait. Are you thinking *Paul* stole Marty's books? Paul wouldn't do something like that."

"Just look."

"No!" Her cheeks were burning. It was the first time she had ever refused to do something I asked. "Why would you even think that?"

"When I saw Paul a few days ago at the sale in Queens, he made reference to not finding a Hemingway there. That's one of the missing books."

"So? He's not exactly an obscure writer. It's like making jokes about the Gutenberg Bible."

I stood up. "Okay. It was just an idea."

She pushed up from the table as well and I had a vision of how pregnant she would look in a few months. "His dresser's the only place. I never go in there."

She didn't invite me to come with her, and was back several minutes later, her face glowing with relief. "I didn't find anything anywhere!"

Then I thought about where I left the books I wasn't thrilled about. Sometimes they stayed in the back of my van for weeks.

"Does he take his car to work?"

"Well, we only have one. When I have to take it to the bookshop, he gets a ride. Unless he has somewhere special to go, then he drops me off."

I couldn't imagine Susie not noticing rare books in her car, but I said, "The car's outside?"

She chewed at her bottom lip. "We never lock it."

At first look, the trunk of the old Plymouth seemed to hold only the usual detritus of ice scrapers, a red gas can, a carton of books worth very little. Feeling foolish, I pulled back the fuzzy gray covering that hid the spare tire. Only, where the tire should have been was a package wrapped in a black plastic garbage bag.

I looked at Susie and she stared back helplessly at me.

I reached for the package and pulled it out. *Heavy.* Exactly the way a collection of books should feel.

"Let's take it inside," I said.

"Why? Put it back and I'll talk to Paul when he gets home."

"Susie." I hadn't planned the way it would sound, but it was the voice my father had used when he was trying to bring me back to reality. It was a voice that you didn't argue with.

"Yes, all right. Whatever."

She followed me unwillingly into the house.

I OPENED THE bag on the kitchen table. Pulling out the books was as shocking as uncovering a cache of stolen jewelry.

Susie sank onto a kitchen chair and burst into anguished tears. "I can't believe it. How could he do this to me? Even if he hates my working at the shop. He was trying to get me fired!"

"At least he didn't sell the books."

"How could he? I'm the only one who knows how to do that."

I looked at her. It was the bitterest I had ever heard her sound.

Finally she wiped at her eyes. "I thought when we changed the locks it would stop, and it did. But Paul must have made a new key without my knowing. He sometimes takes my keys when he can't find his. Having a key made at Home Depot isn't exactly hard. Delhi, what am I going to do?"

I thought. "I'll tell you what I would do. I'd take the books back to the shop and put them on the counter and say I found them there. And then kill Paul."

She laughed at that. "Done. But what was he thinking?"

"I don't know." I didn't want to tell her how crazy I thought her husband was. To do such a thing over and over again in the hopes your wife would be fired and be forced to work at home to build the business you were dreaming about? I remembered the destroyed Christmas windows. What kind of a creep would do that?

"Oh, gee, I can't kill him, we're having a baby." Susie gave me a damp smile. "But I'll tell him if he ever touches another book, I'll be on the next plane home to my folks."

Sitting in her tiny vintage kitchen, I realized that going home was what she secretly wanted. I wondered if that was what would happen.

Chapter 50

THE LAST WEEK in March was Hannah's spring break and she decided to come home, getting a ride with friends and arriving about 8 p.m. I had kept her posted on what was happening with Caitlin, but she didn't seem very interested. I tried to put myself in her place and imagine what she was feeling. She had gotten past the idea that we were trying to replace her, but was still concerned with the impact it would have on her life.

In fact, she wanted us all to be there to talk about what she called "my sister problem."

Jane took the Long Island Rail Road to Stony Brook and Colin met her train. They got to the house just before seven. I had a pot of vegetarian chili on the stove and I'd made a quick version of cornbread and a green salad. This way we could eat whenever Hannah arrived.

"You're going to be so happy," I told Raj when I fed the cats their dinner. When Hannah was home he was constantly curled up with her or butting his head against he chin to be petted.

"What do you think?" Jane asked as she hugged me. Perhaps because of the time we had spent together and what we'd been through, she seemed softer, closer to me.

"I don't know what to think about anything," I told Jane. "What do you think Hannah has to say?"

"Hard to tell with her."

When Colin kissed me I held on to him for several moments. He was still tracking Ethan and Sheila and had learned from a colleague that Dr. Crosley was out on "emergency medical leave" and had gone to his home in Barbados to recover.

"He has to come back sometime," Colin growled to me. "And I'll be waiting. John Eliot promised to let me know when he comes sneaking back into the country."

"I thought John was his good friend."

"Not as much as he is mine."

We waited in the living room with wine, olives, and several kinds of cheese. Jane pulled out her phone and began texting. Colin picked up the *New York Times*. I reached for *TransAtlantic*, Colum McCann's latest book, but it sat untouched on my lap like one of the cats waiting to be petted. Why couldn't I be happy with the children I had raised, the family I loved so much? Why was I yearning for a young woman who didn't even want a connection with us?

Because she is one of us, no matter what. Because we have important gifts for her that she can get from no one else.

I had replayed the scene of her visit often, mostly with regret. If I had only been able to convince her, if I had only been able to find the right words. Still, Caitlin had listened intently to the story of her abduction and seemed intrigued that she had a twin. Even when I refused to promise amnesty for Sheila and Ethan, she hadn't stormed out. But she had closed the door with a finality that made me sure I wouldn't see her again.

Just before eight o'clock, there was the sound of tires on the gravel driveway, a flash of headlights into the room.

"She's here!" I was surprised. Usually Hannah called en route, when she was about an hour away. I wasn't sure what that meant. *Just be happy she's coming home at all.*

The car continued around to the back and I thought I heard several doors slam. If her friends wanted to stay for dinner, that was fine.

The kitchen door opened. "Hello?"

"We're in here." I jumped up and went to meet her, but saw two girls through the entryway.

I looked again and put my hand to my mouth.

Colin and Jane rose as if jerked by puppet strings.

Caitlin spoke finally. "Well, I couldn't have a twin without meeting her! I'd always wonder what she was like. After I came here and saw her photo again, I had to go to Cornell to find her."

My brave girl.

Hannah, only a little fuller-faced than her sister, couldn't stop smiling. "As soon as I saw her, I *knew.* It was only last week, but it's so cool. I didn't know it would be so cool. We wanted to surprise you. So did he."

Jason stepped around her and winked at me. "I was curious too. When Hannah called me, I had to see."

I stared at them and then was reaching to hold all three.

"Get your camera," Jane murmured behind me. "It's time."

I nodded. We might never be so happy again. The path would be tortuous ahead. But just for this moment, for right now, we were safely under the dome.

CAITLIN STAYED TWO nights in Hannah's room, then flew to Barbados to be with the Crosleys. The morning she left I sat at the old kitchen table, devastated, as Colin tried to console me.

"She let me know that her visit didn't change anything," I said bitterly. "All she wants is for them to be able to come back into the country without being arrested."

"What did you tell her?"

I shrugged. "Not that all is forgiven." I looked into his deep blue eyes, lined from too many hours in desert suns. "Colin, I couldn't! Even apart from what they stole from us, they *killed* somebody. They're murderers. When they set everything in motion, they may not have meant that to happen, but it did. I don't think Caitlin will ever accept it as the truth though. If we could get someone to write the story, to publicize what they did, it would—"

"No. We said we wouldn't do that." He stood up and put a comforting hand on my shoulder. "I told you, I'll take care of this. I will."

Years ago I would have believed that he could rearrange the world. Now that I was as old as he had been, I knew it couldn't be true.

There was nothing he could do about the barrier between Caitlin and me. We eyed each other over the wall of mixed purposes with challenge and longing, longing at least on my part. But there was no barrier between Caitlin and Hannah. Ironic that Hannah, the one who had been most opposed to finding Caitlin, was her gateway back into the family. They planned to spend alternate weekends at each other's colleges. I was sure that would die down as the amazement of it wore off, but I hoped Hannah wouldn't get hurt. *Magic or tragic.*

IT WAS SUNDAY morning, the first weekend in May, and Caitlin was visiting Hannah at Cornell when I clicked on the *Newsday* website to see what was happening on the Island. The main story was about a fire in a vacation home on Main Street in Southampton. The fire had burned hot and fast, evidently too rapacious for the couple who owned the house to be able to escape. Dr. and Mrs. Ethan Crosley had just returned two days earlier from Barbados for their daughter's college graduation.

The white letters on the ocean-blue background leapt and bounced in front of me. For a moment I believed I was filling in the name I wanted to see. But the names did not change as I stared at them. What had Ethan and Sheila been doing on Long Island? He taught at Brown and their main home, I knew from Colin's trip up there, was in Providence. They had fled from there to the estate in Barbados.

Vaguely I remembered that Ethan's parents had owned a home in the Hamptons when he was growing up, that Colin may even have visited there when they were in grad school, years before I knew him. Could the house Ethan inherited be the one that had burnt down? All I knew about his parents was that the family had become wealthy from owning a farm machinery company in Pennsylvania.

I scrolled down. Arson was suspected. There had been another fire in the neighborhood earlier in the month, though that house had been vacant. Despite their grandeur, many of the homes were seasonal, lived in or rented out for the summer months. Police speculated that the arsonist may have believed that the owners were still away. The Crosleys had not been targets, just unlucky. The Arson Squad was focusing on finding individuals with a compulsion to set fires.

There was a photograph of the beautiful clapboard house, now a ruin. A long-established residence, the kind you see on South Main Street behind hedges. It was also secluded enough so that you might not notice the fire until too late. I shivered in the cool air of the barn. Had Ethan and Sheila known what was happening? In their last moments had they realized that everything they had plotted out was over, that there were some things that money couldn't save you from?

Colin. I had to tell Colin. My hand moved toward my iPhone, then stopped. What would I say? I was suddenly dizzy, the room swimming as if I was seeing everything through wavy glass. Was this what a heart attack felt like? What if this had been Colin's "way of taking care of this" as he'd promised? Did it mean the Arson Squad would soon be at our door? And yet, why would they? They would have no reason to connect us with the Crosleys of Southampton. Colin's ban on publicity, his insistence that we tell no one, had ensured that.

Unless Caitlin . . .

For the next hour I couldn't do anything but sit in my desk chair, stunned, imagining what Colin might have done, how the tragedy would affect Caitlin. How would it be any different from actually losing your parents, if that's who you believed they were? What would it do to her relationship with us? Would it pull us closer or set her on a path of independence away from the whole family, even Hannah?

Ironically, their deaths had resolved the sticking point between us. There would no point in pursuing criminal charges against Ethan and Sheila now. I would have to let DCI Sampson in his cozy office in Stratford know. He could go back to apprehending pickpockets and persecuting street performers dressed like Anne Hathaway and Romeo.

I was still staring at my computer screen which had gone dark from inattention, when the phone rang. Colin?

I grabbed it up. "Hello?"

"Mom? Something terrible's happened. Elisa's parents were in a fire!"

Hannah. "I know. I saw."

"It was down on Long Island." There was something accusatory in her voice, as if I had somehow lured them here.

"I know, the Hamptons. How did they find Cait—Elisa to tell her?"

Silence. "I think one of her dormmates told the police she was visiting me. Anyway, she wants to talk to you."

I thought my heart would stop working. "Okay," I said slowly.

After a moment I heard, "Hi, um—Delhi?"

"Yes. Elisa. I'm so sorry about—the Crosleys." Even in death I could not call them her parents.

"I can't believe it yet. I *don't* believe it. They never should have come back if this was going to happen!"

"They came for your graduation?"

"They wouldn't have missed that. They were staying at the beach house; they were afraid to go back home." Another twin, a stronger accusation: If you hadn't been hounding them, threatening them with arrest, this never would have happened. But then she said, "Anyway, I made a vow to them. I'm going to find out who did this and I won't give up until I do!" Her voice was ragged, close to tears. "Whoever it was is going to pay! And—Hannah told me that you sometimes investigate murders, that you're better than the police?"

Before I could agree or disagree, she added, "Would you help me?"

How could I say no to Caitlin, my long-lost child, when it was the first thing she had asked of me in nineteen years?

"Of course," I said.

Not ready to stop sleuthing with Delhi Laine?
Read on for an excerpt from Judi Culbertson's

AN ILLUSTRATED DEATH

Now available from Witness Impulse

And stay tuned for Delhi's next mystery, coming
Fall 2014!

When Deihi Laine gets the opportunity to appraise the library of Nate Erikson, a famous illustrator, she jumps at the chance, despite the mysterious circumstances surrounding his death. But when another Erikson is found murdered, dark family secrets come to light leaving Delhi determined to solve the crimes once and for all. But digging up truths can get you dirty . . . and Delhi is about to discover just how far some will go to keep them buried.

WHEN CHARLES TREMAINE stepped out of his Town Car and moved down the hill toward the silver gray building, other dealers were on him like butter on bread. Most carried empty cardboard boxes which they hoped to fill with treasure. I had my two vinyl boat bags tucked under one arm, my money hidden in my jeans front pocket to leave my hands free. We couldn't have been more excited than if we were lining up for Shangri-La. I didn't believe Charles's dismal prediction that we were headed for Newark instead.

Judging from the Model-T weathervane on its roof, the building had probably been a stable, then a garage. It had not been well-maintained. The green paint was peeling from its oversized window frames, and one of the panes had a long vertical crack. Dealers took turns peering in, but the windows were too dusty to see anything but long tables of books.

Back on the gravel path we sorted ourselves into one-two-three order. Except for me, the other buyers today were men. I recognized Marty Campagna talking earnestly to Charles Tremaine. *Of course.* Marty was always one of the first three in line at good sales. Rumor had it that he paid someone to stand in his place overnight.

Today he wore a red T-shirt advertising "Joey's Cadillac Repair."

His black-framed glasses were duct-taped at the bridge of his nose, his cheeks stubbly. Although Marty was tall and well-muscled, I knew his brawn came more from leaping over furniture to grab prize books than from workouts at Planet Fitness. But it didn't matter how he looked, he had that elusive gift known as *Finger-Spitzengefuhl*, the tingling in his fingers that comes whenever a rare book is nearby. I didn't know if *Finger-Spitzengefuhl* was real or not. I was still waiting for mine to kick in.

Marty had wasted his money if he had paid to reserve a spot here. Once we were inside and had a chance to examine what had been laid out on the tables, I saw that Charles Tremaine was right. Someone in the family was a Danielle Steel fan. Someone else was parting with a stack of mathematics textbooks. I raced up and down the long plank tables to make sure, but there were no art books, no Erikson-illustrated volumes at all.

Yet the sale wasn't a total loss. From underneath a table I pulled out a grimy carton of older first editions still in dust jackets: *The Bean Trees, The Circus of Dr. Lao, The Heart Is a Lonely Hunter.* And—yes—two Ayn Rands! I didn't even stop to see if the books were inscribed, just shoved them into my green-and-white vinyl bag. A dust jacket can increase a book's value by up to ninety percent. Ayn Rand, like Mozart, never went out of style.

I was moving toward the cash table to pay when Marty stepped into my path. "Hey, Blondie. Find anything good?" He reached down and rummaged through my bag, dislodging books to see what was at the bottom. I held my breath. More than once he had examined my stash, seen something he wanted, and tried to force me to sell the book to him.

Today he jerked back his hand as if to avoid contamination. "*Dreck.*"

"No, it's not." I felt a moment of doubt, then remembered the Ayn Rands in dust jackets.

"Know what I bought? Three books. What a waste!"

Then why are you hanging around?

"I need to talk to you." Evidently his *Finger-Spitzengefuhl* extended to reading minds. "Naw, too complicated. I'll call you later."

And he was off to another sale.

When I reached the gravel area, the dust from the ancient Cadillac Marty drove had long settled. Instead a young woman sat off to the side in a director's chair, arms crossed. A lanky, bespectacled man stood protectively behind her. *Nate Erikson's children?* They were definitely a matched set: gingery hair, pale freckled skin, high aristocratic noses. They had the look of money—her peach sweater was cashmere, her designer jeans fashionably white at the knees. His plaid flannel shirt and Levi's had a deliberately worn-out air that hadn't come from shooting deer.

They studied me, then exchanged a look.

If I had been anywhere but the Hamptons, I might have been worried.

"Hey there!" the woman called, as if I were her neighbor's pet dog.

"Hi."

She pushed up from the canvas seat and the pair edged closer.

"Are you a book dealer?" he demanded.

"Yes." I had run into owners who were hostile to professionals, the last time a month ago. As I left a tag sale carrying a stack of profusely illustrated books on Wedgwood china, a woman in a denim skirt had stopped me.

"How much did you pay for those?" she'd asked.

I could tell from the pinched look of her eyes and mouth that my acquisitions had once been hers.

I should have made up something, but I'd told her the truth.

"That's all you paid? I hope you feel good, profiting from someone else's tragedy."

I started to offer her more money, then realized that no amount would be enough to make things right for her. Still I could not shake my guilt, though I told myself that if I hadn't bought those books, someone else would have. *Sure.* Like rationalizing it was okay to wear a fur coat because those particular animals were already dead.

I reminded myself that the Eriksons had sought out bookstore owners.

"Do you assess books too?" he wanted to know.

"Yes."

"You can tell how valuable—"

"What did you think of these books?" she interrupted him, pointing to my bag.

What could I say that wouldn't insult someone they were related to?

"Well, I bought some."

Her pale blue eyes probed my face. "Were they what you wanted?"

Another trick question. "Not what I was hoping for, maybe, but I did find some good fiction. No art books though."

"No. That's what we want to talk to you about." She looked at the man and he nodded. "We need someone to appraise my father's books. His library is good, but we need to know how good."

Be still, my heart. It was a dream I hadn't known I had. "I could do that." Yet a part of myself asked, *Why me?* Why not Charles

Tremaine or someone who looked like an authority? I knew they had invited only professional booksellers, perhaps for that reason, but something about it made less than perfect sense.

"What's your fee?" plaid-shirt demanded.

My fee? "Forty-five dollars an hour." That sounded like a lot of money for something I would have done for nothing. Just to have the opportunity to look at Nate Erikson's books . . .

"Forty-five dollars?" The woman sounded scandalized. "Mechanics get *ninety*-five an hour. Lawyers are over three hundred!"

"Plus gas and expenses," I added hastily.

She laughed then, a clear note that carried out over the early September landscape. "Fifty-five dollars an hour, none of this nickel-and-dime stuff. When can you start?"

I made myself breathe. "Monday?"

"Fine. Come around nine. I'm Bianca Erikson, by the way, and this is my brother, Claude. The books—"

"How long do you think it will take you to tell us what they're worth?" he interrupted. "This horse has to run."

"Well—it depends on how many there are."

"We have no idea," Bianca said. "They're in his studio covered in dust. The door's been padlocked since the day it happened."

"The studio's been locked since the accident?" It came out before I could censor it.

She rounded on both of us. "Why does everyone keep saying what happened was an accident? It was no damn accident!"

Claude made a protesting sound in his throat.

Bianca gave her brother a scornful look, her eyes as pale and hard as my amethyst birthstone. "Go on, just sweep it under the rug like everything else." Then she strode away, pushing the director's chair over backward as she went.

Claude righted the chair quickly. "I don't know why she says crazy things like that," he muttered. "Even the autopsy said they drowned." He started down the hill after her.

If this had been a Nate Erikson illustration, a serpent would have peered out of the bushes with a quizzical look.

I drove away feeling lightheaded, either because I would be spending time with Nate Erikson's books *and* getting paid, or because it was nearly ten o'clock and I had not yet eaten anything. I decided to stop for a bagel and cream cheese, something I could eat on my way to the next sale.

More than anything, I was shocked by what Bianca Erikson had said. If what happened wasn't an accident, what were the choices? Surely a man with Nate's talent and sensibilities would not have committed suicide, much less drowned his own granddaughter. Even if in despair, I couldn't imagine him inflicting that pain on his family.

That left murder.

Yet as Claude Erikson had pointed out, the police had been satisfied. Something else occurred to me: Had it been *her* daughter who drowned? Maybe Bianca was unable to accept the fact that life was so precarious that a single moment of inattention could have fatal and permanent results.

Tell me about it.

About the Author

JUDI CULBERTSON draws on her experience as a used-and-rare-book dealer, social worker, and world traveler to create her bibliophile mysteries. No stranger to cemeteries, she also coauthored five illustrated guides with her husband, Tom Randall, starting with *Permanent Parisians*. She lives in Port Jefferson, New York, with her family.

Visit Judi online at www.judiculbertson.net.

Visit www.AuthorTracker.com for exclusive information on your favorite HarperCollins authors.

CPSIA information can be obtained
at www.ICGtesting.com
Printed in the USA
LVHW041306050920
665030LV00016B/1658

9 780062 296368

SEP 16 2020